MIDNIGHT MOVIE

ELLIE JORDAN, GHOST TRAPPER, BOOK FOURTEEN

by

GW00499171

J. L. Bryan

Published February 2021

JLBryanbooks.com

Acknowledgments

Thanks to my wife Christina and my father-in-law John, without whom I would be a full-time parent struggling to write at odd hours.

I appreciate everyone who helped with this book, including beta reader Robert Duperre (check out his books!). Thanks also to copy editor Lori Whitwam and proofreaders Thelia Kelly, Andrea van der Westhuizen, and Barb Ferrante. Thanks to my cover artist Claudia from PhatPuppy Art, and her daughter Catie, who does the lettering on the covers.

Thanks also to the book bloggers who have supported the series, including Heather from Bewitched Bookworms; Mandy from I Read Indie; Michelle from Much Loved Books; Shirley from Creative Deeds; Lori from Contagious Reads; Kelly from Reading the Paranormal; Lili from Lili Lost in a Book; Heidi from Rainy Day Ramblings; Kelsey from Kelsey's Cluttered Bookshelf; and Ali from My Guilty Obsession.

Most of all, thanks to the readers who have supported this series! There are more paranormal mysteries to come.

Chapter One

"I wish we had a convertible," Stacey said from the passenger seat. She wore sunglasses against the bright morning daylight, her short blonde hair streaking across her face as springtime air blasted in through her open window. "This is totally convertible weather."

"I don't think we could transport all our gear in a convertible," I said.

"Well, they should invent a convertible van, then. Or a convertible station wagon."

"Sounds practical." I nudged the accelerator down, since the road was clear and wide open. We'd just left Savannah for Highway 204, lined with tall pine trees sprouting from sandy soil, a lesser-used road ever since they built the interstate not far away.

We could've taken the interstate ourselves, but I'd opted for the more scenic route, passing a few farms and empty, tumbledown houses. This road ran parallel to the train tracks, heading westward and inland, away from our coastal home of Savannah.

Not far away, though. Easy commuting distance meant no grimy cheapo motels, no sleeping in the van, and no camping with Stacey, who was always too chipper about sleeping in a tent.

We were headed toward tiny Pembroke, Georgia, a little railroad town that had been a much bigger deal a century or so earlier. We didn't have to drive all the way into town, though, because our client's location was out on the highway.

"Wow, there it is," Stacey said. "That really didn't take long. I barely had any coffee." She sipped from her pink Hydro Flask tumbler.

I slowed at the turn-off. It was a sign I'd passed countless times but barely noticed, an overgrown relic of a bygone time.

Now the overgrowth had been hacked away, the weeds mown down, and for the first time in years, its giant art deco letters were plainly visible to the highway:

NITE-LITE DRIVE-IN
NOW PLAYING: LABYRINTH
COMING SOON: GRAND RE-OPENING!
EST. 1955

Just in case we weren't sure where to go, a lightbulb-studded arrow pointed the way. The bulbs weren't lit, and likely hadn't been in many years.

I turned off the highway and slowed to a crawl, following a long, curved driveway toward an area hidden behind a wall of high pine trees supplemented by spans of privacy fence.

"Check out that screen tower." Stacey, a film-school graduate, shook her head in awe.

She gaped at a concrete building three stories high. The

side facing the highway sloped up from the ground at a steep angle, forty-five or more degrees, all the way to the top. A huge red Coca-Cola logo was painted across it, still faintly visible after decades of sun and rain. A steel door was built into the side of the tower.

"That's a movie screen?" I asked. "It looks like a warehouse."

"Oh, yeah. The screen will be on the front side. I can't wait to see it! Why are you driving so slow?"

"That's what the signs say. Five-mile speed limit." I eased the van around the constantly curving blacktop.

"That's probably for when there's, like, actual other cars here, though? The box office looks cool."

At the ticket booth, a candy-striped arm blocked the road. The booth was freshly painted in cheerful, funky purple with bright white trim. Strings of matching pennants made the whole thing look extra festive. David Bowie stared at us from a *Labyrinth* poster in one of the booth's windows.

"This place was definitely not open when I was in college, or we would have checked it out," Stacey said, while I texted the prospective clients that we'd arrived. It really had been a quick drive. "Once we went all the way to the Jessup Drive-In, which was totally classic. I mean it's super-authentic from the 1940s, but that was an hour away. Worth it. Nobody ever mentioned this one. I'll have to tell everyone about it."

"That must be Benny." A guy bicycled toward us from the other side of the ticket booth, keeping to the shade of the trees lining one side of the road in a solid wall of vegetation.

"I like his hat," Stacey said. The guy wore a puffy blue cap that would have looked at home on the head of a 1920s newsboy shouting the day's headlines at 1920s pedestrians. *Extra, extra, look at my hipster hat!* He also wore suspenders over a *Last Starfighter* t-shirt. He parked his bike by the ticket stand as I lowered my window.

"Welcome to the Nite-Lite!" He sounded fairly upbeat about it, but he had a tired look about him, as people living in haunted homes often do. He walked around the ticket arm to my driver-side window. "I'm Benny."

"Good to meet you," I said. We'd previously emailed. "I'm Ellie. This is Stacey Tolbert, my tech manager."

"Hi! Great place you've got going here," Stacey said.

"Thanks, we're trying. We're visualizing the outcome and following through." He opened the ticket booth door and raised the arm barring the road. "You can park over in the back row by the concession stand. Meet you there."

We cruised past signs that gave directions and advertised upcoming movies, which were actually decades-old reruns, but interesting picks like *The Goonies.* A sign advertised the concession stand with a purple cartoon dragon munching a slice of, supposedly, *Earth's Best Pizza!*

The deserted parking area had spaces for a couple hundred cars, marked out by little speaker poles. The massive white movie screen dominated the space, nearly blinding me with reflected daylight.

"Where are the speakers?" I asked, looking at the pole beside me.

"Drive-ins use radio now. Let's check it out." Stacey opened her door and hopped out, eager as a kid in a toy-and-candy store on Free Toy and Candy Day. I hoped she kept it professional for the clients. I did my best to visualize that outcome, hoping she'd follow through.

Climbing out, I took a breath of fresh, grassy air. In addition to the trees that walled off the view from the highway, there was a big lawn not far away, behind the two-story concession stand.

A mural on the front of the concession stand depicted a long purple dragon woven between puffy painted letters that read PURPLE PIZZA EATER. The dragon smiled, possibly because of the steaming pizza pies he held in each hand. His tail coiled around an overflowing box of popcorn.

"I swear I can smell that dragon painting," Stacey said.

"You're not wrong." I sniffed; the air was full of rich tomato and cheese sorts of scents. My breakfast had been the private-investigator special—black coffee with a side of nothing—but now my stomach gurgled.

"Callie—my wife—is experimenting in the pizza lab today." Our prospective client caught up to us on his bike. "Movie theaters live and die on their concession stands, so she's a real secret weapon. A nuclear weapon."

"Pizza lab?" Stacey asked.

"She innovates, and she likes to keep it seasonal and local. We planted an organic herb and vegetable garden for ultra-locality." He nodded at the lawn that sprawled away behind the concession stand and ended at a high, rickety-looking fence with woods beyond it. The garden must have been beyond the fence, too, because I didn't see any sign of it.

"You're the owner of the drive-in, correct?" I asked, pulling out my notebook.

"I am. We are. It's a joint effort, Callie and me. And a few of my buds who come out for big projects, like rebuilding the stage." He pointed to the raised wooden platform in front of the shining, three-story metallic screen. "That'll be ideal for the *Rocky Horror Picture Show* crowd. We can have live music while we await nightfall. Like my band. We're the Bluegazers, exploring the space between the sounds of blues and shoegaze. I'm sax and backup vocals."

"Right," I said, feeling like I was writing down too many details. Benny was enthusiastic. He looked about my age, late twenties. "How long have you owned the drive-in?"

"About three months now," Benny said. "It's been out of business for years, obviously. Finding it was ninety-eight percent kismet. One day Callie and I were out for a drive, doing some casual photography of Georgia's lost highways for this website I was going to make. Then, boom. We saw the marquee sign with the big arrow and had to check it out. It was fenced off, but not all that well, so we snuck inside. Not that we were talking about buying it, no way, not then. We just wanted some pictures.

"It was rundown and overgrown, but it wasn't *bad*, you know? And walking around, I got obsessed with it. Bringing it back to life. I had all these ideas, like the place was really speaking to me. And boom, next thing you know, here we are."

"And you're already open?" Stacey asked.

"We're soft-opened," Benny said, still straddling his bicycle. "We turn on the lights, and if anybody shows up, great. We're focusing on older movies. They're cheaper to license and better suited to the nostalgia tinge on the whole drive-in experience. We're still ironing everything out before we start advertising and drawing in crowds." He scratched his thin beard. "Well, hopefully drawing in crowds. But I think we have the *concept* to make it work. And Callie's pizza will keep them coming back. You can't get it anywhere but here."

"It does smell awesome," Stacey said.

"She might guinea pig you with some samples," Benny said.

"Yeah, twist my arm." Stacey eased closer to the concession stand.

"Didn't you mention you lived on the property, or nearby?" I asked.

"We do." He pointed to the screen tower. "Behind the magic screen, like the Wizard of Oz."

"You live in the screen tower?" Stacey gasped. "No way!"

"Ayuh," he said, in his slight New England accent. "The owner had a private apartment in there. These old-time screen towers had plenty of room inside. Look how big this one is. One over in Claxton had a local radio station on the upper floor. Anyway, the last owner kept up the screen tower apartment better than the old farmhouse." He nodded again at the privacy fence. "For now, Callie's pretty much just using it as the garden shed."

"Are the disturbances in the old house or in the screen tower?" I asked.

"Pizza! Pizza!" A small girl in a floppy sunhat burst out of the glass front door of the Purple Pizza Eater. She was around kindergarten age, five or six, wearing a tie-dyed dress. She raced toward us, past weathered picnic tables shaded by new beach umbrellas, bare feet slapping the cracked blacktop. She held one hand aloft, smeared in red sauce.

"Did you help Mommy make pizza?" Benny scooped her up off the ground.

"Try it, Daddy!" The girl attempted to cram her sauce-covered hand into his mouth, but he managed to turn away at the last second. She painted a tomato-red clown smile across his face.

"Daisy June!" A young woman pursued the girl out the front door but stopped short when she saw Stacey and me. She touched her face self-consciously and looked down at herself. Her hair was back in a kerchief, and she wore an apron splattered with ingredients and small tomato-sauce handprints. She blushed. "So I guess the detectives are here, Benny? Thanks for the heads up."

"They're here and entranced by the aroma of your latest creations," Benny said. "As anyone would be."

"Daddy, try the new flavor!" The little girl again attempted to shove sauce in his mouth, getting it up his nostril instead as he jerked away.

"Thanks, kiddo." Benny set her on the ground and pointed to us. "Say hi to our guests."

The girl looked at us and jumped, as if noticing us for the first time. She held up a sauce-covered hand at Stacey. "Want to taste?"

"No, thanks!" Stacey said. "I just ate breakfast off somebody's hands a few minutes ago, so I'm all full."

"I'm Ellie," I said, stepping toward the blushing woman in the kerchief. She was in her twenties, too—hey, that made all of us, except for Daisy June—but came across as on the younger end, or maybe she was just shy. "You must be Callie."

"Yeah. Hi. Sorry, I'm in the middle of a few experimental pizzas right now." Her accent was soft and languid, definitely not New Englandish like her husband, and told me she was from somewhere in the South but not Georgia.

"A *few* pizzas?" Stacey looked past her toward the concession stand. "They smell great. For sure. A lot."

"Maybe they should go inside with you," Benny said to Callie, raising his eyebrows. I recognized that signal between parents who didn't want to discuss their haunted house problems in front of their kids. It makes sense because they want to protect the kids, but usually kids are the first to know something's wrong. "They could try some of your new pizzas. Hit 'em with a taste test."

"I'm sure they don't want to be bothered with that,"

Callie said.

"Uh, I do!" Stacey said. "I cannot emphasize this enough, in fact. I had nothing for breakfast except for some eggs and tomatoes and toast and cereal, and that was a couple hours ago."

"Okay, sure. Come on in." Callie turned back toward the Purple Pizza Eater, and Stacey ran ahead to hold the door open for her as she walked back inside, adjusting her green kerchief. Stacey was not kidding about wanting some pizza.

"Let's race, Daddy!" Daisy June ran to her blue *Frozen*-themed bicycle. Benny jumped back onto his bicycle, and father and daughter raced each other across the deserted parking lot toward the movie screen.

Looking at the big screen and the cheerful cluster of bright little buildings centered on the concession stand and its picnic tables, I thought the drive-in theater seemed like a perfectly fun place, evoking a sort of nostalgia for a time when I hadn't even been alive.

Looking the other way, though, I couldn't help but have a darker feeling about the tall, rickety fence along the back of the sprawling lawn, its weathered posts like a thousand sharp teeth waiting for something to bite, the shadowy woods waiting on the other side.

I followed Stacey into the concession stand.

Chapter Two

If the faint smell of pizza had been enticing outdoors, the aroma inside could only be described as painfully delicious.

The Purple Pizza Eater's interior continued the overall retro theme, with shiny surfaces and touches of chrome. They had painted the walls multiple hues of purple— purple stripes, purple polka dots—and decorated with vintage movie posters in brass frames dotted with tiny lightbulbs.

"Sit anywhere you like." Callie dashed behind the long counter to a brick oven in the kitchen. A big popcorn popper trimmed in red and polished brass at one end of the counter was currently empty but exuded a ghostly odor of butter and salt that lingered in the air. The menu board was adorned with images of dancing cartoon drinks, popcorn, and ice cream cones that looked like they'd originated in advertising reels of the 1940s or 50s, freshly printed in bright colors.

Stacey and I took one of the diner-style wooden booths that looked out through large windows so patrons could watch the big screen when eating indoors, listening to the speakers mounted above us. The framed, lighted movie posters nearest us featured a black-and-white *King Kong,* plus *Rocky* and *Muppets Take Manhattan.*

"How cute is this place?" Stacey snapped pictures with her phone. "Jacob is going to freak out."

I traced my finger over the wooden table, etched with years of scraped and carved graffiti, teenage declarations of love and hate, a tic-tac-toe game, stick figures, and other hieroglyphs of lost time and forgotten days.

"Okay, I admit this is a little crazy," Callie said from behind the counter. She set out three pizzas on wooden platters. "One Greek style with olives and feta, and one egg roll pizza with cabbage, carrots, all that, with a kind of soy-sesame. Then I have this Southern-style pizza with collards and chicken, which is really completely experimental. Do either of you want to try? It's totally okay if not. Like I said, these are really weird and bizarre—"

"I'll have all of it," Stacey said. "Those look amazing."

The girl blushed and swiped her pizza cutter, slicing out wedges for us. "I get wacky ideas. But I figure, if we're doing a drive-in, we could do kind of a high-end version of that classic drive-in food. The drive-in is where America met pizza and fell in love." She brought the food over on metal dishes the size of hubcaps.

"Holy cow," Stacey said after biting into the collards and chicken. "This is… amazing. The best… are you a witch or something?"

"No," Callie said. "Well, on Halloween, a couple times."

I tried the Greek one. Jaw-dropping. Unbelievably good.

"No, seriously, you're like a master chef," Stacey said.

"Definitely not." Callie was redder than ever. And really, given how that pizza tasted, she could've been as arrogant as a stereotypical French master and gotten away with it. "I mean, I went to culinary school, so it's all just practice. Anybody can do well with practice."

"Where did you study? Paris?" I asked.

She laughed. "Just the Art Institute. Over in Atlanta? It was…pricey, but worth it." She bit her lip. "I met Ben while I was living in Atlanta, too."

"Where are you from originally?" Stacey asked.

"Little Rock."

"I've got a cousin in Arkansas!" Stacey said.

"When did you move to Atlanta?" I asked.

"For school a couple years ago. Atlanta was much bigger than Little Rock, which I liked. I wanted a big city to explore. It was scary at first, though. It got better after I met Benny. He's more outgoing than I am. You know, he meets people easy, he knew the interesting spots around town. I probably would have holed up and had no social life without him."

"When did you move to Savannah?"

"After I graduated, I got a job here. We wanted to move here, anyway."

"Where do you work?"

"It's called Napoleon III."

"Only one of the best restaurants in the city," Stacey said. "And you're making pizza for the drive-in. Your husband was right—you really are the secret weapon here."

"Sure. What do you want to drink? We have Cannonborough sodas from Charleston. Honey basil, raspberry mint, blueberry vanilla. Or iced tea, or water."

"Water's fine," I said, and Stacey gave a thumbs up, her mouth full of egg roll pizza.

Callie brought iced water glasses and sat in the booth with us, nervously twisting a napkin in her hands. "I don't know where to start."

"Your husband said you've been hearing things late at night. And seeing things."

"We both have. He told you that, right?" Callie asked.

"He didn't get into details." I eased my notebook onto the table.

"Great." She sighed, twisting the napkin tighter, like she was about to rip it in half. "It started with the voices. They came late at night. From… out there." She gestured at the parking lot and movie screen. "It began a few weeks ago, when we started screening movies."

"Are you showing a movie tonight?" Stacey asked.

"We are. Have you ever seen *Labyrinth*? It's a classic."

"It's been a while," I said. "Can you tell us what you experienced?"

"The first time was the night we screened *Bedknobs and Broomsticks* for Daisy, and for whoever else showed up that night, which turned out to be nobody. We all went to sleep around one in the morning. It was still dark outside when they woke me up."

"Who woke you?"

"These weird, echoing voices, like a movie soundtrack blasting over the outdoor speakers back here at the concession stand. I don't know what movie. I couldn't make out what they were saying. I assumed the sound system was going haywire. I also thought Ben would eventually wake up and go deal with it, but he just kept snoozing. I went to check on Daisy. She was sleeping through the voices, too, but Gumby wasn't on his usual rug in her room."

"Gumby?" I asked.

"Our chocolate lab. I looked all over for him. Usually,

he stays close to Daisy at night."

"Gumby was okay, right?" Stacey asked, plainly worried. "Nothing bad happened to the dog?"

"I finally found Gumby on the ground floor. He was growling at the door to the outside. Gumby's usually a big marshmallow. I'd never seen him growl before.

By the time I finally calmed him down, the voices had stopped. It was silent outside."

"So, the chocolate-and-marshmallow dog was fine," Stacey said, relieved.

"I checked that the door was locked before going back upstairs to bed. I told myself it was just a bug in the sound system. If not for Gumby, I would have thought it was just my own mind playing tricks, something I dreamed while I was still half-asleep."

"Oh, wow, that's crazy," Stacey said.

"It was eerie."

"No, sorry, I mean it's crazy how good this pizza is. Collards, chicken…do I detect a note of cornbread in the crust?"

"Just a note," Callie replied. "You don't think it's too weird?"

"Mm-mmm." Stacey shook her head emphatically while chewing the last bite.

"What happened next?" I asked Callie.

"I went back upstairs. Gumby came with me, sticking to me like bubblegum, like he used to when he was a puppy. He was shaking pretty bad. I was, too."

"Did you have any other occurrences like this?" I asked.

"It happened again a few nights later. The voices were louder. A woman and a man, yelling. Fast-paced, back and forth, like in a stage play.

I woke up Benny, and we went downstairs. Gumby was

growling at the closed door again."

Stacey leaned forward, plainly worried for the dog again.

"We didn't see anything out the window, just our little side yard. Benny slid open the deadbolt. I told him to wait. It's a solid fire door, no peephole or anything. Someone could have been standing right outside, waiting for us. Benny opened the door anyway, and Gumby bolted out, barking."

"Oh, no!" Stacey said. "Not Gumby."

"Benny ran out after the dog. Daisy started crying upstairs, and I was torn because I wanted to go up to her, but I didn't want to take my eyes off Benny. I could barely see him in the dark. The voices stopped, though."

"Did Benny see anything outside?"

"Nothing. He wanted to check the sound system for electrical problems, but I told him to wait 'til morning. I wanted everyone locked inside together. Upstairs, Daisy was still crying, saying she had a bad dream about an evil man. We all stayed in the same room that night."

"That sounds frightening," I said, scribbling on my pad. "Did he ever check the sound equipment?"

"Yeah, the next day, but nothing was wrong." She shook her head. "It was quiet the next night, and the one after. We didn't talk about it, like that was the key to the whole problem—just don't talk about it, pretend it didn't happen, and it would go away. Like that ever works."

"Did you have any other problems?"

"Oh, yes. The worst was one night as I was breaking down the kitchen." She gestured toward the brick oven behind the counter. "I'd told Benny to go ahead and put Daisy to bed. I like squaring away the kitchen at the end of the night myself, making sure everything's where it's supposed to be, ready for a new day.

"I turned off the lights, locked the door, and started skating on my board across the parking lot, heading home to the tower." She looked out at the rows of speaker poles. "I have a little flashlight on my keychain, but I didn't need it because of all the moonlight.

"As I was a few rows into the parking lot, passing that crumbling old projector house from the fifties—which is a hazard we need to remove, but that's another story—the voices started up again. Loud, but totally garbled, like the man and woman were arguing again. Like a man and a woman in a heated argument.

"Then the sky turned dark. Clouds, I guess. That was when I saw them, up on the screen, larger than life. They were just barely visible, but I could make out the glowing ovals of faces, a couple of faces yelling passionately at each other. Like a movie was playing at low resolution, projected with barely any light at all. Ghost lights, that's what I thought. Chilling and cold.

"One of the ovals, who I took to be the yelling man, closed in on the other, like he was attacking her. Or kissing her, aggressively.

"The moonlight came back, reflecting off the screen, drowning out the faint images. The voices stopped, too. All of it stopped. Like I'd gone crazy, but only for a minute, then right back to normal. Though I guess you never really hear of crazy people abruptly 'going normal,' do you? Not that I'm anybody's idea of normal.

"Anyway, the whole event with the voices and the images, the ghostly movie playing up there, might have lasted ten seconds. After it ended, it was hard to force myself to keep going toward the screen tower where I'd just seen the strange images. But my family was in the tower, and I sure didn't want to be alone anymore.

"I looked up at the projection booth—" She pointed

toward the concession stand's second floor above us. "It was all dark. Nothing happening, nobody in there, as far as I could see.

"As fast as I could, I skated the rest of the way to the tower, ran inside, and locked the door. Gumby was right inside the door, whining. He calmed down once I took him upstairs.

"I couldn't sleep. I just kept remembering the voices and the phantom shapes on the screen. I'm sure this all sounds strange to you. I promise we are well within our gourds, not out of them." She sighed and looked around. "Except maybe for buying this place. There's an obvious reason it's been out of business for years. It's a drive-in theater. But with Ben, it was always going to be *something*. At one point, the dream was a coffee shop where he and his band could play. Then he talked about a vintage record store, which seemed like a bad idea to me. He looked into opening a CBD oil place. He kind of has a mad-artist approach to life. Like with college. He started out in music at Chapel Hill, then cultural anthropology at Georgia State, but ended up getting his degree in social media from A-Plus Online Technology University."

"Well, I think y'all are doing a great job," Stacey said. "I can see this drive-in being a fun night out for anyone."

"I hope so. But can we convince enough people to come? And will they keep coming back?" Callie frowned at the blank white screen towering over the empty parking lot, like she was counting all that it had cost them so far.

"They'll come back for the pizza," I said, and she smiled a little. She wasn't wrong, though. They were taking on a type of business that had peaked and declined long ago, and obviously they knew it, or at least Callie did.

I'd assumed Benny and Callie were rich kids, or at least one of them was, with money to burn on iffy business ideas. Callie's face looked strained, though, like someone attempting to balance too many things at once while trying not to collapse from exhaustion. Maybe they'd put themselves at great risk for a dubious business idea, and she was trying to support them both with her job at the restaurant.

"Have you had any other unusual experiences?" I asked.

"I thought I saw someone watching me from the old farmhouse, back behind the fence, when I was working in the garden. A shadow. It vanished when I blinked. I always feel like someone's watching me there, maybe from the windows of the house, though I never actually see anyone.

"Out here in the parking lot, I've smelled smoke a couple of times. I mean tobacco, a cigarette or cigar. But we don't smoke tobacco. Graham and Marcia—those are Benny's friends who came out last week—they smelled it, too, when they saw the man."

"What man?"

Before she could answer, a pair of double doors at the far end of the room flew open, making us jump.

"Foosball, snoozeball, Daddy's gonna lose-ball." Daisy June skipped out through the double doors, Benny following. Behind them was another large room, empty aside from movie posters on the wall and a foosball table in the middle.

"How do you like our fabulous arcade?" Benny gestured around at the mostly empty space. "The future to-do list includes pinball and retro video games. Maybe ping-pong."

"Those can wait." Callie gave a short, tight smile that faded quickly. "After the digital projector, resurfacing the screen with new aluminum, restoring the buildings, we're probably good for now."

"Definitely. And air hockey. A jukebox, obviously. All part of the time-warped package experience." Benny looked out at the enormous white screen and smiled. "It's all happening. Maybe we should rename this place The Time Machine. What do you think?"

"Well, it already came with a huge sign calling it the Nite-Lite, so that's paid for," Callie said. "I was just telling them about when Graham and Marcia came to see *Princess Bride*. Maybe you can fill them in on that. Daisy June, want to play foosball?"

"Foosball!" the little girl shrieked, running back through the double doors, her voice echoing in the nearly empty arcade room. More framed posters decorated the wall, many of them black and white—a 70s-horror looking thing called *Manos, Hands of Fate*; a *Commando Cody* poster featuring a helmeted superhero; a noir-ish looking black-and-white flick called *Pocketful of Aces*, featuring a pinstriped gangster with cards in his hand and a beautiful woman on his arm. The woman's large, expressive gray eyes made the *Aces* poster stand out from the others.

Callie followed. She cast a worried look at us, and out at the theater screen, before closing the doors behind her.

Chapter Three

"Hey there, buddy." Benny petted a chocolate lab that came up to him as he stepped outside the concession stand. The dog regarded Stacey and me cautiously.

Stacey put out her hand and made little clicking noises at Gumby, who sniffed her palm dubiously.

"We plan to fence off a dog park." Benny swept his arm across the lawn behind us. "That'll be something people can do while they wait for the movie. People like it when they can bring their dogs places."

"Callie mentioned your friends had an unsettling experience here," I said. "Something to do with cigar smoke?"

"Yeah, for sure. Graham and Marcia came out from Atlanta for our *Princess Bride* screening. They parked up in the front row." Benny started across the rows of parking spots, toward the screen tower. The tower's reflective surface glowed in the daylight. "You know, at one point back in the sixties, drive-ins were more popular than indoor theaters. Families came every week. But you know what wrecked it all?"

"Cable TV?" I guessed.

"Flatscreens? Broadband?" Stacey asked.

"People not wanting to sit around in their cars?" I suggested.

"All those, and more," Benny said. "But the first big blow was Daylight Savings Time. You start the movie an hour later, the customers get home an hour later, it's not so convenient. Your standard drive-in experience is a double feature, but we're shifting to a movie *palace* type experience instead."

"Ooh, so you have a cartoon?" Stacey asked. "A newsreel? A serial?"

"We're skipping the newsreel," Benny said. "But yes to an opening cartoon, a short film, or some vintage serial, and *one* feature. If we're screening *Superman: The Movie,* we could start with a 1940s Max Fleischer Superman cartoon, follow it with a chapter from a 1950s Superman serial, then boom, right into Marlon Brando's end-of-the-world, you-complete-me monologue to baby Superman. Everybody gets a full, classic experience, but you also get home by midnight."

"Can you tell us more about what your friends experienced out here?"

"Sure, back to business, right." He took off his puffy hat, unleashing a tumble of long dark hair, and wiped sweat from his brow. "No other customers showed up that night. We screened *The Princess Bride*, and I led into that with an early Bugs Bunny—*Buccaneer Bunny*, 1948, because it has Yosemite Sam as a pirate. Then an episode of *Manhunt of Mystery Island*, an adventure serial from Republic, 1945.

"Anyway, they were watching the serial when Marcia

smelled smoke. In her rearview mirror, she saw somebody right behind the car, a man in shadow, outlined from behind by the light from the concession stand. He was just standing there, like he was spying on them.

"But when she turned to look out the rear windshield, nobody was there. Graham got out and looked but didn't see anyone. He smelled the cigar smoke, though.

"Later, they asked me who the strange man walking around the parking lot had been, but we didn't know. We would have noticed someone hanging around without paying admission. We couldn't figure it out.

"The next night, we had some random pull-ins off the highway, a family with two kids. They left in the middle of *Princess Bride*, hauling out of here like the Fire Swamp had erupted beneath them. Maybe they saw the strange man, too. They didn't stop to explain.

"The same thing happened the next week. Two couples, college-age kids, came in one car. They hauled out of there after about an hour."

"Cigar smoke again?" I asked. "Either time?"

"Maybe. It would have been hard to smell over the burning rubber... the smell of customers who couldn't wait to get out of here. The smell of impending doom for us and our little business, pretty much."

"Have you personally witnessed anything else?"

"The house behind the fence always gives me the jitters, but it's falling apart and overgrown, so anybody would probably say that. Callie really hates it. I think the theater's old owner ended up living in the tower and letting the house rot. Kinda makes sense, if you're on a budget and have to pick. The tower's concrete, and that doesn't rot."

"What do you know about the previous owners?" I asked.

"Stan Preston built it back in 1955 and ran it until it went out of business. He kept on living here even after it closed, maintaining it as well as he could, which is why it's all in relatively good shape. I bought it from his daughter, Leah, who is elderly now and lives in Missouri."

"I'll probably need to speak with her if you hire us," I said. "Did Stanley smoke cigars?"

"I don't, uh…" Benny's eyebrows shot up. "I did find an old wooden cigar box in the office. Tossed out the last few cigars as part of the clean-up, but actually kept the box itself. It was totally vintage, and just too nice a piece of woodwork to chunk out like trash. I thought it might be good for keeping art supplies or something."

"Okay, that's promising," I said.

"And listen," he said, "did Callie tell you about, uh, the ghost movies?"

"Have you seen them, too?"

"Yeah, one night, when I was closing up and Callie was already back home with Daisy. I didn't even have Gumby with me. He usually sticks close to Daisy, anyway.

"I had shut everything down and was heading home for the night, biking across the parking lot toward the tower. Up on the screen, shapes appeared, pale shapes like big faces. I could just barely hear music, sappy string music like an emotional moment in an old movie. The face-shaped glowing spots moved close together on the screen. Then there was a whipping, cracking sound, like back in Maine when a frozen pond breaks in the spring.

"It ended after that. I looked back at the window to the projection booth—" He pointed to the large dark square on the second floor of the Purple Pizza Eater. "—and it was completely dark, nothing happening that I could see, but I was majorly panicked about the idea that someone was up there, messing with the new digital projector. That projector by itself represents literally half our investment here. Buying and rehabbing the place adds up to less than the cost of the projector. So far."

"Oh, you had to buy a digital cinema projector?" Stacey whistled, looking from the projection booth to the giant screen. "Sounds pricey."

"Yeah, very very very. I figured somebody was up there. I ran inside and grabbed a knife from the kitchen—okay, no, it was a pizza cutter, I admit I grabbed a pizza cutter—and I ran upstairs.

"I opened the door to the projection booth… and nothing. Nobody was there, and the projector was all shut down like I'd left it. But that was impossible, I thought. I'd definitely seen something getting projected on the big screen. I even checked the old thirty-five millimeter that came with the drive-in—we happily keep it around for the more authentic retro option. Cold, untouched, definitely hadn't been used recently."

"It's cool you kept the old thirty-five millimeter," Stacey said.

"Technically there's *three* generations of projectors here. The digi is the newest, obviously, and it's amazing. Fully programmable, set it and forget it, 4K resolution, a six thousand to one contrast ratio, and pumps out forty-five thousand lumens of brightness.

"Next oldest is the 1970 thirty-five-millimeter camera. Old Man Preston built the concession stand's second floor to make a projection booth for it. He ran the thirty-five mill until the place closed around the end of the twentieth century.

"But the oldest projector, the truly *original* one from 1955, is actually still here, too, down in the original projection house, but those were fire hazards at the best of times."

Benny led us to a small, sunken brick building like a World War II pillbox located right in the middle of the parking lot. He raised one of two small metal plates at the sunken building's front to show me the interior, where the 1955 projector, a hulking mechanical monstrosity taller than I was, sat back in the shadows like a titanic trapdoor spider waiting for curious prey to wander too close. The interior of the building was dark and tomb-like, some of it underground, with no windows other than the two portholes with metal plates at the front.

"Wow, cool," Stacey said, lifting the other plate to peer inside along with me.

"I mean, to be clear, I wasn't down here, I was up there." He pointed to the big window on the second floor of the concession stand. "Once I saw the digi projector was fine, I locked up the concession stand and pedaled like a maniac to the screen tower to check on Callie and Daisy. Usually, it's nice to be isolated out here, surrounded by farms and woods, miles from town… except when you're worried about an intruder prowling around the joint."

At the screen tower, Benny unlocked the metal fire door in the side. A recently mowed lawn, consisting mostly of clover and wildflowers, grew in the open space between the screen tower and the monument sign out by the highway, where a lone UPS truck rumbled past.

With the steep ramp for its rear wall, painted with that long-faded Coke logo, the screen tower resembled a three-story concrete lean-to, propping up the big screen against the hurricane-force storm winds that sometimes blew in from the ocean.

"Gumby was right inside," Benny continued as we entered the tower. "He was acting nervous, like he knew something was up, and that is not his normal personality. Usually, he's a real optimist."

We crossed a mud-room area where jackets were hung and dirty shoes stashed. Rollerblades, another bicycle, and a kid's scooter hung on nails on the wall, with camping gear stacked below that.

The bottom floor was arranged shotgun-style, one room opening into the next. Past the mud room lay a long, cluttered office wallpapered with years of faded movie posters and promotional fliers for the Nite-Lite Drive-In. A sizable desk was nearly lost under dusty paperwork. Cabinets and boxes everywhere held wires and lightbulbs and loose nails and screws and a heap of changeable letters for the marquee sign. Much of the clutter had been unceremoniously shoved against the side of the room where the steeply slanted ceiling met the floor.

"I know it's kinda hard to believe this is the 'after' picture of the office, but trust me, it was way worse before. Plus, we first had to clear out the second-floor apartment, which had, like, old-man clothes, old-man socks, all of the previous owner's personal stuff… yeah."

"Anyway, that night I came in here and checked on everything. Everybody was cool but the dog, but even he started to relax after a while."

"Have you had any similar disturbances since that?"

"No, but Callie thinks something weird is happening here, and I am with her on that. And you guys are supposed to be the local paranormal experts."

"We do specialize in these kinds of cases," I said.

"What do you think about this one?" He leaned against the edge of the desk, scattering yellowed paperwork but paying no mind as it spilled onto the floor. "Is this place haunted? Could it be?"

"I don't like to rush to conclusions. If you want to hire us, we'd set up observation equipment and stay on-site overnight, seeing what we can find."

"Sounds good to me, but Callie will want to know what it costs. She's always worried about that stuff. And granted, we both have student debt, too."

"That's reasonable." While we discussed it, I looked over the movie posters on the walls, including cheesy creature features like *The Blob* and *The Crawling Eye*.

The posters and fliers clustered in front of the desk mostly advertised vintage crime and spy movies. *The Nightingale Job. The Chicago Hustle. Murder in Morocco.* All seemed to feature the same guy in roughly the same fedora, with a mustache big enough to shame Yosemite Sam, a cigar smoldering at the corner of his mouth.

"This guy was a major Chance Chadwick fan, huh?" Stacey said, looking over the same pictures. "And Adaire Fontaine. Ooh, look. *A Soldier's Dame*. Ever seen it?"

"Nope. I'm not caught up on the latest films of…" I squinted to read the fine print. "1954."

"How can you not have seen *A Soldier's Dame*?" Benny seemed genuinely shocked, like I'd told him I hated rainbows and puppies.

"Seriously." Stacey looked similarly offended on behalf of weather phenomena and juvenile canines. "Adaire Fontaine almost won an Oscar for it."

"Who?" I looked at the poster for *A Soldier's Dame*. A woman in a nurse's uniform embraced a strapping, handsome soldier while he gazed past her into the distance. Rows of crosses behind them indicated a graveyard.

"Adaire Fontaine?" Stacey gaped.

"Famous movie star from Tifton, Georgia? Starred in a little epic called, I don't know, *Legend of the South*?"

"Okay, yeah. She's the one with the big red hair, right? And big gray eyes?"

"She only had the big red hair for that movie. But the eyes, yeah, that's what everyone thinks of."

"Great, glad you have so much background on this," I said, looking at the faded image of Adaire's large, captivating eyes as she agonized over her fallen soldier. "As old as this poster is, Stanley never pinned anything over it, not even slightly overlapping."

"It's the same with the Chance Chadwick posters." Stacey nodded at the detective-or-secret-agent posters. "Maybe these were his favorites."

"Maybe. Benny, we can come back anytime after you and Callie decide. We don't have an active case right now, but that could change." That was my best attempt at being salesy. Not one of my top skills.

"Yeah, sounds good," he said. He picked up a loose pair of tiny sneakers from the office floor and tossed them into the next room, which was brightly painted, its walls decorated with giraffes and bunnies. Toys, books, and craft supplies were crammed onto a kid-size tabletop. "Thanks for coming out. It was good to meet you. Real paranormal investigators, huh? I bct you guys have some wild stories."

"Most of them have to kept confidential," I said.

"Oh, yeah, sure, makes sense."

"The theater's totally great," Stacey told him. "I'm definitely spreading the word and coming back as a customer, regardless."

"Thanks. We're planning our grand opening in a couple of weeks, and it would be nice if the drive-in would stop running off guests before that." He led us out and locked the screen tower door behind us, then returned to the concession stand while we returned to our van.

Chapter Four

"I hope they call back," Stacey said as we exited the drive-in for the highway. "I really want to hang around there for a while, see the old place hopping with guests and popping with corn at night. Like when they have the grand opening."

We drove to our office, a fairly bleak cinderblock building where Calvin Eckhart, the founder of our tiny detective agency, had originally set up his shop and home. He spent most of his time in Florida these days, leaving me to manage the agency along with Stacey.

I parked the van in the ground level workshop that took up most of the floor. There was a shabby reception spot with an empty desk and chairs out front, but we kept that area locked if we weren't expecting anybody. Our clients came through recommendations or found us on the internet. Nobody just walked in through the front door out here in this rundown industrial area, with the dulcet sounds of the car crusher at work in the junkyard next door. It was probably best that clients rarely saw our offices, actually, or they'd probably think twice about hiring us.

"I'll just upload today's pictures." Stacey set her handheld camera down next to the server. "Want to grab a bite?"

"No, thanks. I'll head home in a minute." I dropped in front of a desktop, ready to add my notes into a client file in case they hired us. "No point spending too much time on this unless they hire us."

"It would be nice having a case that isn't wildly far out of town this time. See ya." Stacey gave me a hug where I sat in my chair, which she sometimes does at random times, and I returned it awkwardly, reaching back with one arm.

I watched her leave, then let out a breath when she was gone. I'm more of an introvert, and she's not, and sometimes that's a little much.

I hung around, typing up my notes to this case in detail, playing some Claude Debussey. I must have been in a plinking-piano mood.

Writing my notes led me into some preliminary research, looking up what I could find on the Nite-Lite Drive-In, and on the famous Golden Age actress Adaire Fontaine, since I was apparently a drooling barbarian for not knowing more about her. I'd surely heard of her, but I wasn't into classic movies like film-school graduate Stacey, or her bad-movie fanatic boyfriend Jacob. I had to catch up.

The building grew quieter in the evening, as the car crusher went into its nightly slumber and, I assumed, the junkyard boys punched out for the day.

It startled me when my phone rattled. Michael.

Got fresh blue crab, he said. *You should come over tonight. I'm cooking stew. And I make it very spicy.*

I smiled. *I don't know. I was hoping for a peanut butter*

sandwich and a quiet night at home.

You need to have a festive and loud night with me.

Sounds exhausting. The festive and loud part.

Quiet and unfestive, then. I can be completely boring. I'll start now.

Give me time to swing home. I'm still at the office.

I wrapped up my work and headed home to my studio loft in a long-defunct glass factory. Cramped but convenient, and cheaper than average due to the landlord's poor maintenance and overall crummy customer service.

My mostly black cat Bandit greeted me at the door, crying like he was starving.

"You poor little guy," I said as I entered the kitchen nook to find his bowl of food only one-third full. "How did you survive in these conditions?"

He meowed plaintively. I ripped open a bag of food and poured it into the storage column jutting up above the bowl. I used pet dishes that refilled as the cat ate and drank, but the feeder had run out.

The bowl refilled, and Bandit began snacking contentedly, dismissing me with a flick of his tail.

I could have gone as I was, in my professional black meeting-a-new-client suit, but we were having a night in, not out… a night involving stew that could seriously damage my good suit. I switched to jeans and a light t-shirt. Much more comfortable, much better for dealing with shrimp peels and crab shells. I unleashed my hair from my ponytail, watched it fall into an unflattering rumple, and tied it back again.

"Later, gator," I said to Bandit when I finally left. He was lying on the couch by then. He flicked the tip of his tail at me once again, perhaps in response.

At Michael's house, a three-story, nineteenth-century Queen Anne divided into apartments, I stepped up onto the big wraparound porch on the first floor. The unoccupied porch swing creaked, pushed by a gentle evening breeze. Or maybe a ghost was swinging there. The house had been haunted by a monstrous entity when I'd first visited it, and while I'd dealt with that problem, this was still Savannah. If a ghost had been passing on the sidewalk and decided to step up and sit for a spell, I wouldn't have been the least bit surprised.

I pressed the call button next to a side door trimmed in panes of colored glass. "Anchovy's Pizza."

"Right on time," Michael's voice replied, not that we'd set a time. The door buzzed to let me in.

I ascended the wide, dark stairs, rounded the second-floor landing, and continued up to the third.

When he opened the door, it reminded me of the first time I'd met him—right here, at his door. A particularly nasty ghost had been menacing Alicia Rogers, a client who lived in another apartment in the house, and I'd met Michael while canvassing the neighbors, seeing whether others in the building had witnessed paranormal activity.

Here he was again, tall and strapping in his plain white t-shirt and jeans, green eyes taking me in, a cocky smile on his lips. The smell of spicy broth bubbled out, along with some scratchy Delta blues album singing about the "heavy water" of the Mississippi. The whole scene was soothing and welcoming.

"Not many would dare make a crab boil in a white shirt with no apron. Bold move." I entered his place, a former attic full of irregular ceilings and little nooks, rugs on the hardwood floor, sea critters in a gurgling saltwater aquarium. The lighting was soft and inviting, because it was only candles.

"We're going to crack shells by candlelight?" I followed him into the brick nook of the kitchen, which smelled like sea salt and bay seasoning.

"It's more romantic," he informed me.

"Aw."

"Because you don't see as many crab guts."

"Maybe I'll just have a salad."

"There is no salad, only slaw." He stirred the gigantic steel pot on his stove. The crabs floated among ears of corn and fat chunks of Vidalia onion.

I leaned against the counter. Most of the room had been restored by Michael himself, over a few years, in exchange for lower rent. The cabinets and drawers had antique knobs and pulls that looked like they'd fallen out of a Gilded Age penthouse.

The walls and ceiling dipped and sloped here and there, following the house's irregular roofline. Michael's bedroom was dominated by a giant bay window. I glanced toward the closed door to his room, then at another closed door.

"Is Melissa home?" I asked, figuring it would be great to stray out onto some delicate ice, conversation-wise.

"Soccer practice," he said. "She might show up for dinner. Might not. I texted her. It's not like I cook all the time. We might have to invite Alicia and her kids to help eat all this."

"Melissa's okay, then?"

He shrugged. "She's a different person now. Quieter. More serious. It definitely changed her."

"I'm sorry."

"It wasn't your fault."

"Sure." We both knew it was, that my personal demon, the ghost of a murderous, long-dead plantation owner named Anton Clay, had taken her as part of a plan to renew himself, to make himself into something dangerously powerful, a true devil.

We'd stopped the malevolent spirit and sent him on his

way, but we'd all paid a personal price for it, one way or another.

"What's new with you? Any new fix-it projects?" I glanced at the closed door to his room again; his little workshop area was also in there.

"Just the big chess-piece one," he said.

"I thought that had moved permanently into the corner."

The tall, massive clock, made of dark walnut wood and carved to look like a castle, was currently my least favorite feature of his room, even with its faceless bishops and knights hidden away inside. Those chess-piece characters emerged on the hour, or at least they did when the clock functioned. It presently did not.

"Yeah, I'm looking for something else. Maybe a nice small cuckoo clock. Something simple."

"To restore your clock-repair confidence?"

"Exactly. The chess clock has blown that out of the water."

"Like I'm about to blow through your crabs," I said. "Are they ready yet?"

"Almost."

A door creaked open. Melissa entered, nine years younger than I was and about that many inches taller, at least at the moment in her soccer cleats.

"Oh, hey, Ellie's here." Melissa's tone was completely neutral. She advanced on Michael, trailing mud clots across the hardwood. "Is the food ready?"

"Cleats!" Michael shouted.

"Way to turn into Mom," she grumbled, backing up to the door.

"One of us had to," Michael said. "And Mom would tell you to change clothes before you get dirt on the kitchen chairs."

"Too bad." Melissa elbowed in front of him and dipped boiling stew into a bowl. Mud fell from her soccer practice uniform.

"How's school?" I asked her, attempting to be friendly, but I instantly cringed at the boring parental question that came out of my mouth. Was I really that old now?

"Fine. Just holding my breath until graduation."

"Looking forward to that?"

"New city, new state, new school, new people. My own life, finally." She cracked open a crab leg and slurped down the meat while looking me in the eye. "I wish I could leave tomorrow. What about you? Any exciting ghouls and ghosts invading people's brains?"

"Not lately," I said, hoping to avoid talk of the supernatural. I'd brought too much of that into her life.

"Ellie went to that old drive-in theater in Pembroke," Michael said, oblivious to my stance on the topic. "Was it haunted?"

"No idea yet." I ladled out crab, corn, and potatoes for myself.

"This stew has not been cleared for ladling, people," Michael said. "You haven't let it simmer. If it doesn't simmer, it doesn't thicken."

"What was the theater like?" Melissa asked me, surprising me with her interest.

"It has a lot of character, I guess. The previous owner seemed obsessed with certain Golden Age movie stars, so I've been reading up on those."

"Like who?" Melissa asked.

"One called Chance Chadwick. That was a stage name," I said.

"Obviously." Melissa sat at the kitchen table, watching me over her steaming soup.

"His real name was Carlos Gonzales." I took the seat

across from her, happy to try to bridge some of the dark gulf between us. "He made movies in the 40s and 50s. He had a pretty wild reputation. He was an amateur pilot and liked racing cars. That's how he died, actually, driving his Rolls-Royce too fast along Mulholland Drive and flying off the road into a canyon. There are graveyards of cars off that road."

"Oh, I've heard of him," Melissa said. "Who else?"

"Adaire Fontaine," I said.

"Your case involves her, too? Really?" Melissa drew closer.

"Well, no, I'm just saying the theater owner had a number of posters of her. I doubt she's directly involved. But everyone seems to know all about her, so I'm catching up—"

"You've seen *A Soldier's Dame*, though," Melissa said, a corn cob forgotten halfway to her mouth.

"No, but I'm sure Stacey has—"

"You have to see it. It was one of my mom's favorites. It's really sad. A total classic."

"Okay," I said. "I'll watch it sometime."

"Yeah, like *now*," she said. "How can you not have seen it? You cannot be part of this household without seeing it."

"Oh." I was surprised by her phrasing. Pleasantly.

"Grab your crabs and *come on*." Melissa headed for the living room.

"Stay off the furniture, Melissa," Michael said. "Your practice clothes are dirty."

"You can just steam clean it later, Mom." Melissa rolled her eyes and dropped onto their couch, shedding dirt.

I sat beside her, definitely not complaining about the dirt, glad for this sign of her drawing me into their family a little bit. We'd all lost our own. My parents died in the fire. Michael and Melissa's father abandoned them not long after

Melissa was born, and their mother had died of cancer a few years earlier.

Michael eventually gave up complaining and came to join us, his bowl piled with two crabs, which he'd arranged so that they gripped sausages and potatoes in their claws. They were freaky looking critters, but growing up by the ocean meant I was accustomed to eating creatures with claws and tentacles and eye stalks and shells.

Sandwiched between Michael and Melissa, I ate my stew and watched the 1954 movie. *A Soldier's Dame* was in black and white, and it really was a tearjerker, helped along by the orchestral accompaniment.

Essentially, it was the film promised by the poster, the story of young lovers during World War II. He became a soldier, she a nurse. He died in the war—or so she thought! She returned home and married. Only years later did she learn he had survived and eventually come home, too. But then he died in a coal mining accident, a true American tragedy.

The final scene had Adaire Fontaine's character brooding in the cemetery at her lost soldier's funeral, dark hair arranged in elaborate coils around her face, long black dress rippling in the wind, violins filling the air. She read the letter he'd written to her not long before his death. The camera zoomed closer and closer on her face as she brimmed with emotion at the soldier's voice-over.

"...*when I finally returned from the prisoner of war camp, I heard you'd married J. P. van Rockevelt. I went to pay you a visit, but then I seen you through the window of that big ol' mansion on the hill, surrounded by all them fine things. What could a no-good chump like me ever hope to offer you next to all that? I'm just a no-good bum without a penny in my pocket, a fella without future, a soldier without a war. That's why I never knocked on that door. I moved on. But I'll think about you every day 'til my last. I'll never love another woman as long as I live, and that's all right. It's enough for me to know you're happy and safe. That's why I fought in that war, after all."*

As the sad violins rose to a melodramatic crescendo, Adaire looked from the letter to the fresh grave of her long-lost boyfriend. She spoke to his headstone.

"Today, I may be Mrs. J. P. van Rockevelt, wife of the noted industrial magnate," she said, clutching the letter to her chest. *"But in my heart, I will always be… a soldier's dame."*

Melissa was sobbing next to me. "They missed out on everything," she whispered. Wiping her eyes, she looked at me and whispered, "They could have been so happy together. But she never even knew."

"It's okay." I put an arm around her, with as little awkwardness as I could manage.

Michael looked at us and shook his head. Having sat patiently through eighty-five minutes of lost love and heavily emoted tragedy, he clicked the remote, ending the schmaltzy sad music of the closing credits, and jumped to his TV's main menu. "I'm picking next," he said.

Chapter Five

I was in a good mood the next day. With no urgent need to go into the office, I could sleep late. I spent the afternoon straightening up my little apartment, my window and balcony door open to catch sunlight and fresh air from our city's lovely tree canopy. My cat tiptoed out onto the tiny afterthought of a balcony and watched bicycles and pedestrians below.

Benny finally called me from the drive-in.

"Yeah, we slept on it, and the paranormal investigation is a go," he told me. "We don't have a ton of room, budget-wise, but we can't live with this craziness. We're approaching it like one more renovation problem, like the plumbing or the electrical."

"Great, we'll be glad to help. What day would be most convenient for us to begin?"

"Literally ASAP," he said, pronouncing the acronym as one word. "With our grand opening coming up, we can't afford to delay."

I checked my phone. "The weather's on our side today. We could set up this evening, monitor things tonight."

"Okay, but the drive-in's open tonight. We'll be running from sunset to about midnight. Is that a problem? Should we shut it down?"

"No, just carry on as planned. Maybe your parking lot phantom will show up while we're there."

Afterward, I texted Stacey to let her know we'd be on duty that night.

Jacob wants to come ASAP, Stacey replied.

Does he pronounce ASAP as four letters or all as one word? I'm doing an informal survey.

I don't know, we're texting.

We aren't ready for the psychic yet, I sent back. *We have procedures.*

Grrr. OK but LMK when we can invite him. And then we have to bring the whole Bad Movie Club. Which you should join.

I see enough bad movies by accident, I replied. *I'm sure our clients will be happy to have us bring customers later, though.*

Can't wait, see you at the off.

The what?

The office. It's a new abbreviation I'm trying out. The off. Meaning the office. Cool huh?

No.

At the office workshop, we did a standard pre-job check of our gear and found no issues. We were ready to watch for ghosts.

Stacey and I drove separately to the theater, me in the van and she in her Escape.

At the drive-in, we parked in the first row. Benny bicycled over to meet us.

"We'll set up to listen, watch, and record here in the

parking lot, where people saw the apparition," I told him after I climbed out. "It would be nice to have a wider, more panoramic view of the place. Could we put a camera in the projection booth?"

"The projection booth's pretty cramped already." He cringed, probably at the idea of us hanging around his pricey new projector. "You could put something in the concession stand's arcade area. Just don't block foosball access. Or if you really want to get up high… well, that's probably not a good idea."

"I'm open to bad ideas," I assured him.

"She always is." Stacey nodded a little too enthusiastically.

"The old farmhouse," he said. "It has one of those rooftop walkways, with the railing, you know?"

"A widow's walk?" I asked.

"Right. Way back in the day, the drive-in owners could sit up on their roof and watch the big screen from home. That had to be a pretty sweet arrangement. There's a speaker pole up there for sound, too. This was 1955, so it was like having a large-screen TV decades before anyone else. Of course, they were probably too busy working the drive-in to really kick back and enjoy it too often."

"We should probably check out the farmhouse." I looked past the cheerful purple concession stand to the wide lawn behind it, stretching away toward the high, gnarly-looking wooden fence.

"Okay." Benny pedaled reluctantly in that direction while Stacey and I walked behind him. "But fair warning, it is rundown, and there is definitely no power in there, no light. I'm pretty sure any attempt to turn on the electricity would burn it down."

"We'd better go while there's still daylight, then."

He checked his phone. "I can't come with you. Callie's

leaving for work, so I have to watch Daisy. I'll open the gate first, though. It's hard to find if you don't know where to look." He biked on ahead.

The gate was indeed a nondescript chunk of the fence, with no visible handle on this side. It had to be pushed open by someone who knew the right spot. It reminded me of a jib door, a design usually found in extravagant homes with serving staffs. Such doors vanish completely among the wall paneling when closed.

Benny waited for us, having pushed open the gate, and looked glumly into the area beyond.

"Callie's got the garden beds going pretty well back here," he said. "Stuff grows fine, but she doesn't like it because of the farmhouse. I just told her to think of it like the world's biggest garden shed, but she doesn't like to go inside. She leaves her things here on the porch."

I stepped through the gate and into an area beyond it that felt a little dimmer, a little cooler.

Garden beds brimmed with vegetables and herbs, their spicy scent filling the air. A broken brick path twisted through them, from the gate to the decrepit ruins of the house.

"I can see why she doesn't really like it here," Stacey said, shaking her head at the overgrown building.

The farmhouse was indeed in poor shape, sagging and rotten, thick with vines and undergrowth. On the porch, shaded by thatches of ivy, a set of crumbling wooden shelves held new hand tools and a bag of potting soil.

A railing had been added on the top and sides of the front porch roof, which was slanted and clearly not originally intended for pedestrian use, creating the widow's walk area for film viewing. A speaker pole jutted up like a lightning rod, the rusty speaker still attached after all these years. Next to it lay the weathered, broken-down remains of a wooden bench.

"Have you been inside at all?" I asked Benny.

"Oh, yeah, and it's bad. Water damage. Rotten furniture. Vines growing through the windows."

"Are the floors intact enough to walk on?"

"They're creaky but solid. Kind of. I'd be careful in there. When you're done, you can swing by the concession stand. Popcorn's on at eight. The movie should start by nine, earlier if it gets cloudy."

He left through the gate, seeming to be in a hurry to get away.

"I can see why they're living in the screen tower," Stacey said. "This house is a total tear-down. You couldn't restore this."

"Nope. Nor would you want to, really." The house was large, but that was probably the only positive thing I could say about it. It had an unpleasant, cagey look, with so many of its windows shrouded by vines. "We'd better grab some cameras."

We made a round trip to the van, returning with utility belts and thick jackets and backpacks, like a team-up of Batwoman and Batgirl, sort of. We don't enter spooky old houses without high-powered flashlights and other basic defenses. These only run off the specters temporarily, so their usefulness is limited, even counterproductive when trying to observe and learn about the ghosts that are haunting a client.

The front porch didn't feel all that stable under my feet, and the porch roof sagged, making the railing on top of it uneven. While the drive-in had been kept up to some extent until the owner's death, it was clear nobody had lived in this house in many years.

A foul stench greeted us within the house. Plant life was indeed actively growing up the walls in the kitchen, having invaded through a broken window. Water-damaged paintings and framed posters advertising theatrical performances from decades earlier adorned the walls.

"Hey, this used to be pretty posh," Stacey said. "Too bad about the leaks."

"It's definitely not like any farmhouse I've seen."

The living room had been decked out in decadent Hollywood Regency fashion. A long, low, screamingly green couch heaped with the remnants of bright, brocaded cushions was flanked by immense faux-Grecian black and gold urns decorated with horses and bulls. Everything that wasn't marble or black lacquer was instead puffy, bright, thick with fringe and busy striped patterns. It was a weird, dreamlike environment.

We headed up the warped, wobbling stairs. For our safety, Stacey waited until I was at the top before she started up.

On the second floor, vines and tree limbs had grown in through broken windows. Several doors surrounded the rickety banister at the top of the stairs, where one could look over and easily imagine falling to the first floor.

The large bedroom at the front of the house was furnished in a similar fashion as downstairs, and again had been left in neglect for many years, with a leaky roof feeding mold and mildew.

My eyes danced dizzily over the extravagant decay. The black lacquer bedframe was virtually buried in a heap of golden tassels the size of horse's tails. Matching black lacquer mirrors trimmed in gold flake hung above the headboard. Water damage had wrecked the zigzagging bright green wallpaper. The fluffy zebra-striped rug hadn't fared well over the years, either, physically or stylistically.

In front of the enormous, gold-leaf-encrusted dresser mirror was an array of dried-up cosmetics, left open ages ago. A pink coffee mug full of black filth sat at one end of the dresser.

"I don't think the last person to live in this room moved out," I said. "It seems like they might have died here."

"Well, thanks for that eerie comment." Stacey took snapshots and electrical readings.

A row of framed family pictures stood atop a boxy white and black dresser with door pulls that looked like golden camels. I studied a wedding picture—the man was tall, his face pitted with little scars that were visible despite attempts at makeup. His smile was barely visible under his huge, swooping mustache. His gaze was strong; he wasn't particularly tall or large but exuded some intense energy. His wedding attire was a canary yellow fedora and suit, not the most traditional formalwear for a Southern wedding.

His bride's dress was an ivory lace column gown with golden Grecian designs and a high empire waist. Her elbow-length gloves were a sparkling gold, as were the feathers on her wide-brimmed hat. They certainly struck me as people who might have redecorated this simple, boxy farmhouse into what we saw around us. Clearly, the house's original structure was much older, dating to sometime in the 1800s.

In another picture, the former bride, now a few years older and in a midi dress with thick, colorful stripes, knelt with her arms around two elementary age children, a girl and a boy in their Sunday best. In this case, that was a teal suit with a cravat for the grumpy-looking boy and a colorful, copiously poofballed dress and big glittering bows for the girl.

The husband stood stiffly off to one side, sticking with his 1950s-style fedora and suit instead of embracing quirky 60s fashion like his wife. This picture's fedora-suit combo was gray plaid instead of canary yellow. He still sported the giant mustache that covered much of his face.

The oldest photograph that I found showed a stern-looking older man and woman of an earlier generation, dressed in much more conservative church wear, the woman in a long dress and pearls, leaning on a cane, though she wasn't elderly in the picture.

A woman's clothes hung in the closet. Poking around, I found a couple of bright dancing dresses far in the back, but most of that wardrobe had given way to more practical items over the years, looser things made of flannel with more flexible waistbands, and more comfortable shoes without narrow spikes for heels. I got the sense that the party-girl bride had grown old here in this house, in this room, among these echoes of her earlier life. But where were the possessions of her overly mustached husband?

"Hey, look at this weird door." Stacey drew back immense window curtains that looked like they'd been purloined from an actual theater, thick and crimson red with miles of golden fringe, so long they puddled on the rotten carpet. Stacey grimaced as she knotted the slimy golden ropes of the curtain ties, then wiped her hands on her jeans.

There had once been a dormer window here, looking out over the front porch, but it had been replaced by a narrow glass door. The glass was shattered, the door ajar, the thick shag carpet all around it blackened from years of rain and decay.

Carpet squished under my boots as I stepped over. I eased open the door and slipped out onto the sloped roof, emerging in the area marked off by the railing. Loose shingles slipped under my feet. If I lost my balance, I could easily crash through the crooked railing and land in the front yard, on the weedy ground if I was lucky, the brick walkway if I wasn't.

The remnants of the bench where Stan Preston had watched movies from home slumped next to the speaker pole.

"This thing's long dead, obviously." Stacey gently lifted the speaker from its latch. A cable trailed from the back of the speaker and down inside the pole. "You'd hang this on your car window. Normally, I mean. They probably didn't park their car on the roof. This was just the type of speaker they had handy."

"This isn't a bad vantage for our cameras. A little overgrown." I could see over the fence and across the lawn to the buildings and parking lot, a pretty solid manager's-eye view of the drive-in, partly obscured by tree branches around the house.

"The movie on the big screen could blind the night vision camera."

"Set up a conventional camera, too. Put them both on timers so they click over to night vision at midnight, after the movie ends." I looked at the rust-splotched speaker, which Stacey had replaced on the pole. "Maybe a microphone, too. Just for fun."

"Aye aye, sarge." Stacey got to work, setting up tripods and battery packs inside the broken glass door of the dormer, so they'd be somewhat protected against the weather.

I nosed around the upper floor. There were three additional bedrooms, none particularly large.

Two were stripped down, lacking much furniture or decoration beyond the tiger-striped walls in one and jazzy geometric wallpaper in the other. I found an antique model airplane parked on the upper shelf of the closet in the striped room, and a long-abandoned dollhouse and mildewed stuffed animals in the wallpapered room.

At the back of the house, the largest bedroom was cool and dark even during the day, its windows overgrown with vines that filled it with the smell of earth and vegetation. A trace of cloying, flowery perfume hung in the air, as though it had become ingrained in the woodwork over many years. A strong, unexpected scent could also be an olfactory manifestation of something paranormal—often they were pretty gross, like the smell of decay, so even a sickly-sweet perfume was a better odor than most.

There wasn't a touch of lacquer, gilt, or bright zigzags in this room. The dresser and nightstand were thick, heavy wood. Everything looked handmade to me, possibly original to the house. This older, plainer furniture had survived the ravages of time and abandonment far better than the floofy stuff in the other bedroom and downstairs.

A dusty, unadorned walking cane reminiscent of a shepherd's crook hung on the closet doorknob. A number of overlapping small circles, about the size of the round base of the cane, were stamped into the hardwood floor by the bare iron bedframe, near yet another leaking window.

"Done!" Stacey popped into the doorway, beaming. "Ooh, looks like you found the house's gloom room. Wanna bet somebody died in here, too? Like that first room? How do you like when *I* say it, Ellie?"

"It's possible," I said. "My sense is the kids grew up and moved out. These both look like women's bedrooms. Who exactly lived here last?"

"I don't know. All I know is Stanley lived his final years in the screen tower apartment."

"We're going to need more location history. Hopefully, his daughter will feel like talking."

"It's getting dark. You feel like maybe leaving the creepy old house now?"

"You really don't like it here, do you?" I looked at some

yellowed pictures on the wall, depicting this area as a working farm, with a chicken house and goat pen and rows of crops, those features long gone now. The earlier generation of farm family had no time for fancy hats with golden feathers. The father wore a straw hat and overalls, the mother a starchy-looking calico dress, the children patchwork clothing. The faces of the past had been left here in this abandoned place, to be remembered by the shadows and the wind blowing through cracks and holes in the walls. I wondered how many had lived here over the years, and how many had died.

I snapped pictures with my phone before we left.

Outside, the garden was gloomy as the sun crawled down out of the sky.

Chapter Six

We set up some cameras on the wooden stage Benny and his band had built under the screen. They looked out at the parking lot and the buildings beyond, giving us a reverse angle from the cameras back at the farmhouse. If anyone snuck up on us while we watched tonight's movie, hopefully we'd catch them coming or going.

By the time our gear was ready and recording, the sun was down. We caught up with Benny in the Purple Pizza Eater concession stand.

"Ready for the show?" Benny stepped up behind the counter. Popcorn burst deliciously in the popcorn machine. "Callie left a few pizzas prepped in the fridge. You guys want me to bake one?"

"That sounds really great, but we probably shouldn't eat pizza every day, no matter how good it is."

"Speak for yourself," Stacey said. "I'm getting some popcorn, too."

While Stacey waited for the popcorn, I wandered into the game room with its lone game, a foosball table that wasn't even configured to take money from customers.

"Isn't that Adaire Fontaine again?" I asked Stacey, pointing at the *Pocketful of Aces* poster. An alluring woman in a black chiffon gown and wide-brimmed, feather-adorned black hat clung to Chance Chadwick. Chadwick, clad in dark pinstriped suit and fedora, fanned five aces in one hand. The fifth ace had a five-pointed star as its symbol, since the four real suits were already taken.

Stacey glanced at the poster. "Oh, yep."

"I watched *A Soldier's Dame* with Michael last night," I said.

"Really? That's awesome. Did it bring out his soft and sensitive side?"

"It brought out his sister's."

"Yeah? She's okay since the whole…" Stacey trailed off, making vague gestures with both hands. We both knew she meant Melissa's possession by the diabolical spirit Anton Clay.

"I don't know, but she's getting along okay. Eager to dive into her future and leave the past behind."

"That's probably for the best. We all have our ghosts from the past." She stretched and looked at the foosball table. "You any good?"

"At foosball? I've played it before."

"That's not what I asked."

"I'm probably not that good."

"I bet I can whip you at it."

"Well, I concede the point."

"Oh, you think you can take me? Come on." Stacey picked up the rubber ball and held it over the little chute. "Loser buys at the concession stand. Ready?"

"Yeah. Fine." I took control of two rods, and Stacey

dropped the ball into play. She started whacking the ball easily past my little characters, expertly shifting hers back and forth until they smacked the ball into my goal, right past my ineffective attempts to block. I managed to make the goalie turn a flip, but not at a useful place or time.

"Boom! Point!" Stacey held up both hands as though calling a touchdown.

"I noticed." I tried to play a little more seriously, as I grew to understand that my lack of foosball experience would in no way dissuade her from razzing me if she beat me.

"Hey, ghostbusters, I'll leave the popcorn out for you." Benny appeared at the door with an iPad in his hand, displaying a security-cam view from the front of the theater. "There's an actual customer at the ticket booth for some reason, so I'll zip over there and collect admission."

"Thanks. We'll be done here as soon as I totally own Ellie," Stacey said.

While she spoke, I saw my opportunity and gave the little ball a hard kick with one of my guys, zinging it down the unprotected gullet of Stacey's goal. My characters flipped around and around with the force of the blow, as if cheering the point they'd scored.

"Hey, no spinning," Stacey said. "That doesn't count."

"You can't just make up rules mid-game."

"Everyone knows about the no-spinning rule."

"I didn't."

"You should have."

Stacey beat me by six points out of ten. Though I would argue it was only five.

By then, Benny was back from the ticket booth, and Stacey added a strawberry jalapeno cola to her order. And popcorn. And a slice of pizza. All on my tab. She was taking me to the cleaners.

"Enjoy the show." Benny tapped his tablet; he could monitor the ticket booth camera and control the theater projector from it. "Tune your car radio to 89.3 FM. If you forget the channel, just check one of the ten signs that mention it. Here we go… this evening's cartoon begins in three… two…"

"We're missing it!" Stacey said.

We hurried outside, laden with snack foods and related beverages. A van holding a family with two parents and four kids had parked in the third row, not far from the sunken brick structure of the primitive projection house of yesteryear. That low, tomb-like building lay dark and lifeless as the movie was projected from the second-floor window of the concession stand far away.

We clambered inside our van on the front row.

"Oh, my gosh! *Powerpuff Girls*? Good choice." Stacey settled into her seat, arranging her popcorn and drink.

I tuned the van's radio, and the evening's cartoon played over our speakers. Blossom, Bubbles, and Buttercup found themselves in a maze-like jungle temple. The episode seemed like a good set-up for the eventual feature, *Labyrinth*.

After the cartoon was a clip from a Muppet movie I'd somehow never heard of before, *Billy Bunny's Animal Songs*. Words on the screen guided the audience in singing along with a group of musical frogs and Billy Bunny himself as he made his way through a treacherous, puppet-infested swamp.

I wondered if the kids in the van were singing along with the Muppets.

Stacey certainly was.

When that was over, we got a literal song and dance from animated drinks and popcorn boxes reminding us to visit the concession stand. The cartoon probably dated back to the 1950s.

A second cartoon, with more of a 1970s feel, featured a flying-saucer pizza, its pepperoni glowing like red portholes, zapping grumpy cartoon kids with a red pizza ray that placed slices in their hands and turned their frowns upside down.

Something moved in my sideview mirror. The other van opened, and a dad herded four kids to the Purple Pizza Eater. They returned with purple-striped cups, pizza slices, and a giant tub of popcorn.

"Here we go," Stacey whispered as the feature began.

My memories of *Labyrinth* were vague and distant, so I quickly got sucked into the tale of the stolen child and his sister who had to seek him out in the goblin realm. Also, David Bowie.

As Sarah, the teenage girl in search of her kidnapped baby brother, descended into the well of hundreds of hands that formed into unsettling faces when they wanted to speak, a bright light flared in my sideview, jarring me out of my popcorn-and-movie-induced trance.

The family van behind us had activated its headlights and started its engine, even though the movie wasn't over. Maybe the parents had gotten fed up after the puppet sing-along. Or maybe…

Stacey and I hopped out, recognizing the parallel to other situations where theater customers had run off during the feature.

We approached cautiously, leaving the first ring of cars for the second. The van tore out of its parking spot on the third ring, tires squealing and leaving tracks on the pavement.

The front passenger window lowered, and a lady yelled at us in Spanish, gesticulating wildly. Unfortunately, I had no idea what she meant. The four kids screamed inside the van.

The dad laid on the gas and they hauled away, fishtailing down the exit drive for the highway.

"Another satisfied customer," Stacey said, watching their taillights fade through a haze of tire smoke.

Benny raced out from the purple pizzeria to join us. "What happened? Why'd they leave?"

"We're not sure." I stepped into the spot where they'd parked. "Does anybody smell cigar smoke?"

"Kind of hard to tell through the car exhaust and burned rubber." Stacey waved her hand in front of her face.

"Yeah, true." I recalled how Benny had described it as the smell of their business failing.

The runaway customers had parked next to the sunken, tomb-like old projector house. I knelt in front of the two hinged metal plates, lifted one, and peered down into the projector porthole. It was like looking into a basement window, or maybe a sewer drain where a killer clown might pop up and offer balloons.

Nothing clawed my face off, or tried to lure me with a free balloon, but the smell of cigar smoke oozed out from down there.

Clicking on my light, I saw the hulking antique fire hazard of the 1955 projector, the shelves full of film spools and assorted junk, and that was it. Nobody was in there.

"It must have been a job back in the day," Benny said. "The carbon arc burned hot, about six thousand degrees. You had to keep it burning and keep the coolant system watered, too, in between constantly swapping out reels. The carbon burned down after twenty minutes. That's why the reels were twenty minutes long."

"Are you sure nobody's been down here recently?" I asked.

"Nobody but me, and only at our first walk-through. It's a sad spot to me because everything's rusted or rotten down there. Forgotten stuff. It's locked, but I have the key if you want to go in."

"I'll take it."

He sighed as he handed over the key, looking down the exit drive where the customers had gone. "This cannot keep happening. Did you catch anything on camera?"

"We'll be checking that soon," I said. "In the meantime, just keep the movie rolling. Maybe the apparition will come for us next."

"I'm having a great time, by the way," Stacey said. "Great selection of shorts for the lead-up."

"Oh, thanks!" Benny scratched at his beard. "Yeah, I thought the Muppet sing-along would be a fun group activity. That's what the drive-in's all about, the social side of movie watching."

"Stacey certainly enjoyed it," I said. "Let's go back. I want to see how the movie ends."

We returned to the van in time to see the final showdown, the inept goblins' wacky attempts at war.

I kept glancing outside. Our windows were open so we'd catch any whiff of cigar smoke. We waited for the entity to come for us next.

Unfortunately, it did not make an encore appearance, at least not by the time the movie ended and the screen went dark.

"Hey, guy, come haunt us!" Stacey shouted into the empty, darkened parking lot. "Are we not worth haunting or what?"

Her shouts, not surprisingly, didn't help.

"Let's check the footage," I told her. "Maybe we caught a visual of whatever chased that family away."

We clambered into the back of the van. Stacey pulled

up the video recording from the moment before the van had fired up and roared away.

"Here it is!" Stacey said, momentarily triumphant, but then frowned. "There's not much, though."

She turned her tablet toward me. Our van was in the foreground, the shapes of ourselves visible inside.

Farther back sat the family van, the shapes and faces less identifiable behind their more distant windshield.

"Here it comes," Stacey whispered.

A shadowy form appeared several paces away from the van. It approached, moving with a jerkiness, blinking in and out of sight.

It appeared at each of the van's windows, as though it wanted to look in at every individual person inside the van.

The van's headlights flared, blinding our night vision.

"Can you grab the subsequent moments—"

"From the conventional? Yes, obviously." Stacey went to work. I waited impatiently, looking among the live feeds on the little monitors mounted in the back of our cargo van, our handy mobile nerve center for paranormal investigations. "Yep. Here we go. Again, not much, but…"

The regular camera showed the family van starting up and peeling out. On the video, Stacey and I climbed out of the van. The lady in the passenger seat shouted at me in Spanish as they drove away. Trying to warn me, maybe.

"There's nothing there after they drive away," Stacey said. "But we know that, because we were there."

"Reverse it to the exact moment the headlights come on," I said. When she did, I pointed at the area where we'd seen the shape on camera. "Enhance."

"Enhancing." Stacey zoomed in close to the driver's side of the van. She cropped the glowing headlight out of the frame and monkeyed around with the light levels a bit.

"There it is," I whispered.

"You're right," she whispered back. "It's barely there, but… it's there."

What we saw in that frame, in the first flare of the van's headlight, was even less substantial than the shadow on the night vision camera. It looked like a few filmy brown blobs, barely suggesting the shape of a person next to the van.

"Re-enhance," I said.

"Ooh, so technical." Stacey zoomed on the face. It was too blurry to have any clear features, even with Stacey's enhancements, but we could discern a rough blob of a head.

"It's like it's looking back at us," Stacey whispered, shivering. "I wonder what that family saw when it walked up to them—"

Something pounded on the side of our van, making us jump. I nearly screamed, honestly, after staring closely at the dead thing we'd caught on camera, trying to make out its face, its eyes.

Footsteps sounded outside.

I grabbed my tactical flashlight and slipped up to the driver's area. A hand knocked on the window.

"Hello? Ya there?" Benny looked into the van, straddling his bike, which had enabled him to approach us swiftly and silently.

Relaxing, I opened the door. I wanted to complain about him startling us, but being a jumpy scaredy-cat is not a good look for a paranormal investigator. "Hiya," I said, swinging for casual and calm.

"I'm closing down for the night. Callie should be home soon."

"Where's Daisy?" I asked.

"Zonked out." Benny pulled a video monitor the size of a cell phone from his pocket, with a night vision view of the little girl asleep. "I can keep an eye on her from anywhere around the theater. There's an intercom so I can talk to her if she wakes up." He touched a button to show me, but lightly and carefully, as if it were a detonator on a bomb.

"Well, we caught something. Want to see it?" I asked.

"Definitely, yeah."

We climbed out, and Stacey showed the video of the filmy shape approaching the vehicle. After a quarter of a second, the shape disappeared like a soap bubble, or like a brittle filmstrip breaking on the projector.

"That... is freaky," he said, looking at the still frame of the blurry shape. "I knew it. There's something wild happening at the drive-in."

"It came from the direction of the original projection booth, where we smelled the cigar." I nodded at the sunken brick pillbox structure. "That could be Cigar Man's lair."

"Seems like a natural ghost habitat," Stacey said. "Silent and untouched for years, full of memories. Partly underground, even."

"In the olden days, that booth would have been a real center of action," Benny said. He lifted one of the metal plates at the front, revealing a dark porthole. "Those early projectors needed constant attention. You had to watch the movies for that changeover signal. And they were a fire hazard. Around 1970, Old Man Preston left this one to rot and installed a more modern thirty-five-millimeter projector up in the concession stand."

"Looks like we'll need to put some eyes and ears down there," I said.

"I left the concession stand unlocked for the night, so you guys can access the drinks cooler, you know, the facilities. Just make yourself at home. There's a bag of leftover popcorn, too."

"Thanks so much," I told him. "Go get plenty of rest.

We'll keep watch."

He smiled and touched the brim of his hat before pedaling off behind the screen tower.

"Wow, it sure gets dark out here at night." Stacey turned slowly. Beyond the puddle of light from her tablet, we couldn't see much. With the projector shut down, the concession stand dark, and all the lights off, the place was a silent ghost town.

I looked over at the sunken projection booth on the third row, abandoned for decades. In the gloom of night, it looked remarkably like a crypt. Its small, square door was impossibly short. Anyone bigger than a child would have to sit down and slide inside, as if wriggling down into a sewer drain under a sidewalk, perhaps to meet that killer clown.

"Maybe we should wait until daylight to go in there," Stacey whispered.

"Maybe." I slid the key into the lock of the little Hobbit door. It swung inward, into a pitch-black space.

I knelt at the edge of the doorway and pointed my flashlight inside.

The interior was larger than the pillbox structure above and went down several feet. It had a cold, dank cellar feeling. A brick floor was barely visible under a layer of sandy mud.

Two bulky projector support pedestals sat at the far end, bolted to the floor, one for each of the building's front portholes facing the movie screen. One pedestal held only remnants of the machine that had once been there, but the other still had the hulking antique projector I'd glimpsed from outside.

"I don't smell the cigar anymore," I said. "And that's not a smell that generally disappears in a hurry from a closed environment."

"Olfactory manifestation, maybe?" Stacey asked, and I

nodded.

Searching the shelves with my flashlight turned up small hand tools, a film splicer, and scraps of damaged film. Electrical wires hung loose from the ceiling; I hoped they weren't attached to anything live.

"Yep, let's wait until daylight," I decided, then pulled the door shut and locked it. Standing to brush dirt off my jeans, I said, "I guess we just head back to the van, continue the night in stakeout fashion—"

"Ellie." Stacey's voice was low and hushed. She pointed.

Someone stood on the stage under the screen, watching us from behind our cameras, as though he were a director and we were actors performing for him.

"Is that Benny?" I asked, even as I realized it wasn't. Benny didn't inspire this kind of dread.

A spot of light glowed in the darkness, illuminating the figure's face.

It was all in black and white, the small light glowing from the tip of a cigar.

The spot-lit face was dashingly handsome, despite the huge old-fashioned mustache that covered much of it. He wore a pinstriped coat and fedora, like in the *Pocketful of Aces* poster.

"It's Chance Chadwick," Stacey whispered.

When the cigar went dark, the figure vanished into the deep shadows of the stage and screen.

Chapter Seven

"Why would Chance Chadwick haunt this old drive-in?" Stacey wondered as we ran toward the stage. "He died in a car crash out west, thousands of miles from here."

"Good question." I jumped up onto the stage, swinging my light around. Nobody was there. The cameras hadn't been damaged, which is always a plus. I thought of how Benny had immediately worried about damage to his projector, and I sympathized.

The apparition had stayed behind our cameras, out of view, like it was quite familiar with life around cameras and didn't want to be caught on one.

"Maybe the owner guy, Stan, played a bunch of his movies here?" Stacey walked around the stage, as if looking for clues. Footprints or ghostly cigar ends, maybe. "It doesn't make sense. Ooh, maybe they built the drive-in on top of a forgotten cemetery. Or some eighteenth-century witch put a hex on it. Or a werewolf was killed here by a vampire during a zombie outbreak—"

"Let's just hope Stanley Preston's daughter feels like talking about the past."

We waited out the night in the van, hoping the ghostly movies our clients had described would appear on the screen. A pair of headlights appeared—Callie's small, elderly Honda, trundling up the entrance drive. She parked by the screen tower and trudged out, looking exhausted from a late night at the restaurant, barely casting a look our way before walking out of sight around the side of the tower.

"She looks wiped out," Stacey said.

We continued to sit and wait, watching the blank screen, but nothing appeared up there except moonlight.

Stacey pulled up footage from the camera in the farmhouse, hoping its overview perspective had caught Chance Chadwick's appearance on the stage, but the distant camera had failed to do that.

We replayed what the woman had yelled at us in Spanish. Neither of us were fluent enough to catch much of it, especially shouting at us from a passing vehicle.

After a few listens, we agreed the main phrase she used was *los muertos*, which she repeated twice.

The dead.

The sky finally began to lighten, from black to deep blue, and the sprawling space of the drive-in started to grow visible again. That was our cue to head home. We collected the cameras from the stage but left those in the farmhouse where they were. Timers shut them down at sunrise.

Back home, I drew the blackout curtains tight against the morning sunlight. My cat meowed repeatedly for no real reason while I tried to sleep, as cats do.

I awoke at noon, made coffee, and sat in a square of

sunlight on my bed to continue my Chance Chadwick research. It was nice to work from home, sitting on my bed in my pajamas.

Carlos Gonzales, known to his many fans as Chance Chadwick, had grown up in eastern Los Angeles, close to the burgeoning movie industry. After a stint in the Navy during World War II, he'd returned home and pursued acting.

He'd been a minor Hollywood heartthrob of his era, known for his dark eyes, his handsome face and cocky smile, his cold-steel attitude in assorted crime and caper movies, where he typically had time to romance a leading lady in between his plots and schemes, or as part of them.

His death in 1957 had been a shock but cemented his place as a Hollywood legend. The untamable, devil-may-care rebel, racing his Rolls-Royce into a canyon, the fire burning for hours before they put it out and pulled him from the wreckage.

An interesting life story, maybe, but one with zero obvious connection to a random drive-in theater outside Savannah, Georgia.

I texted Stacey to meet me at the lovely Bull Street Library, one of my personal favorite places in town.

On my way there, I stopped at another favorite spot, the Sentient Bean, to treat myself to a stronger, darker, and perhaps more flavored coffee than I had at home. The interior was as welcoming as ever, cheerfully bright walls and a soaring woodwork ceiling, the smell of brewing coffee and baking sweets.

As I waited in line, someone tapped my shoulder, startling me. I turned, preparing to drop into a kickboxing stance in case I had to defend myself there among the pastries and college kids.

"Hey." Stacey gave me a big wave as if spotting me

across a huge distance, though she was in line right behind me. "Guess we had the same idea. Since you're here, am I officially at work now? Or still off the clock?"

"Why? Do you want to complain about work?"

"I have this one co-worker who drives me crazy. She's always sending me down in spidery cellars or up into haunted attics full of creepy artifacts."

"She sounds like a monster."

"She is. She drinks her coffee solid black. And not just when she's camping."

"I heard she hates camping," I said.

"I bet I could change her attitude with a weekend in the woods."

"I bet not," I told her, as the customer in front of me, who'd had way too many questions about the difference between a latte and a frappe, finally moved off so I could step up and order. I'd been toying with getting something sweet, maybe even a mocha, but I went with solid black dark coffee instead, lest I ruin my tough-guy image in Stacey's eyes.

We bought our coffees, filling our respective portable coffee tumblers. Stacey's was a high-end REI model that could probably keep molten chocolate bubbling hot in Antarctica. Mine was from a local gas station chain whose logo had already worn off in the dishwasher.

We headed outside and strolled toward the library.

"I started reading a biography of Adaire Fontaine last night," Stacey said. "Downloaded an ebook. She was considered a wild talent in her day, a dangerously free spirit. No wonder she dated Chance Chadwick. And they both had the tragedy of dying young, in their prime."

"Wait, how did Adaire die?"

"You don't know?"

"Yeah, we've established I would not win any prizes at

Golden Age Hollywood trivia night. So spill it, Film School."

"She was murdered. Strangled to death in her Beverly Hills mansion."

"By who?"

"Some people suspected her director at the time. Antonio Mazzanti. He was rumored to be romantically involved with Adaire on the side. Of course, everyone was rumored to be romantically involved with her. He was directing her in *House of Gold*, a movie set in the Italian Renaissance. She stormed off the set, quitting in a rage, and it was never clear whether her reasons were personal or professional."

"Wow." I sipped coffee as I processed this. "I must have heard of Mazzanti before. Sounds familiar."

"Uh, yeah. Mazzanti was later identified as the Silk Strangler. He murdered two other actresses after Adaire, strangling them with silk scarves. That was years after Adaire Fontaine's murder, but one of the actresses had also starred in one of his later, much less successful movies, a cheesy horror flick called *The Body in the Basement*. That's two actresses who starred in his movies, both strangled to death."

"Yikes. He was arrested for those?"

"No, because he was dead of a heroin overdose by the time the police eventually figured out he was the Silk Strangler. Oh, there was evidence of occult ritual aspect to the murders, too, which made Mazzanti even more of a suspect, because he used a lot of occult and Satanic references in his movies. Maybe they were all ritually sacrificed."

"That's awful!" I thought it over. "What about Chance Chadwick's car crash? Anything suspicious about that? Bear in mind I'm accepting gossip, innuendo, and conspiracy theories at this point. We can analyze and fact check later."

"I'll check. I can't believe you didn't know about Adaire
—"

"Yes, no one can believe how little I know about Adaire
Fontaine. I don't suppose this biography mentions any
connection to our drive-in theater."

"Not so far, but Adaire's earliest stage roles were in
Savannah and Atlanta, before she moved on to New York
and Hollywood."

"Keep reading. Maybe she knew somebody from the
Preston family who owned the drive-in. Speaking of which,
I still need to get in touch with his kids. That'll be my first
job. Yours is to find every *Savannah Morning News* article
about the Nite-Lite Drive-In, back to its opening in 1955."

Stacey frowned, but only a little. She doesn't love
research, but at least she'd be reading about a theater.

We reached the imposing Bull Street Library, designed
like a temple of the ancient Greek world—like the Library
of Alexandria, I like to imagine, probably inaccurately—
and headed inside.

Our clients had provided contact information for Leah
Williams Banford, Stanley Preston's now-elderly daughter
from whom Benny and Callie had purchased the theater. I
called her first and left a voice message. I noticed Preston
wasn't part of her name; maybe she was a stepchild, or
maybe she'd dropped it.

While Stacey fished through microfiche and microfilm
for news stories, I opened my laptop at a table next to a
floor-to-ceiling window looking out onto oaks dripping
with Spanish moss. I accessed my data-fusion service,
available to law enforcement, licensed private investigators,
and other restricted groups, so I could dredge up records
from recent years.

Stanley Preston, the drive-in's creator, had died five

years earlier, and the drive-in was his last known address. His family members included wife Nancy Jackson Williams Preston, deceased twenty years before him, and stepchildren Leah, who I'd attempted to contact, and Zebadiah, deceased. Leah appeared to be the only living relation to the original theater owner.

Stacey brought over a sheaf of warm printouts showing images of old newspapers. "There's a lot," she said. "And I haven't even dug into the *Pembroke Journal* yet."

I flipped through years of advertisements for the Nite-Lite Drive-In. Cowboy and war movies gave way over time to cheeseball films about teenagers from outer space and Annette Funicello beach parties. These in turn gave way to rough-looking biker movies, oddball psychedelic stuff, and lurid horror movies. A couple of these, like *Sacrifice of Souls* and *The Body in the Basement*, were by Antonio Mazzanti, the director-turned-serial killer suspected in Adaire Fontaine's death.

The theater's newspaper advertisements decreased in size over the years. Full-page splashes in the 1950s featuring happy families in convertibles shrank down to postage-stamp remnants by the 1990s, barely large enough to list that week's double feature in the newspaper's smallest font. There were no more ads nor any mention of the drive-in after 1999.

"The rise and fall," I said. "Do you think Benny and Callie's plan to revive the theater could actually work?"

"Who knows?" Stacey said. "It's super risky, but it has a better chance if ghosts aren't actively chasing away the guests. That's great for spooky season in October, but there's eleven other months to think about. Any chance I can get back to researching the murdered movie star?"

"You think you can solve the murder of Adaire Fontaine?" I asked. We were keeping our voices low, but a couple of elderly librarians were within earshot, and they both looked over with interest at the late motive star's name.

"If I can solve it, it'll surely happen by being the hundred thousandth person to read this book about her," Stacey said.

"I realize you're just trying to get out of the old-newspaper job," I said. "But okay. I'll look over these."

While Stacey dug into her Adaire Fontaine biography, I found my way to a lengthy article about the drive-in's original grand opening in 1955. It had been a two-page feature, with plenty of pictures, headlined SAVANNAH'S LATEST AND GREATEST NEW ATTRACTION. The theater's large ads in the papers had likely encouraged the gushing positive coverage.

> "The drive-in is unarguably the way of the future," explained Stanley Preston, enterprising owner of the majestic new theater on the highway between Savannah and Pembroke, in a location convenient to all. "Soon the indoor film theater will be a bygone relic. Americans love to spend their leisure hours in the familiar comfort of their own automobiles, free to chat and to smoke without disrupting other theater-goers. The drive-in is the nearest thing to hanging a movie screen in one's own home. While the adults relax without a care, children can run off and play on the picnic lawn, and teen-agers may enjoy social visits with school chums."

"It'll be fun while it lasts, Stan," I murmured under my breath.

A photograph showed Stan and family outside the monument sign with its giant arrow, its marquee advertising a Chance Chadwick film, *The Chicago Hustle*, along with *Abbot and Costello Meet the Mummy*.

I'd seen the family before, in pictures in the farmhouse.

Stan Preston, the drive-in's creator and our suspected cigar-smoking ghost, once again wore a suit and fedora, with a mustache that covered much of his pockmarked lower face. His wife Nancy stood by him in a flashy red dress, her hair elaborately curled, smiling for the press. The two elementary-age stepchildren were also finely dressed, looking scared and overwhelmed.

More photographs showed the drive-in packed with rows of cars. Kids ran wild on the lawn. A family ate fried chicken and hot dogs at a picnic table by the concession stand. It certainly looked like the popular and wholesome place to be, at least if you didn't think too much about what goes into making hot dogs.

In contrast to the newspaper's huge splash about the drive-in's grand opening, its shuttering decades later barely rated a back page mention, a single paragraph wedged into a slot between a plumber's advertisement and a mattress sale, with the unceremonious headline OLD DRIVE-IN CLOSES.

The Nite-Lite Drive-in, a remnant of the 1950s, has screened its last show. "People just stopped coming," said the owner, Stan Preston, calling it quits after decades of declining attendance. "I guess I ought to retire, anyhow."

That was all.

Preston had died years later, in his nineties. His obituary was short, as if there had been nobody left to say anything about him. He'd been survived by a lone stepdaughter, as we knew.

Before that, Stanley's stepson Zebadiah Williams had died, age sixty-one, out in Louisiana. Prior to that, Stanley's wife Nancy had died in her early seventies, preceding her husband by a couple of decades. I wasn't clear about her cause of death.

Stanley had run the theater from its creation down to the bitter end, when he was living there alone.

My phone rang—Leah, the stepdaughter, calling me back. I hurried out of the library as I answered, drawing a scowl from a balding man with thick glasses reading *The Economist*, who clearly didn't care for me talking on the phone in the library.

"I understand you called me about the Nite-Lite," Leah told me. Her voice was gravelly and faint. "But I sold it. I can't tell you anything new about it."

"I'm researching the history of the place, ma'am," I said, standing on the library's front steps. "I understand your family built it."

"It was Stan's doing, mostly. My stepfather. It was never as glamorous as he thought it would be, though. What's this about, again?"

"I'm researching the history of local drive-ins for an article I'm writing," I said, which was a total lie, unless you wanted to count my final report to the client as an article, a news report for an exclusive audience of two. But telling people you're researching ghosts risks derailing the conversation quickly and permanently.

I finally convinced her to discuss the drive-in theater with me, and once she got started, she had plenty to say.

"A line of cars came up from Savannah every night. In those days, everybody went to the drive-in all the time. Hardly anybody had TV. The drive-in was almost like church, except our congregation met at night, under the stars."

"How did your family end up building a drive-in on your farm?" I asked.

"My stepfather had a love of the theater and the movies. That was what he cared about the most in life, I think."

"What kind of person was he?"

She hesitated before answering. "I don't know why you'd need this for a newspaper article."

"It's more of a deeper academic look," I said. "For a small history journal. I doubt many people will ever read it."

"Oh, I'm so sorry to hear that. If you really want to know, my mother was charmed by him. She would have given him the moon from the sky if he'd asked for it, or died trying. Stanley had a way of casting a spell. He wasn't handsome, but he had a little bit of charm and glossy talk. He'd flatter you if he wanted something from you. It appealed to some people."

"When did you first meet him?"

"My mother brought him home for supper," Leah said. "Grandma Ruby—my mother's mother—she hated him right then, day one. Said he was nothing like my daddy, my mother's first husband."

"Were your parents divorced?"

"Oh, no, Daddy died when I was little. Tractor turned over on him."

"I'm so sorry."

"I only have one real memory of Daddy. He was showing me newborn goats out in the barn. Daddy was a serious man, Grandma Ruby always said. Pious and hardworking. She hated how Stanley wasn't."

"She thought Stanley wasn't serious?"

"Don't think ill of Grandma, because she was right. Stanley came in during my mother's wild streak," Leah said. "I don't wish to speak ill of my mother, either, of course. But my mother married my daddy when she was just nineteen, mostly arranged by Grandma Ruby."

"Arranged?" I asked.

"Grandma Ruby may have been sickly in body, but she had a will of iron, and as long as she breathed, she was a force to be reckoned with. Now, the Williams family, Daddy's people, had a nice house and a lot of land, and I think maybe that's why Grandma Ruby wanted Momma to marry Daddy. She moved in right along with Momma and lived there the rest of her life."

"So, your grandmother lived with you and your parents when you were growing up?"

"Oh, yes. Grandma Ruby had the back bedroom. She'd rap her cane on the floor when she wanted someone to come see her, to take orders from her, or go fetch her something. She just about ruled the house with that cane."

As I jotted furiously in my notepad, I thought of the back bedroom in the farmhouse, with all the circular dents in the floor by the bed. "At what point did your mother end up with Stanley Preston?"

"After Daddy died, Momma's wild streak showed up. She'd leave us with Grandma Ruby while she went to parties and nightclubs in Savannah.

Sometimes she didn't come home for days. Grandma Ruby hollered at her for going into town and carrying on, but Momma didn't pay her no mind. As a widow, Momma felt like a free woman who could do as she pleased, probably for the first time in her life."

"That's when she met Stanley?"

"Yes, she fell in with what you'd call the Bohemian crowd—musicians, theater people, artists, professors, people like that.

Stanley was a local stage actor, and not a successful one. He didn't have a steady job nor any land. Grandma Ruby opposed the marriage. She opposed Stanley's drive-in idea, too."

"But Stanley built the theater anyway?"

"Grandma Ruby was real sick by then, up coughing half the night. When she passed, Stanley acted on his drive-in plans. He sold all the animals, and I never altogether forgave him for that. My sweet goats. He said customers wouldn't like the smell. He sold off everything to raise money for the drive-in, even some land we'd had for generations. Daddy would spin in his grave about that, I'm sure. Grandma Ruby, too."

"Going back to Stanley's acting career," I said. "This may sound random, but I'm just following up on something. Do you know if Stanley ever met the actor Chance Chadwick?"

"I doubt it. He enjoyed Chance Chadwick movies and was always eager to screen them. He grew the Chance Chadwick mustache when that was fashionable and kept it long after it wasn't. It helped cover his chickenpox scars, which he would try so hard to hide under makeup. The bigger the mustache, the less makeup he needed. He smoked Chance Chadwick's brand of cigars, too."

"Is there any chance Stanley knew Adaire Fontaine from his acting days?"

Leah laughed. "He may have said he did, but he told a

lot of lies, said he used to know a lot of famous people. He was the sort of man who could invent his own version of the truth, and start believing it if it was entertaining enough, if it drew him enough attention."

"Adaire did get her start in Savannah's theater district."

"I can't say my stepfather knew any real movie stars. I think he looked up at that big screen and saw what he wished he could be. Heroic, handsome, confident. Instead of a failed actor stuck out here in the boonie-sticks."

"You think he was unhappy?"

"He could be happy. When everything was going his way. And he could rage when it didn't. But as long as he was working, seeing himself as the local movie king, he felt like he was somebody. As the drive-in got less popular in later days, it became harder to keep up that image of himself."

"Was he ever violent?"

"Sure. When we were young, he'd pop us. As we got older, he disappeared into his work. I could tell Momma felt abandoned by him. Eventually, he started living out in the screen tower and left Momma alone in the house. He never acted like he cared about anyone. My baby brother, Zeb, tried hard to buddy up to Stan, when he was still little —he missed Daddy so much, and after the wedding I think he misunderstood, and thought Stan would be kind and loving to us like Daddy used to—but Stanley never really took to him.

"Stanley did make us work at the drive-in. At first, I enjoyed it, because it was like all the kids came to my house to have fun. But I had to work there, serving hot dogs and sodas, dressed in these striped uniforms with bow ties. I'd be hot and sweaty, and I felt like all the girls from school were making fun of me. My brother got resentful, too, once he realized Stanley was never going to care about us.

"I went on to college and never looked back. I'd visit Momma in that house as it was crumbling around her, but she wouldn't move. 'This is where I was happiest,' she always said. 'When you and your brother were little, my little angels. That was the best part of my life.' Of course, she was out dancing and partying a lot of that time. Anyway, Momma never wanted to leave, even though Stanley stayed out at the screen tower and she was pretty much living alone in the house. But she said it was like living with her mother and her children, even if we were all just memories."

"Would you say your mother and stepfather grew apart over the years?"

"Stanley cared more about the movies and less about her. I sometimes wonder if he ever cared for her at all, or if he just saw her as a naive young widow with a lot of land. I never visited the place again after Momma died. By the time I heard Stanley died, I hadn't spoken to him in years. I was surprised he left the place to me, really, but he just didn't have anybody else. I didn't want the empty wreck of a drive-in. Who would? I always assumed somebody would buy it in order to demolish it and put up a gas station or a Wal-Mart."

"The family who bought it is trying to bring it back to life," I said.

"Well, bless them, but I wouldn't hold my breath. The drive-in era is long past."

"Did your brother stay in touch with your mother and stepfather?"

"He moved off to Louisiana and hardly ever returned. I know Momma wished he'd visited some. He'd call her once or twice a year. And he didn't care about Stanley any more than I did. I last saw him at my mother's funeral, oh, twenty years ago. He died nine or ten years after that."

"I'm sorry to hear it." I took a deep breath and plunged in. "I have another question that might be kind of strange. Did anyone ever report unusual experiences at the drive-in?"

She laughed. "Unusual? Sure. Pretty much every weekend. Oh, goodness."

"Anything that would have been considered paranormal?"

"Paranormal?" She repeated the word like it was foreign. "We did have Halloween nights. A Casper picture as the early show for the little ones, then a vampire or Frankenstein movie for the late show, when the littles were supposed to be asleep in their parents' back seats."

"Aside from Halloween promotions, did anyone ever report seeing strange things like ghostly figures or apparitions?"

"It almost sounds like you're asking whether the farm was haunted."

"Yes, ma'am."

A long pause on her end, and then, "I don't appreciate having my leg pulled."

"I'm not—"

"That farm was my Daddy's pride and joy. It was in our family for generations. Stanley Preston wrecked it all, and now it's an ugly ruin. If anybody haunts it, it must be Daddy, cursing my momma for marrying such a shiftless second husband. I do not care for these kinds of questions you're asking. Do not call me again. Good day and God bless." She hung up before I could say anything more.

Chapter Eight

"How'd it go?" Stacey stood beside me on the steps, holding her tablet and our folder of printouts from the newspaper microfilm. "And before you answer that, can we get some lunch?"

"I was planning to visit the Bryan County courthouse in Pembroke next," I said, and Stacey sagged visibly.

"Property records?" she asked.

"I think we can delay that for now, though. Leah, Preston's stepdaughter, told me it was in her father's family for generations. She grew up there, working at the drive-in. She got offended when I asked if it was haunted. But also the question seemed to catch her off-guard. She didn't react like a person who'd grown up having paranormal experiences there. Just bad memories. Stanley wasn't the warmest stepfather."

"Does that mean no property record research?" Stacey perked up. "Just straight to lunch?"

"Unless we discover signs of a haunting that precedes the twentieth century, going to the courthouse might be a waste of time."

"But going to lunch is never a waste of time, so…" Stacey took my arm and steered me down the sidewalk.

"There's some possible links between the creators of the drive-in and Adaire Fontaine, after all. Stan Preston was an actor for a while in Savannah, but his career never went anywhere. His wife Nancy, the widow who owned the land, liked to party with the theater crowd in Savannah. That's how they met."

"And Adaire was a major partygoer all her life."

"We need to find out whether Stan knew Adaire or not," I said. "We need a complete list of plays he was in, or any theater where he worked in any capacity. And hers. The list of his plays will probably be shorter but harder to find, because he was obscure."

"Whoa," Stacey said. "Maybe we really will solve the murder of Adaire Fontaine!"

"If you do, let me know," said a random elderly man in a baseball cap, startling us. He was walking his schnauzer toward Forsyth Park. "My wife's been trying to solve it for forty years." He continued past us down the sidewalk, never breaking his stride, never glancing back to see our reaction, his schnauzer trotting dutifully alongside him.

"See?" Stacey said. "*Everyone* has heard of Adaire—"

"I get it."

Over lunch at Bull Street Taco—my taco had red chile tempura cauliflower, hers had tuna, and she was finally mollified to be eating lunch—Stacey dished the dirt she'd been digging up about the late great Adaire Fontaine. "She may have been denied Oscar recognition more than once because of her wild behavior," Stacey said. "A real party girl in the more restrained era of the 40s and 50s. There were so many rumors of scandals and affairs, it's hard to know which ones were real."

"Any connection to Chance Chadwick?" I asked. "Other than co-starring in that poker movie?"

"You mean *Pocketful of Aces*? Technically, that was a caper movie, because they were robbing the big boss while distracting him with a poker game—"

"But did Chance and Adaire date?"

"Yes, when they made *Hotel Island*. He had a lead role, she had a bit part. Then they co-starred in *Pocketful of Aces* the following year, but their careers diverged from there. She went on to make critically acclaimed films like *A Soldier's Dame* and *Legend of the South*. He never really broke out of the hardboiled stuff—*The Nightingale Job, Bootlegger Boulevard*. If Chance Chadwick hadn't died in a spectacular crash, he might have faded away altogether. I think his last movie was *The Chicago Hustle*, two years before he died. That was a long time for a leading man to go without a film in those days."

"I thought you were focusing on Adaire Fontaine."

"I'm reading about both of them. Plus, this is mostly common knowledge. At least for film-school dorks."

"Good thing you're one of those," I said. "What else do we know about Chadwick's death? Was anyone else in the car with him?"

"A Spanish fashion model named Julia Garza, who he'd been dating for about a week. They were heading to his house in Malibu but never made it."

"Was he driving under the influence?"

"It's possible. By 1950s California standards, anything less than half a bottle of hard liquor was probably considered fine."

"Was there any suspicion he was murdered?"

"The consensus seemed to be reckless daredevilry."

"And his after-death punishment for that was to spend eternity at a drive-in?" I asked. "Seems excessive. It looks like the only possible connection between Stanley Preston and Chance Chadwick would be through Adaire Fontaine. Did they suspect anyone else in Adaire's murder besides the director?"

"Antonio Mazzanti was always the prime suspect. She was murdered at home, with no sign of a break-in. She'd walked off the set of *House of Gold*, a very expensive period piece about the de Medici family, wrecking Mazzanti's work and breaking up with him all once."

"That's some spicy gossip," I said. "With piles of obvious motivation."

"There were other suspects, generally romantic rivals, the significant others of those she was rumored to have had affairs with, and like I said, there were many rumors on that front. Mazzanti was investigated but never arrested. He never completed the de Medici movie either. His movies after that tended to be shoddy and low budget. Major studios and actors didn't want to work with him because of the suspicion. And then he went on to commit at least two other murders."

I nodded. "We'd better get moving if we want to set up the camera down in the old projection house before dark."

"Which we definitely do. I'm not going in there after dark."

We left the restaurant and split up to claim our individual vehicles.

As I drove the van out to the drive-in, I called Calvin down in Florida.

"The Nite-Lite Drive-In?" He chuckled after I told him about our case. "I frequented it in high school. My ex-wife and I went there a few times. I don't think we ever took Lori. The place was seedy by then. Didn't show decent movies anymore. I'm surprised it's still open."

"Our clients are trying to reopen it—in a non-seedy way with decent movies—but they've got a paranormal pest problem. Something keeps running off their customers, and they can't afford to lose any. I'd love any police or medical examiner reports on the deaths in that family."

"You know who to call downtown."

"Yes, but they always move faster for you. I must lack gravitas."

"That's something you could develop."

"I'll put it on my to-do list. Most of the drive-in owner's family members died locally, but the stepson was out in Louisiana. That could make things less zippy. Though I have no sign the son is haunting the drive-in. The owner was a struggling local stage actor named Stanley Preston. Ring any bells?"

"We didn't attend a lot of plays. Grant Patterson is your man to call for that."

"He's next." I finished our call as I reached the theater.

Stacey and I parked in the third row, our vehicles flanking the low pillbox of the old projection house. If that sunken, partially underground space was indeed the ghost's lair, we wanted to make sure it encountered us first when it came out, rather than any customers who might show up later.

Callie jogged out from the screen tower, plainly distressed, her hair loose and flying everywhere, dark bags under her eyes. She wore tennis shoes and pajamas. Her dog followed on a long leash.

"Hey," she said as we stepped out. "So, there was an incident."

"Is everybody okay?"

"Daisy was scared. She kept saying she could hear

someone walking around on the third floor, above her room. Gumby was acting weird, too, whining and looking up at the ceiling.

"Benny went up to the third floor—there's all kinds of junk up there, and he expected to find a squirrel or a rat. Instead, he saw a man. A shadow. It wasn't moving, and it disappeared when he turned on the light. But… he smelled cigar smoke."

"Sounds like our parking lot phantom is widening his territory," I said.

"I didn't smell it when I went up there," she said. "Benny didn't tell me about what he saw until after the sun was up and Daisy was back asleep."

"That's awful," Stacey said. "Sorry to hear it."

"We'll definitely check out the third floor." I looked up at the screen tower, where the late afternoon light glowed orange.

"Listen, I hate to ask, and it's totally fine to say no, and Benny didn't even think I should ask, but is there any chance y'all can accept partial pay in food? Because it would be easier on us—"

"Yes, please!" Stacey said. "More pizzas!"

"There's other stuff, obviously," Callie told me. "Salad greens, some vegetables from the garden. It's not like I want my family eating junk food every day."

"That works for me," I said, feeling bad for her, but also remembering the exquisite gourmet pizzas. If only charity always tasted so good. "This case might take a while. We have a lot of open questions about who is haunting this place and why."

"Plus, your cheffing is exquisite," Stacey said.

"Thanks." Callie blushed, as if her culinary skill was somehow news to her.

"I'll take movie tickets, too, personally," Stacey said.

"Gift certificates. I really want to see this place happen."

"That would be a relief," Callie said with a relieved smile. "Thank you. Seriously. I'm sorry."

I was a little more dubious about getting paid in movie tickets, but Stacey could do what she wanted. We'd certainly worked for little to nothing before. If the client seemed to be in danger, we'd take the case without much regard for their ability to pay, even if our overdue accounts receivable stack couldn't handle much more. That was my boss's long-established practice, and I was happy to uphold it. Well, maybe not "happy," but I couldn't just leave people at the mercy of the dead.

I saw signs of trouble in this small family, too, a lot of strain and tension, even as they put up a cheerful front for strangers. They were exhausted.

Callie's talents were almost wasted out here at the drive-in, I thought. Unless the drive-in proved successful, in which case, great for them. It's nice when people's dreams come true. So far, though, with Cigar Man haunting the parking lot and weird ghost-movie apparitions on the screen, the place was more of a nightmare.

"We'll get started," I nodded at the sunken projection booth. "We'll be out of the way before all the customers show up, I promise."

"Oh, sure, before we get flooded with all the customers." She shook her head and headed away toward the Purple Pizza Eater.

Stacey and I opened the van and got to work, hurrying before the sun went down.

I sat on the ground in front of the too-short door to the sunken projection house, shoved it open, and peered into the earthy darkness. Reluctantly, I wriggled down inside and dropped to the floor, my boots crunching in damp, sandy earth atop the uneven bricks of the floor.

"This place is a kill box," I said, pointing my flashlight into dark corners. There was no electricity—Benny had assured me the loose, dangling wires were attached to nothing. "There's no getting out of here fast."

"Well, great, I look forward to it." Stacey passed me down the tripod, the thermal camera, and the other monitoring gear, then sat down and scooted inside to join me. She landed nimbly on the floor beside me, though it was an unpleasantly long drop. I didn't look forward to climbing back out.

Our flashlight beams moved across brick walls slick with dampness that wept in from the surrounding soil. Metal shelves held bric-a-brac, rusty hand tools, and spare parts for servicing the projector.

Stacey approached the mechanical monster of the antique projector itself, like a slumbering dragon in its lair, but surrounded by useless junk instead of treasure. The stump of the second projector beside it lay in ruins, the years having been less kind to it.

Movie posters covered the wall behind us, pasted onto the brick, badly wrinkled and discolored from years of creeping dampness. The distorted faces of deteriorated, long-dead movie stars watched us explore their domain.

The rotten face of Chance Chadwick, reduced to a barely-visible mustache under a fedora, looked out from a decayed *Hotel Island* poster, surrounded by palm trees, a biplane careening overhead. Adaire Fontaine had been in that movie, though at that point in her career she hadn't yet risen to the level of being mentioned on the poster. She was certainly featured in the following year's *Pocketful of Aces* poster, on display in the concession stand in much better condition.

A *Legend of the South* poster from 1956 had Adaire Fontaine front and center on the veranda of a mansion inundated by floodwaters, clad in a lavish antebellum gown with cascading layer after layer of lace, her mountain of hair—curly and red for this particular film—blown back as she stared into the wind. I remembered vaguely that the movie involved a massive Mississippi River flood, based very loosely on actual floods that had devastated the region.

"This thing should be in a museum," Stacey said, looking over the projector. "I guess it's nice they didn't throw it away altogether. Easier to just leave the old dead beast here, I guess." She tapped a tiny glass window on the side of the projector. "The light came from two burning carbon rods. The early film was nitrate, too. All very flammable. You know the whole thing about not shouting 'Fire!' in a crowded theater? There's a reason they say 'theater' and not 'sports arena' or even 'restaurant' where there's plenty of hazards. Projection equipment used to start fires all the time."

"Stanley's cigars would have increased the risk of fire, too. Keep your nose open for that smell. It could be our only warning if he decides to lash out."

We set up cameras and cleared mildewed magazines off a small table in the corner to place the audio recorder and motion detector.

"Okay, well, I hate it down here," Stacey said, after double-checking the thermal camera in the back corner. "Can we go now?"

"Yep." I started for the door.

A few stairs leading up to the gnome-sized door would have been helpful had they existed, but instead we had to scale rusty, sagging rungs bolted into the wall. They looked quite tetanus-inducing and were generally much looser than I liked my wall-mounted rungs to be.

I followed Stacey out, flopping fishwise onto my belly, my upper body sprawling across the ground outside the little door. There was no way to exit gracefully, or even quickly. I wriggled the rest of the way up and got to my feet, brushing dirt off my jeans.

"Look at that, Mommy!" someone shouted. A boy of nine or ten in a baseball cap stood two rows behind us, next to an SUV that had parked backward in its spot and raised its back door. He pointed at us, having watched my graceless, wriggling exit. The loud, pointing boy was accompanied by two older women and a girl of twelve or thirteen who stared at her phone. "There's a secret passage in that little building! Look, Billie!"

"Shut up," said the girl, in the tone of someone who was absolutely never going to listen to anything her brother said, her voice slushy around her braces.

"Can I go explore it?" The boy eased toward us. I shook my head, not that he was asking my opinion.

"That's employees only," one woman said, barely glancing our way. "Stop lazygagging and give us a hand."

The boy reluctantly returned to help them. They looked like experienced tailgaters, with multiple coolers and a card table with a tablecloth, all decorated with University of Florida Gator insignia. They set out boxes of Popeye's fried chicken and biscuits with buckets of mashed potatoes and coleslaw.

They weren't the only customers. Three carloads had arrived and parked, widely spaced from each other, and a fourth crept uncertainly down the driveway toward the lighted ticket booth, like a motorist tentatively entering a strange and ancient land in which the customs were unknown.

It was nearly dusk, and soon the projector would spring to life, playing the Powerpuff Girls cartoon again.

I double-checked that the tiny door was locked before we walked away, in case the kid got bored and tried to explore later. He could still lift the metal plates over the portholes in the front of the projection and peer inside at the dead projector and rusty junk, if he was into that.

Stacey and I grabbed more gear from the van and walked around to the door on the side of the screen tower. I knocked, and Gumby exploded into furious barking somewhere inside.

Callie answered after a minute, looking frazzled as usual. Daisy stood several feet away, red-faced and pouting, arms crossed and back turned to her mother.

"Did we come at a bad time?" I asked.

"It could be worse. You're ready for dinner?" Callie asked us. "I'm working on it."

"We were actually going to investigate the top floor," I said.

"Any chance that could wait until after bedtime?" She pointed at Daisy, who re-crossed her arms and turned farther away with a "hmph!" sound. "We were just about to have a late dinner and right to bed."

"No bed!" Daisy said.

"It's almost bedtime *now*," Callie said.

"We'll be happy to join you if that's easier," I said. "Or we can just skip the whole food thing—"

"No, I made a lot, and it won't be good tomorrow. Come on, Daisy. We're eating dinner, and we're being polite to our guests."

"No!" Daisy turned another rotation away, toward the posters for *A Soldier's Dame* with Adaire Fontaine and *Bootlegger Boulevard* with Chance Chadwick hanging above the cigar-stained desk.

"All right, stay down here by yourself. Gumby, come!"

The dog bounded along at Callie's side. Stacey and I followed Callie through the long, narrow office. Just before the open door to the colorful playroom, we turned aside to find a long set of concrete stairs. A freshly painted rainbow of bright colors cheered up the stairwell, with the walls painted to match. It was like walking through a pack of LifeSavers.

Gumby lingered on the bottom step, waiting until Daisy came running to join us, having decided she wasn't so keen on being downstairs by herself.

"Mommy, wait!" Daisy scrambled past us to grab her mother's hand and walk up with her.

Stacey and I dropped our gear on the stairwell's second-story landing, since it was bound for the third floor, and followed them into their apartment.

The apartment had the same general look as the first floor, with one steeply sloping wall, but narrower with even less floor space. We'd emerged in a kitchen, next to the floor's only visible windows. At the far end of the apartment were a couple of closed doors, presumably to bedrooms and such. A string quartet crackled softly over a record player, near wall cubbies full of instruments—a ukulele, hand drums and maracas, a small violin. The intoxicating smell of fresh-baked bread hung in the air.

We sat at a heavily scratched dining table. Daisy, after some cajoling by her mother, took the seat across from us, on a booster chair under the low slope of the back wall.

"Were there any more customers?" Callie asked while passing around a gigantic bowl of salad greens and a platter of sliced homemade bread.

"I saw four cars of them," I said. "One family looked like they were having a picnic."

"Let's hope they bought a food permit from Hector."

"Who's Hector?"

"The bassist from Benny's band. He's volunteering at the ticket booth tonight. Benny's running the concession stand."

The homemade meal was as good as the pizza, but healthier. I asked general background questions, not wanting to scare Daisy with talk of apparitions and hauntings. The little girl's mood improved as she ate. She hummed as she danced a little stuffed tiger on the empty chair beside her.

"…we've fixed up this floor a lot, and a little bit downstairs to turn that back room into Daisy's play area. We added the glass door so we can keep an eye on her when she's by herself in there. Her room up here isn't much bigger than a closet with a window, but it's cheerful and close to us. Benny says we'll eventually renovate upstairs into a guest room and bigger room for Daisy—"

"I don't want to live upstairs!" Daisy said, suddenly upset again.

"You might have a different opinion when you're a teenager," Callie said.

"No, I won't!"

"Oh, look, it's past bedtime." Callie stood up.

"No, it isn't!" Daisy argued, falsely.

"Just leave your dishes on the table and head upstairs whenever you're done," Callie told me. "We'll catch up later. Say good-night, Daisy."

"Good night!" Daisy sang and waved to us with sudden cheerfulness, as if she hadn't been angry and sullen most of the time. They departed through a door at the far end of the apartment.

Stacey and I hurried to finish and to clean up our dishes, despite Callie's admonishment not to do so. I grabbed a small piece of the homemade bread and carried it out into the stairwell with me. It was like a rare delicacy.

"Okay, then." Stacey looked up along the dimly lit concrete stairs to the dim, uninviting third floor. No happy rainbow colors had been painted here; it was grim cinderblock gray all the way to the top, where a black metal door awaited us. "This is sure to be a happy place."

We gathered our gear and hiked up, supplementing the weak overhead bulbs with our flashlights. I unlocked the door and pushed it open, revealing the darkness of the uninhabited third floor.

Chapter Nine

The tower's third floor was, as expected, even narrower than the one below it, like a long walk-in closet with a low ceiling and clutter that made it feel claustrophobic and difficult to navigate. It was exactly the kind of dark, forgotten space ghosts liked to inhabit. Most of the overhead lights were burned out. Junk was crammed into both sides of the narrow space. A faded sign advertised hot dogs for a quarter, Cokes for a nickel. A pile of outdoor speakers rusted away next to a cigarette vending machine.

"Look, it's the murder movie," Stacey whispered and pointed, though there was no need to whisper.

One of the movie posters tacked to the wall advertised *The Body in the Basement*, featuring a patchwork wooden door, slightly ajar, with dirt-covered fingers reaching out from behind it.

"That was made by Mazzanti, the serial killer movie director?" I asked after reading the poster's fine print.

"Yep. A few years after they made this, he murdered the leading lady, Portia Reynolds. That's why it's sometimes just called 'the murder movie.' It's actually hard to find, since distributing it is considered extremely poor taste."

We walked single file, working our way past advertising stand-ups made of wood and cardboard. A giant, faded cartoon mouse face promoted some long-forgotten kids' movie. A dusty Santa mannequin slumped in a sleigh, near a wooden Christmas tree cutout dotted with colorful lightbulbs, many of them broken.

"Lots of Halloween stuff over here." Stacey slowed down to study a life-size coffin covered with dust and spiderwebs, heaped with oversized skulls and a jack-o'-lantern painted on plywood. "They get kinda dark back there. Look."

Behind the plywood jack-o'-lantern was a caged gibbet with a fairly realistic zombie inside it, one plastic hand reaching out through the bars. There was a black iron candelabra shaped like a pentagram, candle stubs at each point of the star. A lifelike plastic goat statue with red glass eyes. Severed limbs and assorted torture implements, hopefully fake, were piled nearby.

"This isn't fun Halloween, this is bad Halloween," Stacey said.

Ahead of us, blocking off the rest of the third floor, loomed a hand-painted plywood flat depicting a haunted castle, with a little ghost in the arched window. The tall piece of plywood looked as though it had been designed to frame a door, maybe the concession stand entrance. A dusty red curtain hung inside the door area, obscuring the view beyond.

I drew the curtain aside.

Beyond lay a final narrow room. We'd reached the back end of the tower's top floor.

A table against the low, steep ceiling was heaped with jumbles of small film spools and reels, all covered with dust. The previous owner had plastered the wall with images of his favorites, cut from posters, magazines, and newspapers, wrinkled and curled and stained nicotine yellow by cigar smoke. Chance Chadwick and Adaire Fontaine were most heavily represented, among other actors of their generation.

Stacey looked through the film reels. "These look like eight-millimeter film."

"Which means?"

"Homemade movies, most likely." She picked up a spool and frowned. "Can you read this, Ellie?"

I tried. I squinted. The writing on the label was faded and looked like random geometric figures to me. "I can't tell if it's bad handwriting or a secret code."

"Why not both?" She picked up a boxy portable film camera from a shelf, wiped the lens that took up half its body mass, and peered through the viewfinder. "He probably filmed them on this Super 8. The first home movie camera. He has an eight-millimeter projector over there. It looks like he watched his home movies here, too." She unrolled an age-cracked screen on a movable stand, and I covered my nose as dust swirled out. "A screening room inside a screen tower. Wacky. Should we pop in a reel and have a look?"

"Maybe later," I said. "Tonight we have to sit out in the parking lot and try to get harassed by the ghost."

We set up gear to monitor the third floor.

By the time we emerged from the tower, night had fallen and the cartoon was playing on the big screen. A few more cars had arrived, including some rowdy teens who sat in the back of a pickup truck, vaping, talking loudly, laughing. If they missed important *Powerpuff Girls* plot points, it was their own fault.

Stacey and I split up; she went to her Escape while I sat in the van. We were working parking-lot phantom security tonight.

I texted Callie, updating her about the top floor and letting her know we'd be watching and listening for any further activity up there.

Then I waited, hoping to see the dead thing that came out at night to terrify the movie audience.

Chapter Ten

Having already seen the cartoon, I spent my time in the back of the van, checking the monitors, particularly watching the sunken, disused projection room and the third floor of the tower. Daisy was sleeping down in her bedroom, and while her parents could watch her remotely over the baby monitor, I was glad to provide some extra eyes and ears on any activity in the tower while her parents worked.

The teenagers in the truck looked like they were having a good time, though paying no attention to the screen. The tailgating family had moved on from fried chicken to pie. The boy watched the movie from his lawn chair, while the middle-school girl paced around outside the car, holding her phone, frequently stealing long glances at the wild older teens across the way like she wished she could join them.

As far as I could tell, nothing stirred in the sunken projection house just outside my van, or in the dark upper reaches of the screen tower.

Billy Bunny's song and swamp show played, followed by dancing hot dogs and pizza slices promoting the concession stand. People drifted over to the Purple Pizza Eater and back, returning with popcorn and soda and pizza boxes. Foot traffic continued into the opening sequence of *Labyrinth*.

See anything? I texted Stacey, while looking across the top of the abandoned projection house at her car.

Nothing except some major tight pants on David Bowie, Stacey texted.

Let me know if anything sneaks up on you, I texted back.

I would probably notify you of that, yes.

I waited and watched a little *Labyrinth*, the tale of teenage Sarah crossing into the Goblin Kingdom to rescue her brother. The story echoed some of the world's most ancient myths, going back to the Sumerian story of the goddess Inanna—her descent into the underworld, the land of the dead, a place of darkness and monsters, and her victorious return to the world of light.

Seemed like it would set a good tone for ghosts to come out.

Yet the monitors showed little sign of activity. The sunken projection house was a little colder than the above ground area, but nothing had changed. No cold spots, no movement. Nothing happened up in the tower, either, which I watched closely.

After a while, I started to wish I'd grabbed some popcorn.

Finally, the closing credits rolled. The theater's outdoor lights showed the way to the exit. Car engines started, headlights flared to life. The words GOOD NIGHT! glowed on the screen, surrounded by colorful cartoon stars.

The cars of the theater patrons made their way out the

exit drive, disappearing onto the midnight highway beyond. When they were gone, all the theater's exterior lights snuffed out.

Benny emerged from the darkened concession stand. Callie had skateboarded home earlier to join her sleeping daughter in the screen tower.

Stacey and I stepped out of our vehicles as Benny bicycled over to us.

"Any news?" he asked.

"No activity so far," I told him. "We'll keep monitoring all night, and probably take a walk around, pick up some readings."

"Pretty good crowd, huh?" He looked at the exit driveway. "Considering all we have is the sign out front and a basic website. When the big rollout happens, boom! Am I right?"

"I hope so," I said. "Looked like you sold a lot of pizzas."

"Yeah, we sold a few." He glanced toward the screen tower where his family waited, then back at the empty parking lot and darkened concession stand. "No patrons got run off tonight. That's good, right? Maybe things are calming down already. Maybe we just have to convince the ghosts, 'hey, yo, we're just trying to make this place nice again.' And they can just chill with us, watch the movies for free. Right?"

"Maybe so," I said. "Have you spent much time on the screen tower's top floor?"

"Not really, but it looks like some of the old holiday décor is prime."

"Have you looked at any of the film reels up there?" I asked, while thinking he might want to consider taking a closer look at the awful holiday décor before using it.

"Reels?" He was obviously excited. "Like what?"

"Eight-millimeter," Stacey said. "Probably just home movies."

"Oh." His face fell. "Anything interesting?"

"We haven't looked," I replied. "Just wondering if you had any insight. Maybe save us some time."

"Sorry." He shook his head. "There's some old thirty-five-mil reels up in the concession stand. The previous owner's favorites, it looks like, black and white classics, but we still can't exhibit those without paying to license. Which we might do, sometime after I see what condition they're in. We could have Hollywood Golden Age weekends, promote them to the local retirement communities. Hmm. Anyway, have a good night. Text if you need anything. I probably won't answer until tomorrow, though, realistically, because I won't be awake much longer."

"Okay. We'll keep quiet."

"Send a marching band through my bedroom, I won't hear it." He yawned and pedaled away.

"What now, boss?" Stacey asked me. "Shall we commence poking around?"

"Let's stay out here dangling ourselves as bait a little longer," I said. "Maybe the crowd was too large for Cigar Man's taste. Go back and wait. Keep all your lights off."

"You got it. I'll go put myself on the hook, maybe something will bite me." She winced. "But not literally. No bites or scratches, dead guy!" Stacey scolded the sunken brick projection booth, so reminiscent of a mausoleum in a graveyard. The rows of speaker poles sprawling out all around us could have been markers for other graves, ones for paupers, maybe.

I returned to the van and sat in the driver's seat to wait alone in the dark. The starlight from above, plus the faint glow from the monitors in the back of the van, were the only sources of illumination. The low hum of the monitors and speakers was the only sound.

As I was climbing into the back of the van to look over the monitors, my phone buzzed in my pocket. *You're seeing this, right?* Stacey had texted me from her car.

Clambering back up front, I saw what she was talking about. Couldn't miss it. Before I could even look out the window to see whether Chance Chadwick was standing on the brick projection house, or perhaps some gruesome horror had slithered out from the little Hobbit door to creep up on Stacey, I saw the activity up on the big screen.

On the screen tower glowed pale, cloudlike shapes, just barely suggesting two people, like images cast by a projector almost too weak to shine.

I tried to discern what was happening, what the giant ghostly images were actually doing. Arguing? Fighting? Kissing?

Then I heard it—a female voice, faint, barely audible. Her tone was urgent, her words fast-paced, spilling over each other like a waterfall.

The voice wasn't coming from up around the screen, though. It came from right behind me, inside my van.

I felt chills as I listened to the woman, trying to make out her words.

A male voice took over, speaking rapidly, as incoherent as she'd been, and finally I turned to look.

Nobody was there.

Are you hearing the movie? I texted Stacey.

No. You have audio? From the car speakers? I'll try mine.

Stepping into the rear of the van, I found no apparitions waiting to jump out at me, which was nice. I tracked the low sound to one of our speakers and turned up the volume. I double-checked that it was recording. My eyebrows raised at the source.

The voices are coming from the house behind the fence, I

reported to Stacey. *Maybe that old speaker box.*

Ooh, I want to listen. Can I come over?

By the time Stacey arrived, though, the voices in the house had gone silent.

"Aw, the movie's disappeared from the screen, too." Stacey frowned up at the tower. "I wanted to see how it ended. And I think we came in late, because I had no idea what was going on."

Through the night vision camera in the decrepit farmhouse, we could see some of the outdoor seating area on the farmhouse roof, including the rusty speaker box.

"The sound came from there," I said.

"Not that old speaker? Are you sure?"

"Or else from inside the house. Analyze it, kiddo. It's your time to shine."

"On it." Stacey picked up a laptop. While she reversed and replayed the footage, I turned down the volume on the live monitors. "Here it is," she said.

We listened carefully, but even at a higher volume, it was hard to distinguish individual words from the faint voices.

"Did she say 'cane'?" Stacey whispered at one point. "'Wrong cane'? Or 'long crane'?"

I shook my head. "It's a man and a woman, that's all I can tell. Sounds like they're arguing."

"There's something in the background, too. I'll see if I can isolate it." Stacey worked on digital representations of the soundwaves, identifying a repeated pattern of sharp spikes that grew larger.

Isolated from the soft, indistinct voices and amplified so we could hear it, the first row of sound spikes turned out to be three thuds, like someone knocking on a door.

Thump. Thump. Thump.

A gap of silence followed, represented by a long, flat

line on the screen. Then the sounds repeated louder and faster, the sound growing angrier and more insistent.

Thump. Thump. Thump.

Another silent, flatlined gap.

Then came the final set, almost deafening compared to the first knocks.

THUMP THUMP THUMP.

We pulled back, wincing at the loud, angry sound.

"Sorry." Stacey turned down the volume, though the horse had already fled the barn on protecting our ears against those final loud thumps. "The voices cut out after that last knock. I guess the knocks were part of the ghost movie?"

"Unless the knocks were coming from inside the house," I said. "Can you remove the thumping spikes and just replay the voices?"

"I can...try. It'll be a little skippy if I do it quick, so don't mind the blank spots in the sounds..." Stacey hummed to herself as she worked. "Okey-doke, here's what we've got."

The movie sounds played again, going briefly silent at moments where Stacey had removed the knocking. This left the voices a bit clearer overall, and she could finally crank up the volume.

We each held a notepad and did our best to capture whatever words we could. Stacey played it several times.

"I think she said 'fish chips,'" Stacey told me as we compared notes.

"I got 'wish chips' which makes less sense," I said. "But before that, don't you think it said 'wild card'?"

"Ooh, I know the part you mean." Stacey played the first few seconds and nodded. "I was thinking 'mild car' but that sounded dumb, so I didn't write anything. Then I think she said 'long game.'"

"From the man's voice, I think I got 'doll' and 'clubs.'"

"Wild card, fish chips, dolls, clubs…"

"Maybe she's talking about poker chips, not fish and chips," I said.

"You're thinking *Pocketful of Aces?*"

"Featuring Stanley Preston's favorite actors, Chance Chadwick and Adaire Fontaine."

"He did give that poster a prominent spot in the concession stand," Stacey said. "With a lightbulb frame, too."

"Have you ever seen *Pocketful of Aces*?" I asked.

"I actually haven't," Stacey said. "I mean, it's not considered one of her greater works, but I should probably see it. I've seen *A Soldier's Dame*, obviously, and *Legend of the South*—"

"We'll have to watch it."

"Yes! Ellie and Stacey movie night. This is so happening. Your place or mine? Do we invite the guys or nah? We'll need popcorn, obviously. Do you have a bean bag chair?"

"I was thinking of streaming it to my laptop."

"Eleanor Jordan! That's no way to watch a classic movie. You'll miss all the delicate subtleties."

"If it was one of Stanley's favorites, there might be a copy up in the newer projection booth."

"Yes! Thirty-five-millimeter! That's the way to go! It's like listening to the original record instead of streaming digitally."

"They may not be able to screen it because of copyright. Now check for any correlating recent activity down in the old projection house."

"You got it." Stacey worked at her computer. "Okay, nothing on audio, let's check thermal video… what is that?"

On the thermal recording, a deep blue spot occupied

the semi-underground projection house, frozen in place where Stacey had paused it. It was a patch of profound cold with no clear shape.

"It's next to the junky old projector," I said, pointing to the rickety, monster-sized device.

"I'm going to go out on a crazy, hairy limb and guess this entity is responsible for projecting the ghost movies," Stacey said. "Benny didn't find any sign of it up in the concession stand projection booth because it doesn't hang out up there. It hangs out down there, in that terrible, terrible place."

"Back it up some more."

Stacey reversed the video to the moment when the cold spot first appeared, then played it.

Comparing timestamps, we found that the cold spot had appeared about thirty seconds before the ghost movie started playing on the screen tower. It had lingered near the projector until the movie stopped, then faded away.

"The case of the phantom projectionist," Stacey whispered.

"He didn't seem to move before he vanished," I said. "The booth might be his lair."

"You think it's the same entity we saw up on stage? The one that looked like Chance Chadwick? Or maybe the one from upstairs in the screen tower? And which one has been menacing the customers? Is the phantom projectionist in cahoots with the parking lot phantom, or are they one and the same?"

"There's no way of knowing. It's a big drive-in. Plenty of room for multiple entities. And nothing attracts a ghost like—"

"—a haunted house," Stacey finished for me, so I'd probably said it plenty of times to her in the past. Once a place is haunted, it's liable to get more and more haunted over time, drawing in souls as the negative entities claim victims, harvesting energy and even souls from the living. "This could be more than one entity. A paranormal double feature."

"Right."

"Or maybe even a series of specters. An all-night macabre marathon of ghosts—"

"Let's hope not," I said. "The fewer, the better. One would be ideal."

"Do you believe it's just one, though?"

"Between the stage, the projection room, and possibly the farmhouse?" I shook my head. "I doubt it. Leah, Stanley's stepdaughter, suggested her own father might be kicking around, angry about how his family farm was ruined to make way for the drive-in."

"I'm guessing he wouldn't be working the dead projection booth, then," Stacey said.

"She also talked about her grandmother banging the floor with a cane when she wanted attention. The grandmother had some health issues."

"Oh! That could explain the knocking sounds." Stacey thought about it. "Maybe she didn't like the movie, and that's her way of booing."

"That tracks with what Leah told me, too. The grandmother opposed turning the farm into a drive-in."

"Then she must *really* hate the projectionist ghost. The projectionist, that must be Stanley Preston himself, right?"

"Possibly, but it's hard to tell much from a blue blob," I said.

"How many blue blobs are also film connoisseurs, though?"

"Leah mentioned Preston had a Chance Chadwick mustache, so maybe that was who we saw up on the stage, too. They could look similar from a distance."

"I don't know. The one on stage looked like the movie star. Not the grumpy scowling guy from the pictures."

We replayed the audio and video clips a few times, gleaning what we could.

On the live feeds, nothing was happening anymore—nothing in the sunken old projection house, nothing in the overgrown farmhouse behind the fence, nothing but the wind creaking the house timbers and rustling the leaves in the trees surrounding the theater.

We waited and watched and listened, our eyes on our small screens as we sat in the towering shadow of the much larger screen ahead, the one that had presided over past generations as they gathered here to watch and listen together.

Chapter Eleven

Stacey and I pulled out of the drive-in a couple hours later, each in our own vehicles.

The van chugged down the highway, and I felt relief as Savannah pulled into view, the dawn breaking, the sun rising from the Atlantic.

I went home, where my blackout curtains turned the brightest Georgia summer day to darkest midnight, and caught up on some sleep. Phantom voices and glowing, indistinct faces haunted my dreams.

When I awoke, I cleared my mind a little with some strong coffee, and then a lot by heading to a kickboxing class. I'd fallen during out-of-town cases that begat missed lessons and restaurant meals and was trying to make up for it with extra classes. Stretching and working my muscles felt good—well, it felt good afterward, at least—and helped me get some distance from the details of the case, so I could hopefully come back with a fresh perspective.

By the time I returned home, Grant Patterson from the Savannah Historical Association had responded to a message I'd sent earlier. He suggested I call him back, so I did.

"Are you truly facing the ghost of Adaire Fontaine?" Grant asked. "Here in Savannah? Which theater is she haunting?"

"Um, no," I said. "Sorry if my message gave that impression, I was a little tired when I wrote it. We are actually desperately trying to find any possible connections between her and Stanley Preston, the owner of the Nite-Lite Drive-In."

"Oh, I don't know about that," Grant said, in a tone he might use if I'd described eating a meal of insects and arachnids. "Adaire Fontaine did not strike me as the drive-in sort."

"Preston was a local stage actor before opening the drive-in," I said.

"Ah. Then we shall focus on Adaire's brief career as a Savannah stage in Savannah in the forties, prior to her becoming a film star."

"It sounds like you've started researching already. I really appreciate it."

"Ellie, everyone knows these things about Adaire Fontaine."

"I am realizing that as the case progresses."

"Will you be investigating her murder?" Grant's voice dropped into a hushed, conspiratorial tone. "Do you believe the killer was Antonio Mazzanti? The Silk Strangler?"

"That's what I keep hearing, but I have no idea. We're also looking for any connection between the drive-in owner Stanley Preston and the actor Chance Chadwick."

"My goodness, this is a juicy case," Grant said. "I can

tell you Chance Chadwick never lived in Savannah, nor anywhere within a thousand miles, or I would know of it. You'll be pleased to hear that Adaire Fontaine's residence in Savannah, and I suppose her overall Georgia heritage, earned her a special nook in the Historical Association's cultural history display, and we have a special archive of materials related to her performances and personal life, with an emphasis on her time in our lovely city, naturally. You are welcome to have a look. What day would be best?"

"As soon as possible," I said. "It will really help."

"Unfortunately, I have a dinner engagement. Fortunately, it is not far distant from the Association. If you're truly eager to delve into this research—"

"We are!"

"I suppose I could meet you this evening and introduce you to the materials, but I would then need to depart in an ungraciously early manner."

"That would be fantastic," I said.

"I will have to notify our conservator Elma Danford, naturally. She'll want assurance that you will touch nothing in the display room and leave not a speck of yourselves behind."

"Not a problem," I said. "I can bring a snack and a drink into the archive room, right? Maybe a nice crumbly muffin?"

Grant paused for a long moment. "The very suggestion is shocking."

"Understood."

"This is a serious matter. I recently found myself selected for a Steering Committee position that Ms. Danford very much wanted for herself. But I won't trouble you with the byzantine internal politics of the Association. We may as well attempt to unravel the intrigues of Versailles."

It wasn't quite sunset when Stacey and I arrived at the Historical Association's stately, sober gray-brick mansion. The wrought-iron railing of a widow's walk atop the three-story building reminded me of the widow's walk on the decrepit farmhouse at the Nite-Lite, though the one at the Historical Association was in far better condition, with less of a death-trap look, and was an original feature of the house instead of a slapdash addition.

After parking on a shady side street, we walked through the Association's garden. The roses hadn't bloomed yet, but the dogwoods and the pink camellias were out in full.

On the shady back porch, we rang the rear doorbell.

The woman who answered eyed us with a severe look, her eyes bright and blue, her gray hair fluffed and heavily sprayed into a formidable steel helmet.

"I am sorry, but the Association has closed for the day," she told us, but her tone didn't sound particularly apologetic. "We offer public hours tomorrow between one and three p.m."

"Thank you, but we have an appointment with Grant Patterson. Is he here?" I asked.

"Patterson. I see." This information seemed to chill her attitude toward us more. "Such an unusually late hour. All very irregular. I suppose you should come inside to await him. Would you care for iced tea or water?"

"No, thank you, ma'am," I replied quickly, not wanting to make any further demands on her hospitality.

"Come this way. Grant Patterson has not arrived, but you are welcome to wait in the parlor. I am Elma Danford, Association conservator."

We introduced ourselves quickly. "Your work must be so interesting," I added. "Is there anything new coming into the Association's collection?"

"Yes, always. Some would say my role is the most

valuable in the organization, even more than my role as a generous and regular Association donor, but I'm sure such talk is greatly exaggerated." She opened the double doors to the parlor and indicated the stiff wingback chairs to us, each with its own little round table. Oil paintings of historical scenes from Savannah adorned the walls, including colonial and antebellum eras, and one of Bonaventure Cemetery, bright flowers growing thick and lush among the gravestones. Antiques—vases, a hand-painted glass globe, a model sailing ship—adorned bookshelves and nooks around the parlor. "Please avoid touching any items. I'm sure Grant Patterson will arrive soon, if the meeting hasn't slipped his mind, as meetings have been known to do in the past."

She closed the double doors.

"Frosty," Stacey whispered.

I nodded and glanced at the cutaway balcony above. Grant's office was up there, a little farther along the upstairs hall. "It's probably best we avoid stepping into any Historical Association drama. Remember how ruthless Grant said the Docents Committee could be."

"This place scares me sometimes," Stacey said.

We waited quietly until Grant arrived a few minutes later. We heard him outside the door, engaging in a conversation that sounded both hushed and heated with Ms. Danford.

At last, he opened the door, looking flushed, and smiled at us. He wore a finely tailored suit, clearly heading on to a grand night after this. "Good evening, Ellie and Stacey. Wonderful to see you."

"Is everything okay?" I asked as we rose to meet him. "Did we come at a bad time?"

"After hours, certainly," Elma said from the hallway, staring at us with a tight smile, next to a stern portrait of

18th-century evangelical preacher George Whitefield.

"As I've said before, they will certainly not touch or damage any part of the collection in any way," Grant told her.

"Then why did you need the cultural display unlocked?"

"Merely to show them the dress. Right this way." Grant led Stacey and me through a pair of double doors to a sizable room near the front of the sprawling house. Elma lingered silently at the doorway, watching us like a predatory bird.

The room displayed cultural artifacts from Savannah's history, some of it quite valuable, including antique silver and gold jewelry carefully sealed behind glass.

"Oh, wow," Stacey said, drawn immediately to a quite fancy-looking dress displayed in a case in one corner, among other clothing cases that included Civil War uniforms and assorted hats, boots, coats, and dresses of historical notables. The dress flared from its bodice to a wide hem at the floor, though not so wide as an actual hoop skirt, instead made of several heaped layers thick with lace. "That's the one from the poster, isn't it?"

"It is indeed the original dress worn by Adaire Fontaine in the climactic flood scene of *Legend of the South*," Grant said. "Quite an impressive addition to our collection. You may thank our most excellent conservator for that. Funded largely via her own personal donation." He indicated Elma by the door, who gave another tight smile. "It is one of our most popular exhibits."

Framed pictures showed the old-time stage theaters where Adaire Fontaine had grown famous. Lines of fans wrapped around the corner at the Savannah Theatre and the Fox in Atlanta. They were primarily excited young women in professional office-girl wear of the 1940s, their hair cut short and styled into big swoops.

"Wow, she really was popular," I said, looking from the long lines to the name Adaire Fontaine in big letters on glowing marquee signs.

"It's said that she appealed in particular to young working women of the postwar period, perhaps because she embodied so much of what they felt, and of how they differed from previous generations," Grant explained. "Adaire Fontaine, strong and feisty, glamorous and fearless, perhaps represented something they saw in themselves."

"Yeah, she was pretty cool." Stacey looked at an autographed photo of the actress, wearing a black chiffon column gown and wide-brimmed, feather-adorned black hat, her outfit from *Pocketful of Aces*. It reminded me of Nancy Preston's wedding dress; perhaps she'd been an Adaire fan. "Wild life, tragic death."

"Indeed," Grant said. "Personally, I've always suspected Antonio Mazzanti, the film director. A strange, morbid character, and a known murderer, of course. As for his films, he went from a fascinating magical realism in his earlier works to simple horror. I believe one was called *The Dead Body Down in the Basement,* or something similar. I didn't watch many of those, as they were nothing like his earlier work. Played only at the drive-in, I believe.

"Like most men who worked with Adaire, Mazzanti's talent paled next to hers. I'm sure she would have won that Oscar had the competition not been so stiff that year. She faced such luminaries as Ava Gardner and Audrey Hepburn, the eventual winner. Adaire's death was such a tragedy, such a brutal horror to fall upon one so lovely and talented. Surely she would have gone on to even greater performances had her fate not been so grim—"

"Are you finished here?" Ms. Danford asked us. "I would prefer to get going for the evening."

"Yes, sorry. Ellie, Stacey, the documents you'll need are down the hall in the Mimosa Room. To which I have my *own* key." Grant cast a brief but pointed look at Danford, who looked down her nose quietly as we exited the room. She locked the door behind us and strode off stiffly in another direction.

Stacey and I shared a look but didn't say anything until we were in the Mimosa room, lined with polished wooden filing cabinets and shelves on every wall. Large windows let in the purple evening light.

"She didn't seem to want us here," I said after double-checking the hall and closing the door tight behind us.

"Mm." Grant opened a filing-cabinet drawer, his fingertips dancing nimbly across the thick brown folders inside. "Steering Committee. It's best we tread lightly. Here we are." He drew out a thick folder and stepped over to one of the two tables in the room. He clicked on an antique lamp whose glass dome shade glowed softly, putting out lovely light. "You'll be glad to know that we have a small number of documents related to Adaire Fontaine, collected and preserved here for the education and enjoyment of posterity."

I leaned over and opened the folder. Playbills and programs waited inside, stiff and yellow with age, preserved by plastic lamination. The one on top advertised "The Dazzling Adaire Fontaine!!!" starring in a production of *Pygmalion.*

"Regrettably, I must depart and miss what is sure to be fascinating reading," Grant said. "I ask only that you tidy up. The back door will lock behind you as you leave. And should you run into Elma Danford at any time, do not mention that I left you here unsupervised."

"Hey, we're not children!" Stacey said.

"Anyone younger than fifty is considered a child in this

building. Have a good evening."

After Grant left, softly closing the door behind him, we spread everything out across the tabletop. I turned up the lights to help us read the faded print.

The artfully designed theater advertisements and play programs were charming works of a lost era, illustrated with cartoons and embellished with calligraphy. They often included photographs of the cast. Some featured Adaire Fontaine only, with minor mention of the other players.

Adaire's career as a local stage queen had only spanned three years—her innate star quality made her too big a fish for our local theater pond—but she was in a number of productions during that time.

"Bingo!" Stacey held up a program for a production of *Arsenic and Old Lace*, the cover illustrated with a kindly-looking cartoon grandmother holding a teapot. The yellowed program had been preserved in a plastic sleeve, from which Stacey had carefully extracted it. "Hey, do you think 'Bingo' is the dog's name or the farmer's name? Ever noticed you can't really tell? 'There was a farmer who had a dog and Bingo was his—'"

"What did you find?"

"Right here." She pointed to the faded cast list. "Adaire Fontaine as Elaine. Stanley Preston as Mortimer."

"So they *were* in a play together," I said.

"Not only that, but they were a couple. The characters, I mean. Elaine and Mortimer were engaged to be married. Mortimer's a much bigger part, though, if I remember right. He's onstage a lot more than Elaine."

"Maybe this was the beginning of his obsession with her. I wonder if they had a personal relationship, too."

"The biography says she dated a lot of people. Not seriously, more in a social butterfly kind of way. And she was notoriously flirtatious at parties."

"Hm. Take pictures of that program."

We continued looking through them, but only found one other connection, a lucky catch. Adaire had starred in a local production of *The Glass Menagerie* in 1948, just before moving away to New York. She was listed as Laura, one of the small number of characters.

I was just about to close that program when I saw Stanley Preston's name on the facing page, near the bottom, among the crew. He had worked as a stagehand instead of a cast member.

"I guess Stanley's acting career went downhill," I said.

"So he started looking for other ways to make money, like marrying young widows with big farms," Stacey said.

"Which brings us to the drive-in." I took pictures of the *Glass Menagerie* program. "Maybe they had a relationship, maybe not. Maybe he was just an admiring superfan."

"Yeah, or maybe he killed her!" Stacey gasped. "Are we going to solve the murder of Adaire Fontaine after all? My aunt will want to know all about this."

"I wouldn't call your aunt just yet. Remember, Adaire was murdered out in Beverly Hills."

"Oh, I know. And there was no sign of a break-in. That's why she was probably killed by someone she knew. Like Stanley."

"She didn't have any security? A bodyguard?" I asked.

"Oh, no, she couldn't afford it. Even the mansion was a rental. She blew through money like it was water. Plus, she was always loaning money to friends who mostly never got around to paying her back."

"Sounds like people took advantage of her."

"You get that impression from the biography. She was too innocent about the people around her, like she always wanted to see the best in everyone. Her childhood in rural

Georgia didn't prepare her for the shark-infested waters of Los Angeles."

We checked through the rest of the materials, but we didn't find Stanley Preston's name again. We gathered the materials back into the folder before leaving.

The hallway outside was dim. Most of the Historical Association's lights were off for the evening, and it was quiet enough to hear our own footsteps echoing down the paneled hallway. We passed paintings of local gardens, architecture, and historical personages, past bookshelves thick with volumes of local and regional history. We passed through the cutaway balcony area, looking down on the parlor, now full of shadows, the empty chairs still facing each other as though invisible occupants were gathered for a silent meeting.

"Why are you still here?" a voice snapped, and I jumped.

Elma Danford emerged from around a corner ahead, her bright eyes burning with clear disapproval.

"We were just, uh, leaving, ma'am," I said, cowed by her glare, though she was shorter than I was and stooped over.

"Patterson allowed you to remain in the archives unsupervised," she said, then clucked her tongue. "Very interesting. I hope you took great care. Every item the Association owns is unique and irreplaceable."

"Yes, well, we definitely appreciate the help." I took half a step forward, but I couldn't ease around her to the stairs. She'd positioned herself right in the middle of the hallway, blocking my way if I didn't want to literally elbow past her and risk toppling her over. She was using her age and fragility as a weapon, and I think it was deliberate.

"Only dues-paying members of the Association may be left unsupervised in the archives," she told me, really laying down the law here. "Mr. Patterson sets a poor example by flouting the rules. It is conduct unbecoming a Steering Committee member. I shall be writing a letter to the chair."

"Oh," I said, not sure what else to say. She really was steamed about not getting that spot on the Steering Committee.

"I'm afraid I must insist you depart the premises."

"That's pretty much what we're trying to do—" I began.

"Immediately."

"Right. But you're kind of blocking us," I said.

Glaring, she took her time moving one step to the side.

Stacey and I hurried past and clambered down the wide wooden stairs as fast as we could.

"No running!" Elma shouted after us, and we slowed to a fast walk until we finally escaped out the back door and into the night outside.

Chapter Twelve

At the Nite-Lite Drive-in, the big monument sign outside was dark. I almost missed the turn-off.

"No movie tonight?" I asked when Benny and Daisy rode up to meet us at the ticket booth, the headlights and reflectors glowing on their bikes. Stacey waited behind me in her car.

"Callie's at work, and none of the Bluegazers felt like volunteering," Benny said. "We haven't been rehearsing much, either. I'm working on a new song, though."

"Didn't you say you had some old movies that came with the drive-in?"

"Yeah, really old. There's a *Legend of Boggy Creek* in there, hopefully the original and not one of the unauthorized sequels. But like I said, I can't exhibit them to the public without paying a license fee. Plus, some are in really poor shape. They haven't been stored in the most careful condition."

"Are there any with Adaire Fontaine? Or maybe Chance Chadwick?"

"There's one with both of them, *Pocketful of Aces*. I know because that was sitting in the projector when we bought the place. It must have been the last movie Stanley watched before he, you know, kicked it."

"Is there any chance you could play it for us?" I asked. "Since the drive-in's closed tonight, it wouldn't technically be illegal, right?"

"Oh, no, that's more like watching it at home, I think. If nobody's paying and it's closed to the public. I can load the reel and get it going, but I can't guarantee it's in good enough condition to watch. It'll break at least once, probably more. I'd have to hang around and watch for problems."

"Stacey can probably help with any of that."

Benny nodded and pulled the lever to raise the striped arm blocking the road. "Meet me at the concession stand."

We drove on ahead, the circuitous driveway taking us the long way to the parking lot, where Stacey and I again parked on either side of the sunken old projection house in the middle of the lot.

Then we headed to the concession stand, where Benny and Daisy pedaled over to meet us. The majority of the exterior lights around the parking lot were switched off, conserving electricity while the theater was closed.

"Pizza!" Daisy proclaimed, pedaling her bicycle inside as soon as Benny opened the door.

"No pizza tonight," Benny said. "We already had dinner."

Daisy rode through the dining area and on into the game room, where she drove in circles around the foosball table. "Foosball, foosball, Daddy's gonna lose-ball!"

"Right," Benny said. He glanced from me to Stacey.

"The projection booth is, uh, cramped for four people. Is it possible for one of you to stay down here and keep an eye on Daisy?"

"And make pizza!" Daisy said.

"We're not… you already had dinner."

"Snack!" Daisy said, ogling the candy counter with its giant movie-theater-sized bags of Twizzlers and Junior Mints. Her voice rose with a hopeful question: "Maybe it's snack time?"

"It's not snack time."

"Maybe tomorrow?" Her big hazel eyes were still affixed on the Twizzlers.

"Maybe tomorrow. Probably not Twizzlers."

I sighed. "I guess I'll stay with her, since Stacey's the one who'll be monkeying with your projector if needed."

"Oh, yeah, I can shut it all down for the night, too," Stacey said, "so you don't have to come back out after the movie."

"Cool." Benny stooped toward Daisy. "Miss Ellie's going to play with you for a minute while I go upstairs, okay?"

"Foosball?" Daisy cast a hopeful look from me to the foosball table in the next room.

"Sure," I said. "But, fair warning, I'm not very good."

"I am!" Daisy skipped ahead of me into the game room, with its one game. "Foosball, foosball, Miss Ellie's gonna lose-ball…"

I followed her while Benny and Stacey headed upstairs to the projection booth. Daisy scooted a bright yellow two-step staircase out from beneath the foosball table and climbed up on it to face me. A gritty look of determination formed on her face.

"You're gonna lose-ball," the little girl said firmly, trying to intimidate me with her trash talk.

"We'll see," I said.

The ball dropped onto the shiny green playing surface, and we were off. Daisy's hands danced from one rod to another, reaching so far I thought she'd fall off her step-stool, but somehow she didn't, instead balancing on her toe-tips like she was in a ballet.

I struggled to get my little guys to whomp the ball into the wire cage of her goal, but she scored on me twice before I even got it close to her goalie, and then she immediately whacked the ball deep into my side of the table. At one point, she jabbed me in the leg with one of the rods, and she apologized but didn't stop playing while I recovered.

She also knew about the no-spinning rule, so maybe Stacey wasn't making that up.

Chance Chadwick watched over us from the *Pocketful of Aces* poster on the wall, clutching his winning five-ace hand. Handsome as he was in his gangster suit, he paled next to the gorgeous Adaire Fontaine, draped in a famous black gown and gloves, her hat tilted to emphasize the black feathers, her trademark gray eyes, exotic even in black and white, seeming to gaze deeply into me and through me.

"Boom! Lose-ball!" Daisy announced after smashing a winning goal against my hopeless foosball team. The ball dropped away into my miniature soccer goal, disappearing into the foosball table's invisible underworld of gutters and tunnels, the dark places through which foosballs passed between their death at the tabletop goal and their rebirth in the return drop. "Tough turkey! Want to play Frisbee?"

I glanced outside. It was dark, but a few exterior lights were on, and with the theater closed for the night, there wasn't any need to worry about cars driving through. "Sure. I'll just text your dad about it real quick."

Focused on my phone screen, I followed Daisy outside,

where she picked up a green Frisbee featuring Oscar the Grouch from one of the picnic tables and headed toward the parking lot.

"Hey, maybe we should play on the lawn instead of the parking lot," I suggested. It didn't seem like a good idea to encourage her to play where cars often drove.

Daisy frowned, looking past me to the wide lawn behind the concession stand. "I don't want to go there," she said.

"It's probably safer," I said. Then, not wanting to worry her, I added, "For me. In case I crash to the ground trying to catch a Frisbee. I'd rather do that on grass than pavement."

She still frowned at me, but finally sighed, "Well, I guess," as though incredibly put upon by my change of plan. She reluctantly doubled back from the parking lot.

The lawn was spacious and shadowy, enclosed by the woods and the high fence. Fortunately, the Frisbee glowed a radioactive shade of green in the dark, making it easy to see. Daisy and I threw it back and forth. Her throws were more like bowling, rolling it along the ground on its side, usually in a very wrong direction that required me to chase after it.

For my part, I was able to sling it through the air a little more effectively toward Daisy, but I was out of practice. More than once, the glowing green disc swerved unpredictably, wobbling like a UFO on its way to a crash landing in New Mexico.

Daisy enjoyed chasing after it, laughing as she pursued the glow farther and farther away each time, only to send it rolling sideways across the ground toward me like a loose hubcap.

As I sent the green disc away on another long, wobbling glide over the lawn, my phone buzzed in my pocket. Stacey was calling, because she's into voice calls rather than texting more than the average human.

"What's up?" I asked, watching the glowing disc careen to another graceless crash in the distance. *Hello, Roswell.*

"We are good to go. The *Pocketful of Aces* reels aren't in the best shape, but the movie can handle a viewing. Are we definitely going with that one? There's a few other choices up here. I don't recommend *Legend of Boggy Creek*, though."

"*Pocketful of Aces* has both Chance Chadwick and Adaire Fontaine, and if it was the last movie Stanley ever watched here, it might have the greatest chance of stirring up his ghost. Assuming he's Cigar Man."

"Or maybe we'll see Chance Chadwick again," Stacey said. "That would be pretty cool. Especially if Jacob was here to see it this time. Can he join us for the movie tonight? Like I said, he *really* wants to check out the drive-in —"

"Maybe tomorrow night. We can try screening another movie from Stanley's collection, if Benny allows it."

"Ooh, I know which one," Stacey said. "Anyway, we are good to go up here. Benny also loaded in an ad reel to buy us more time before the feature."

"Great. I'll meet you in front of the concession stand." I hung up and looked toward the glowing green disc in the distance. "Daisy, let's go. We're all done here."

The green glow didn't move. From here, it was no bigger than a tiny orb, the kind of thing we might catch on camera as a spirit passed through a room.

"Daisy?" I strode toward the distant Frisbee, getting anxious. The girl was not known for her silence. "Hey, Daisy, let's go back to your dad. Daisy?"

She didn't respond, and the glowing green spot didn't move.

I broke into a run, calling her name, my heart racing.

The Frisbee lay in the glass, glowing green, not far from the high fence at the back of the lawn. I picked it up and looked around, but there was no sign of her. The lights of the concession stand were far away, and there were none around here, just deep shadows and the high fence, its old boards and posts bone-pale in the moonlight.

"Daisy, where are you? Daisy!" There was still no sign of her, and I hadn't strapped on my utility belt for the night yet, so I had no flashlight. "Daisy!"

I walked along the fence, using my phone flashlight to light my way as I approached the glowing flying-saucer shape.

"Daisy!"

Finally, I reached the gate, the one that looked no different from any other section of fence, almost imperceptible until you stood right in front of it.

It stood ajar, open by a foot or so, enough for a small girl to squeeze through.

"Daisy?" I asked. A shiver ran through my spine as I pushed the gate panel open wide. Its hinges creaked loudly in the quiet night. The background chirping of night insects was more distant here, despite the surrounding woods, and the air again felt cooler on this side of the fence.

The farmhouse was a dark, shadowy bulk looming over me, casting everything before it into pitch darkness. I could just discern its bulky roofline against the cloudy night sky above, the broken-down widow's walk railing like a row of broken teeth in the sparse starlight.

As I looked around, trying to see in the shadow of the house, something seized my arm, cold fingers gripping tight.

"Daisy?" I said, still not seeing anything. The hand was small and trembling.

I reached out and touched her small head, her long hair. She was shaking but said nothing.

"Daisy, let's go," I said. "Your dad's waiting."

She didn't budge, though. Her hand gripped me like a claw, and it felt like she was riveted to the spot.

"Come on, Daisy," I said, amazed at how difficult it was to get her moving. I would have to pick her up if she didn't cooperate.

Then I heard her speak, her voice a tiny, raspy whisper: "She's watching us."

"Who?"

"The lady in the house."

I looked across the broken-down house again, the empty window holes, the broken railing. "I don't see anything. What does the lady look like?"

"Scary. Old and scary. Like the house." I felt Daisy shiver again. "I don't think she's alive anymore, but she still walks around."

Then I heard it, the creak of a footstep up on the roof.

It wasn't particularly heavy or loud, but it was clear in the still, quiet night, and Daisy gasped. I tried not to react, even when the second footstep sounded, followed by a small thud. It continued across the roof, in the makeshift widow's walk area, but from where I stood, and with the lack of light, I couldn't see anything beyond the railing.

Step, thump. Step, thump. As if someone were walking across the roof, watching us.

"She looks too scary," Daisy said, as if she could see a person standing up there at the railing. She trembled harder. "She looks bad."

"Let's go. Can you walk?"

"No. My feet are too heavy."

"I understand." I dropped the Frisbee and picked Daisy up, then hurried away from the house.

I stopped only to close the gate behind us. Just before I did, I took another look up at the widow's walk.

I didn't see anything there, but I heard the door leading into the house creak, as if whoever had been on the roof was stepping back inside.

After I shoved the gate closed, I broke into a run across the lawn, barreling toward the distant lights of the concession stand, moving as fast as I could with Daisy in my arms.

Chapter Thirteen

"What took so long?" Stacey asked as I reached the front of the concession stand, still holding Daisy. "You look like you've seen a… wait, *did* you see a…?" She looked from me to Daisy, clearly struggling not to say words like *ghost* with the little girl listening.

"Daisy, are you okay?" Benny asked as I passed the girl over and she wrapped her arms around his neck. "Are you hurt?"

"It was scary," she said.

"What was?" Benny looked over her tiny shoulder at me. "What happened?"

"She ended up near the farmhouse," I said.

"A scary lady lives there," Daisy added. "She's old and breathes weird and her eyes are missing but she can stare at you. I hate that house."

"You're safe now," Benny said, though he had a questioning look that seemed directed at me.

"I heard some strange sounds, too," I said. "Like footsteps. But I didn't see anyone."

"She sounded nice at first," Daisy said. "Then she got less nice."

"Did she speak to you, Daisy?" I asked.

"Yes."

"What did she say?"

"She said, 'oh little girl, dear girl, come see me,'" Daisy said. "But her voice got scary, and then I saw her, and she was too scary, Daddy!"

"Maybe y'all should head home," I told Benny, nodding at the screen tower. "Stacey and I will check out the house right away."

"We will?" Stacey asked. "I mean, yeah. Obviously. Of course." She cast a doubtful look toward the shadowy lawn behind the stand.

"Yeah, good. Good luck with it," Benny said. "Come on, Daisy. Can you pedal?"

Daisy nodded, wiping her eyes. He set her down, and the two of them bicycled away.

"What on Earth happened at the farmhouse?" Stacey asked, and I filled her in while walking to the van.

"Too bad we didn't have the cameras up and running for the night," I said as I strapped on my utility belt with the nice hefty flashlight I'd been missing earlier. "Maybe we'll catch something later."

"You think it was the same entity who made the knocking sounds last night?"

"It sounded similar to me. The obvious guess would be that it's Ruby Jackson, the sickly mother-in-law who used her cane to summon younger relatives. Daisy's description of a scary old lady would fit that, too."

"Okay, well, let's go have a look at the scary dead old lady." Stacey sighed and followed me across the lawn. We carried fresh batteries in our backpacks for the gear we'd already set up in the house, plus an extra night vision camera and tripod.

The gate resisted my first attempt to open it, like the hinges had stuck, but it finally relented and swung inward, admitting us into the darkness.

"Whoa, aliens," Stacey said, pointing to the glowing green Frisbee.

"Grouches aren't aliens. We'll grab it on the way out." I looked up at the roofline where Daisy and I had heard the footsteps. There was nothing moving up there now, as far as I could tell.

We stepped through the doorway onto the creaking floorboards of the house, dodging spindly trees and spiderwebs on our way to the loose, wobbly staircase inside.

Again, we took it one at a time to reduce the risk of the stairs collapsing beneath us. I went up first, then waited at the top for Stacey.

The door to the roof stood wide open, but fortunately the entity in the house hadn't damaged our gear.

While Stacey changed out camera and microphone batteries, I had another look at the bedroom of Stanley Preston's mother-in-law, Ruby Jackson. The cane still hung on the closet doorknob. I looked at all the overlapping dimples in the floor next to the bed, thinking of what Leah had told me about her grandmother banging the floorboards for attention. I thought I could detect the cloying, flowery perfume odor again.

"Got the batteries in." Stacey arrived with the extra night vision camera. "Where do you want it, boss?"

"Ruby Jackson died in the 1950s, but this room still smells like her perfume," I said.

"Well, there's some on the dresser, right?" Stacey nodded at glass bottles arranged next to a framed, faded black-and-white farm photo. Everything lay under a thick layer of dust.

"It's like she remained a major presence in the house long after she died." I rummaged around. In a nightstand, I found dozens of medicine bottles, their labels faded, and an odd-looking device with a large rubber bulb at one end and a clear plastic tube and nozzle at the other. I took snapshots with my phone.

"You think she's the one you heard walking around earlier?" Stacey asked.

"It all fits. Let's set the camera in the hallway, looking into this room."

The house made my skin crawl like I was covered in bugs. I was eager to finish our work and leave. We set up the camera quickly and hurried down the stairs, again taking turns lest it fall apart under our combined weight and motion.

After hurrying out the front door, I breathed easier once we departed the shadow of the house and closed the gate behind us.

Next, we switched out batteries on our other gear, which included an unpleasant visit to the tomb-like sunken projection house in the middle of the parking lot, with its damp floor and walls and the crumbling ruins of the 1950s fire-hazard projector. We hurried, standing back-to-back down there so nothing could come shambling up behind either one of us.

I returned to the van to check that our monitors were receiving everything well. Stacey went to the concession stand to start the movie.

The big movie screen lit up with colorful, cartoony letters surrounding by equally colorful and cartoony stars: WELCOME TO OUR DRIVE-IN! This gave way to more text: COMING ATTRACTIONS! Both of these looked generic, like they'd been made for the use of any drive-in rather than this particular one.

I turned on the van's radio in time to hear "…will be coming soon to this theater!" in a nasal, old-time Walter Winchell kind of radio personality voice.

I settled into the driver's seat to watch.

The screen went dark, and a tense soundtrack began to play, piano in an eerie minor key.

On the screen, a pleasant-looking suburban house appeared, and the view zoomed in slowly over the neatly trimmed lawn and hedges to the front door.

"It looks like any other home, but this house has a secret," a voice said, a sinister Vincent Price-ish voice replacing the honking Walter Winchell-esque one.

The view jumped abruptly into an interior hallway. The house looked pleasantly well-appointed on the inside, too, as the viewpoint moved past open doors, peering into a living room, kitchen, and bedrooms, all neatly kept, perfectly mid-1960s suburban middle class, neither showy nor shabby.

The door at the end of the hall, though, looked completely out of place, not so pleasant and innocent, certainly out of place in this world of Tupperware parties and PTA socials. The door was inexplicably lashed together from mismatched boards, scrap wood, and metal bolts, and it was the only door in the house that was closed.

"A certain sort of evil lurks down below," the Vincent Price guy continued in his overdone spooky tone.

The door rattled like something was trying to get out.

There was a close-up of a woman screaming.

"Coming soon to this very theater," the voice resumed. "A chilling tale of unspeakable terror, *The Body in the Basement!*"

A face appeared in the window beside me, and I

gasped, jerking away from it. By the time I grabbed my flashlight, I realized it was Stacey, smiling and waving.

"Don't sneak up on me," I said, lowering the window.

"What did you think of it?"

"It was a pretty mean prank to sneak up after that house back there."

"No, I mean *The Body in the Basement!* Can you believe they have it?"

"Yeah, I'm pretty sure I never want to see that movie."

"But they have the whole movie here! Not just the trailer. Jacob's going to do a freak-flip when he hears we can watch it on thirty-five-mil at a drive-in. With the whole Mazzanti murder-movie angle, you can't find the movie anywhere these days, like Hollywood decided to completely memory-hole it."

"That looked pretty bad for a supposedly famous filmmaker."

"Well, that's the thing. His later stuff is just *so* bad. It's his early movies that some people considered genius. There were a couple of guys back in film school who said he was better than Fellini, but I think they were trying to be edgy or iconoclastic or just trolling people.

"Point is, when Mazzanti was young he made some very different, visionary films that were considered brilliant. *The Heart of Man*—that's about a priest who follows the devil through an eighteenth-century Venetian carnival, and the devil takes different shapes. An aristocrat, a beautiful dancer, a street criminal. An artist. At least, most people say it's the devil. It's kind of nonlinear and open to interpretation. But when you watch it, you get very drawn in, even if you're not sure what you just experienced when it was over. Then there's *Stanzas for Regina*, which is about an elderly woman remembering her life in hallucinogenic flashbacks. I think. That one was even harder to follow, honestly, yet also considered brilliant.

"But that was the early 1950s. By the late 1960s, Mazzanti was making, well, stuff like *The Body in the Basement*." Stacey nodded at the big screen, where the horror movie trailer had thankfully passed. The opening credits of *Pocketful of Aces* now played, but there was no action on the screen yet, just a series of title cards while jazz crackled on the soundtrack.

"I wonder why his later work changed so much," I said.

"Drugs!" Stacey said. "And alcohol. Way too much of both, and I guess they chewed up his brain. He went in for that side of Hollywood, the parties and reckless living. Just like Adaire Fontaine and Chance Chadwick. You know what they say, live fast and die young. And in his case, murder people along the way."

"How did Antonio Mazzanti die, again?"

"Also drugs," Stacey said. "Heroin overdose. He was living in a cheap Skid Row hotel by then, and they found him dead on the floor."

"You've really dug into the research on this case."

"Yeah, movie star biographies are more interesting than a typical stack of county tax records, believe it or not. Shh, we're missing it."

The movie unfolded, a grim noir film about gangsters and gambling. Chance Chadwick played a handsome devilish rogue of a poker player, in town for the big game —it wasn't clear what town, but it looked like a big industrial city like Detroit. Adaire Fontaine was the girlfriend of the city's most powerful mob boss, who hosted the big illegal poker tournament.

As it turned out, Chadwick's character was secretly out for personal revenge against the mob boss, who'd killed his brother. The real plan was to rob the mob boss blind, and Chadwick had to seduce Adaire Fontaine into the plot, along with other conspirators.

Adaire stole every moment she was onscreen. Her eyes, huge and beautiful and hypnotic, had no doubt entranced audiences regardless of whether they cared about the clunky heist-caper plot.

Stacey and I took turns watching the monitors in the back of the van. Hopefully, the movie would stir up some local spirits, bring them out of hiding, especially if this was the last movie that had played at the drive-in before it closed.

I looked at each haunted hotspot in turn, watching for movement—the projection house, the farmhouse, the tower's third floor. Nothing stirred.

During one of my turns in the back, I heard Stacey shout from up front, "That was it!"

"What?" I scrambled up to look out the windshield, then both windows.

"The movie!" She pointed to the screen, and I looked up to see Chance Chadwick and Adaire Fontaine in a passionate embrace, a neon BAR & LOUNGE sign glowing behind them.

"Yeah, I figured they would end up together," I said.

"This isn't the end. Anyway, I think they just said that dialogue we recorded the other night and tried to figure out. You didn't hear?"

"I wasn't listening, sorry. Can we rewind…?" The word was barely out of my mouth before I knew how ridiculous it sounded. We couldn't just back up the video with the touch of a button. Someone would have to go up in the projection booth and do it manually. And by "someone," I meant Stacey.

"I can go stop the movie and roll it back," she offered, as if reading my mind.

"When you do, make a digital recording as the movie

plays again, so we'll have a copy that we *can* rewind and replay easily."

"Ooh, good idea. Back in a flash. Or probably not a flash, because this could take a while. I can't rush with that fragile old film. I'm surprised it hasn't broken yet." Stacey hopped out and headed toward the concession stand.

I stayed in the van and continued watching *Pocketful of Aces* on the big screen. The movie had tastefully cut away from the Chadwick/Fontaine love scene, jumping ahead to the big mob boss sitting around with his assistant mobsters in a smoky room, explaining their plan to rob all the players at the big poker game. Everybody was plotting against everybody in this movie. Adaire sauntered in, serving drinks, delivering flirtatious lines as she learned their scheme.

Later, she walked down a grim alley in the dark city, a long raincoat buttoned over her black dress, her eyes large and her facial expression complex, tension and fear boiling under a cool surface. Rain spattered her as she walked. It fell slowly at first, then rose to a torrent as she approached the cheap hotel where she would meet Chance Chadwick to pass him the information, the storm perhaps reflecting her character's hidden inner turmoil and the growing dangers of their ever more risky plot against the murderous mobsters. The camera lingered on her face and her walk through the rain for almost a full minute, as if knowing the audience would drink up the stunning visual of her. Bluesy jazz played counterpoint to the rain and thunder.

Lightning flashed, and the screen went completely dark.

I was startled for a moment, before realizing Stacey had shut down the movie. I'd been drawn in, forgetting the real world around me.

In the darkness and quiet, each passing second reminded me of how isolated and alone I was out there. I kept my eyes on the sunken projection house not far away, waiting to see if the parking lot phantom would emerge to stalk me.

Focused on that tomb-like structure, I glimpsed a flicker of white at the edge of my vision.

I looked up and scanned the parking lot, trying to figure out what I'd just seen and where it had gone, but I couldn't spot it.

After disabling the van's dome light, I eased open the door and stepped out as quietly as I could.

A sort of electricity seemed to hang in the air, though no storm was expected that night. Wind rushed through the high trees surrounding the drive-in, the oceanic rushing of leaves like a thousand voices whispering above me.

Then I saw it again, the pale white shape crossing the parking lot, in the direction of the concession stand, as well as the lawn and the farmhouse beyond. I had the impression of a female, perhaps wearing a white hood or veil.

If it had been more solid, I might have thought it was Callie home from work, dressed her in chef's whites. But the figure was wispy and indistinct, barely there at all.

My heart pounded and my adrenaline surged, the way it does in the presence of the supernatural, but I forced myself to remain still, rooted to the spot as I watched, for fear of running off the entity. Perhaps we'd been wrong, and the parking lot phantom was a woman, not Stan Preston at all.

It moved soundlessly across the blacktop, floating like a strand of silk on the wind toward the concession stand, where every light was out except for a single interior one, illuminating the big clear cube of the popcorn machine with a buttery yellow glow.

The pale figure vanished before reaching even the weak

square of light cast from inside.

I hurried into the concession stand and looked toward the game room. If the entity had continued on the same path after turning invisible, it would be in there.

The double doors to the game room were closed tight. Had they been that way before? Maybe Benny had closed them for the night before I'd returned with his daughter crying in my arms.

I touched a doorknob, cautious as a firefighter testing for heat, but I was checking for cold. And I found it. The doorknob was chilly to the touch, as if it were winter inside the game room.

There was a good chance the entity was still in there.

I took a breath, trying to steel my nerves for whatever unknown thing waited within, and slowly turned the knob and eased open the door.

The game room was cold and dim, illuminated only by the weak light spilling over my shoulder from the popcorn machine area behind me.

I slipped inside, touching my holstered flashlight but resisting the temptation to draw it.

Something was in the room with me. I couldn't see it, but I felt it, watching me but lurking out of my sight, staying invisible. I shivered, both from the cold and from that awful sense of not being alone in the room.

Instead of my flashlight, I drew a small voice recorder from my belt. I forced myself to speak against the instinctive fear of the supernatural that tried to close up my throat, that whispered in the back of my mind that I should panic and run away. Even after years of paranormal investigations, I had to fight the basic fear that most people, as well as most animals, feel in the presence of the restless dead.

"Hello?" I said, trying to sound casual and not let my

voice tremble. "Is someone here?" It was almost like the opening gambit of a Ouija board session. "If there's someone here, I'm listening. My name is Ellie. I am here to help you. We can help you move on from here. Would you like that?"

No response. At least it didn't attack—no cold claws ripping into my back, no invisible hands shoving me against the wall. Not yet.

"Is your name... Ruby Jackson? Was that you walking around in the old house?" No answer. "Did you speak to that little girl?"

Nothing. I went fishing with another name.

"Are you Nancy Preston? Ruby's daughter? Stanley's wife? Are you still here, haunting your old home after all these years?" I walked in a long, slow circle around the room, not sure exactly where the entity was located. Maybe it was spread out, diffused throughout the room rather than in a particular place.

"Please tell me your name," I said. "Say anything you like. I'm listening. Do you have a message for the living? A story that needs to be told? Or maybe you suffered an injustice? Or a tragedy?" I was continuing to fish, hoping for a bite.

The first sound was small—a brief metallic rattling.

It sounded again, louder, and one of the metal rods of the foosball table shuddered.

The rod handles moved slightly, one after the other, as though someone were invisibly brushing their fingers across them. The small player figures dangling from the rods rocked and swayed as if touched by a strong breeze.

I put away my voice recorder and drew out my phone to take video, but by the time I opened the camera app and pressed record, the rods and the figures had gone still again.

"Hello?" I said again. "Is someone there? I'm listening if you want to talk—"

All the rods slammed toward me at once. I barely managed to leap backwards before one rod handle stabbed me in the gut. While I avoided major organ damage, I stumbled and fell into an awkward sitting position on the floor near the wall. My phone skittered away from my hand.

"That… wasn't very nice." I reached to draw my flashlight, and with my other I prepared to blast a little Aretha Franklin-powered holy music from the speaker on my belt to drive back the aggressive spirit.

Before I could do either, though, the entire table slid across the floor toward me, threatening to crush me against the wall.

I rolled aside as the corner of the table slammed into the wall just beside me, near where my head had been.

"Stop it!" I shouted, which probably didn't come across as commanding as I'd hoped.

Something large came rushing down from above.

The table had slammed into the wall below one of the movie posters, which came unmoored by the impact and toppled forward.

As it fell, I found myself looking into the stunning gray eyes of Adaire Fontaine. It was the *Pocketful of Aces* poster, swinging down toward me in its heavy lighted frame.

I flinched aside as it smashed face first into the edge of the foosball table. The glass front of the poster's frame shattered into a thousand pieces, half of them raining down onto the green foosball playing field, the other half raining down onto me and the floor.

I clicked on my flashlight and pointed it toward the center of the room, where the table had been, striking the entity with three thousand lumens of full-spectrum white light, trying to defend myself.

In that instant before my flashlight turned on, looking into the dark room ahead, I saw something that I first took for a ghostly afterimage of the movie poster.

She was as pale and misty as she'd been outside, but now so close I could see her face, as beautiful as in all the pictures. Her big, captivating gray eyes drank me in.

An apparition of Adaire Fontaine stood before me— and in my haste to defend myself, I chased her away with a blast of white light.

When I clicked off the flashlight to restore the darkness, she had gone, and the icy chill of her presence had gone with her.

Chapter Fourteen

"Whoa! Are you okay? What happened?" Stacey turned on the overhead lights and ran to my side, helping me up though I didn't really need it. I shook broken glass off my jacket and out of my hair.

"I guess the movie worked," I said. "Another entity showed up to the party, looking for trouble."

"What kind of entity? Any idea who it was?"

"I got a good look at her. And it definitely looked like Adaire Fontaine."

"What? You got to meet Adaire Fontaine?" Stacey drew back in shock. "I am… so jelly. Super jelly. Lime jelly, because I'm green with envy." She looked around the empty game room. "Do you think she's still here?"

"It wasn't great. She threw a table at my head."

"That's so like her! Passionate and impulsive."

"Yeah, she's a real charmer. We need to clean up this broken glass. See if you can find a broom."

While Stacey sought out janitorial supplies, I gathered up my phone, fortunately undamaged after its high-speed collision with the floor, but that was why I paid extra for the sport pack. I stopped the video recording and replayed it. The phone had captured a couple seconds of a dark, blurry partial view of the table lunging at me, following many seconds of a dark, blurry view of the ceiling after it flew out of my reach. Amazing camera work.

Stacey returned with a broom, dustpan, and a big shop-vac so we could suck the broken glass from inside the foosball table.

Before we could do that, though, we had to lift away the poster frame, which was wooden and even heavier than it looked. Good thing the foosball table had blocked it from landing on my skull.

Stacey gave me a hand, and we heaved it away as delicately as we could, wary of the broken glass inside.

The movie poster flopped out facedown onto the foosball rods when we lifted the frame away. Small, yellowed squares of paper dropped out of the frame, having been concealed behind the poster.

Stacey and I shared a look—*this* was definitely something—and hurried to put aside the frame so we could study the unexpected items.

A stiff, faded postcard showed the Lyceum Theater on Broadway in New York, its facade full of bright lights and soaring columns. I turned it over to read the large, looping handwriting aloud: "'Dearest Stanley—'"

"Oh, dear*est*, not just dear," Stacey said. "Interesting."

"'I have arrived safely in New York, and it has been the grandest of times already. It is a world of dreams, and while I suffer awe and fear at the strangeness and size of the city, there are so many theaters, opera houses, playhouses, dance halls, nightclubs—it is all so fine! I do look forward to your visit, when I shall show you the town, and no doubt entice you to join me here. All my love, Adaire Fontaine.' And she wrote her name really big, like signing an autograph." I showed Stacey.

"Ooh, that's probably worth some cash," she said.

"It's dated 1949."

"*Definitely* worth some cash. That would have been just after she moved to New York."

"She sent him this in 1951." I held up a postcard featuring the Hollywood sign in the hills. "Want to hear it?"

"Of course."

"'Dearest Stanley…' There she goes with the 'dearest' again. 'I am having the most wonderful time on set. Film acting is a rather different craft than the stage, as you know, both allowing and demanding greater subtlety. But posh on the stiff stuff—I'm to be in a feature! Watch for me playing a party girl in Hotel Island, with the amazing Chance Chadwick. My part in the film is small and short, as is my dress! Tell me your latest, even if only auditions—your talent is true, and your time will come! Beloved as ever, Adaire Fontaine.'"

"Benny and Callie could probably sell this big autograph for a bundle, too," Stacey said. "Enough to replace a hundred lighted poster frames."

"And there's a letter." I picked up the yellowed envelope, ripped open along one end, and tucked it into my jacket pocket.

"What? We're not reading it now?" Stacey looked outraged.

"Let's clean up the broken glass first."

"Ugh. Fine."

After some effort, we gathered up and threw away all the glass, vacuuming afterward to be safe.

"What happened with the movie?" I asked Stacey as we

put the supplies away in the concession stand's janitorial closet. "Did you make a digital recording?"

"No, I rolled back the reel, but you got all noisy down here with the crashing and smashing before I could start the replay. I'll go do it now."

While she returned upstairs, I stepped outside. The night was warm, certainly warmer than the game room had been, summer clearly just around the corner. The insects were chorusing again. It was dark until the projector flared to life above, creating a glowing square on the second-story window.

On the screen tower, Chance Chadwick and Adaire Fontaine appeared again. This time they stood on the roof of his grungy apartment building, surrounded by other grungy buildings. They were having some kind of quarrel, but Stacey hadn't activated the exterior speakers around the concession stand, and I wasn't back in the van to hear the radio, so it was like a silent film.

Then I remembered I'd attempted an EVP—electronic voice phenomenon—session with Adaire before she'd hurled the foosball table at me. I played that back while watching the large, glowing, silent black and white people on the screen.

Adaire spun dramatically from Chance and faced away from him, while he remained in the background, growing indistinct, continuing to speak without making any sound that I could hear.

A voice spoke on my recorder, too soft to hear.

I played it again, louder. Out spilled a low, breathy voice, like that of Adaire Fontaine in some of her more emotive moments.

"Look at me."

Even as her recorded voice spoke, the image on the screen tower shifted so that the background, including

Chadwick, faded into almost complete darkness. Adaire's face remained, enormous, taking up most of the screen, her eyes wide and imploring.

"Look at me…" repeated the recorded voice from the device in my hand. Then a third time, much more firmly: *"Look at me!"*

Apparently, that was what she'd been trying to communicate while I spoke to her inside the concession stand. When I'd failed to look at her, she'd thrown a table, as one does. And brought my attention to her long-hidden correspondence.

"I'm looking at you now," I told the face on the screen. She continued gazing out at me, the scene behind her darkened and forgotten, her immense gray eyes large enough to swallow me. No wonder she'd been a star.

"Hey, I got it!" Stacey skipped out the front door of the concession stand, waving her digital video camera around. "I bootlegged it, back-row style. Did you watch the scene?"

"Yeah, but I couldn't hear it." Up on the movie screen, the scene had shifted to a paddlewheel riverboat where the mob boss hosted the poker game. It was a swanky black-tie party, everyone dressed to the nines, or whatever they said in the early fifties. White-coated staff circulated with trays of wine glasses and hors d'oeuvres, and there was a live three-piece band, just to let us know this was a pretty fancy gathering indeed.

"Looks like it's almost time for the big game," I said.

"And the big heist," Stacey added.

"Let me see what you just recorded."

"But then we'll miss the next part—"

"You go listen to the movie and catch me up when I get there."

"Deal!" Stacey handed me her camera and sprinted to

the van so she could tune in over the radio system.

I walked more slowly, my eyes on the little screen in my hand.

The hotel rooftop scene I'd just watched played again, filmed by Stacey up in the projection booth as it had played on the distant screen tower. She'd zoomed in, so the image was a bit grainy.

The scene was different this time. For one thing, I could hear what they were saying instead of just looking at their faces. I watched it play out, turning up the volume.

"You can't cash me out like that," Chance Chadwick said on the screen in my hand. "Just deal me back in, honey. That's all I'm asking. Without you, it's like I'm playing without a full deck."

"You're too much of a wild card." Adaire spun away from him dramatically. "I need a man with a strong, steady hand. Who thinks about the long game. Who doesn't put all his chips on the table because he thinks he has to win big every time."

"You mean somebody like *him*? Listen, doll, he may own a few clubs—he may even be king of this town—but I know you. You're not the kind of gal whose heart can be bought with diamonds, not even by a man who's got 'em in spades." He stepped forward and took her arm.

"Oh, I can't keep bluffing like this. I may lose big, but it's the only game worth playing." She spun back toward him, getting in his face. She stared at him, and he stared back, their eyes locked, silent tension palpable through the screen. "I'm upping the ante, and I'm ready to bet it all. But you better not turn out to be some joker."

"I'm no joker, honey. I'm the ace, and you're my queen." He kissed her, and the musical score hit a crescendo as the camera panned away from the lovers to a neon martini glass blinking above a dive-looking bar.

"That was weird," I said out loud, to nobody but myself. I played it again.

When I'd watched it on the big screen, Adaire had turned away for a long, long moment, everything going dark behind her, leaving all in shadows but her face staring out at me.

On the digitally recorded version, when she whirled away from Chadwick, he'd come up right behind her, never going fuzzy and dark, and taken her arm. It had somehow played out differently than when I'd watched it up on the big screen.

"That's not possible," I said, also out loud. How could Stacey's recording of it be different from what I'd seen? We'd been watching the same projection at the same time.

It was as if Adaire had broken the fourth wall, as well as the veil between worlds, and looked out at me personally from the big screen. Perhaps she'd wanted to see whether I'd gotten her message.

When I returned to the van, I wasn't sure how to explain all that succinctly to Stacey. She immediately jumped into catching me up on the movie, anyway.

On the screen, the party boat rolled on, watched by a group of masked armed men on a riverbank, or maybe a lakeshore, who prepared to board a small motorboat.

"Okay, so those guys are going to rob the gambling boat," Stacey explained, "but they're actually the mob boss's henchmen. It's an inside job. But—oh!" Another group of men, led by Chance Chadwick himself, leaped out and ambushed the masked henchmen, literally from behind bushes, in a somewhat improbable fight scene.

Then Chance and the others stole the coats and masks from the henchmen and left them tied to a tree.

"Ah, the old double-reverse inside job that becomes an outside job," I said.

"Yes, so the mob boss, he'll think he's getting secretly robbed by his own guys, and he'll go along with it."

"But isn't Chance supposed to be playing in the big poker game, too? He'll have to move fast to make all that work."

"Indeed he will," Stacey said.

Soon the movie cut back to the party boat, where Adaire entertained her mob boss boyfriend. She stepped away and looked out off the deck, toward the shore. For a moment I wondered if she was going to darken the rest of the movie and stare into my soul again, but she stayed in character this time, signaling the armed robbers with a cigarette lighter. Her character was playing both sides of the fence, a dangerous game, a big gamble. I still wasn't sure where her true loyalties fell—with the mob boss or the charming gambler plotting against him. That was good acting.

I found myself on the edge of my seat as the heist plot unfolded, watching to see if Adaire would throw me another look or another clue. Anything to confirm what I thought had happened earlier.

The heist went awry. Gunshots rang out. Gamblers, gangsters, waiters, and musicians died in the crossfire, strewn around the boat in their tuxedos and fur coats.

It all boiled down to a final gunfight, with Chance Chadwick cornered in a shootout with the mobsters, hunkered down next to Adaire behind a piano.

Adaire lay on the ship's deck beside him, dying from a gunshot wound.

"Maybe we were wrong," she whispered. "We bet too high. You can bluff and cheat for a while, but you can't win the whole game that way. Sooner or later, they call your bluff, they spot the ace up your sleeve, and the house comes down on you hard."

"Don't say that," Chance told her. "We'll cash out here and move on. We'll be playing with a whole new hand of cards after tonight. You'll see."

"Oh, but don't you know?" she sighed. "There are no new cards, not really. It's just the same old cards, being dealt again... and again... and again..." As she died, she released a stack of cards she'd been holding, and the wind scattered them across the boat deck and over the edge into the water.

"That's it," Chance's character said. "If we aren't walking out of here as a pair, I'm bringing down the whole dirty house of cards."

He charged out at the mobsters, a gun in each hand, and they all died in a mutual shootout.

The camera panned to the water below, where the blood-spattered cards floated face up—all aces.

Then the movie faded to black, and the credits rolled.

"That... was bleak at the end," I said.

"Yep, that's noir for you. These days, they'd never allow a sad ending where everyone dies. Maybe they were going for Shakespearean tragedy there, wrapped in hardboiled crime tropes."

"If you say so." I yawned and stretched. "Anyway, it looks like the movie worked. We evoked an entity."

"Yep, I should go shut down the projector." She shook her head. "I can't believe you got to see Adaire Fontaine in person. You had no idea who she was a week ago."

"I'd heard of her," I said defensively. "I think."

"Ugh."

"Want to hear her voice?" I asked.

"Seriously? You got EVP from Adaire Fontaine, too? This case is solid gold. Like classic country gold, with Patsy Cline."

I played the EVP for her, Adaire's husky voice

demanding, "Look at me… look at me… look at me…"

Stacey's jaw dropped; ghostly voices are always a bit startling. "Sounds like something she'd say. She craved attention and praise, hated to be alone. Loved crowds, especially if she could be at the center of them."

"Meaning she would hate life as a ghost," I said.

"Especially a ghost in the middle of nowhere. Maybe she'd enjoy haunting some famous theater that still holds major performances. Maybe even an opera house. But out here… why *would* she even be here?"

"That's the million-dollar question. I was leaning toward Stanley being a psycho stalker, maybe even the real murderer instead of Antonio Mazzanti—"

"That's just what I was thinking!"

"—and maybe Stan hunted her down, perhaps motivated by jealousy, because she went on to become a famous movie star, and he didn't. Maybe he had obsessed over her in some creepy way ever since they worked together."

"You and me, same brain waves." Stacey pointed back and forth between our heads.

"But she went pretty far out of her way to reveal these notes she sent Stanley." I tapped my pocket. "Maybe we've been on the wrong trail. And of course, maybe it wasn't really Adaire Fontaine's ghost. Ghosts can take on different appearances. Some specialize in it."

"Like the *aufhocker* from that necromancer's library."

"Right."

"Only this would be a ghost acting like it was a famous actress," Stacey said. "Disguises within disguises. An actor turducken. An actorducken."

"Possibly. Then again, maybe she really is here, because of her attachment to the man who built and operated the drive-in. We'll find out more when we read her letter."

"Which we're doing right now. Right?"

"Shouldn't you shut down the projector?"

Stacey sighed. "Fine." She opened her door, then hesitated. "You know, after hearing that ghost's voice… and considering how it threw a foosball table at you… I'm not super wild about going in there alone. Even if I could meet Adaire Fontaine."

"Yeah, of course, I'll come with you." I jumped out with her.

"And maybe you can read that letter while I do it," Stacey added as I followed her toward the concession stand.

Inside, I couldn't help glancing toward the game room to see if Adaire was back, but I didn't see any sign of her, nor feel a cold spot anymore.

Stacey led the way to the EMPLOYEES ONLY – DO NOT ENTER door, which she unlocked. "It locks from the outside automatically," she told me.

The door opened onto stairs that led up to the concession stand's second floor, which had a rough, unfinished look, with lots of bare particle board and sheetrock. It was a smaller space than the first level, added years after the drive-in opened, when Stanley had upgraded from the 1955 fire-hazard projector of the old sunken building to the 1970 projector that was still up there.

Metal cabinets held assorted equipment, repair tools, and a number of film reels. The creaky thirty-five-millimeter projector was still turning its wheels, the loose tail end of the *Pocketful of Aces* reel flopping again with each rotation until Stacey turned it off.

"How did you like the movie?" Stacey removed the decades-old film reel, handling it like fragile crystal. "Are you an Adaire Fontaine fan yet?"

"I can see the star quality."

"Then why don't we look at the big secret letter, already?"

"Oh, are you still interested in that?" I pretended to search my pockets. "Where did I even put that letter? Didn't we put it away somewhere?"

"It's in your jacket, that big inside pocket."

"Right." I drew it out and carefully unfolded the stationery full of Adaire's large and loopy handwriting. The return address was an apartment building or hotel in New York City. "Are you sure you want to hear this?"

"Why? Have you read it already? Is it bad?"

"I haven't read it. Just wondering whether you'd changed your mind about being interested in this letter—"

"Ellie, quit it! That could be a major historical document, revealing new secrets the world will want to know."

"Maybe it's not totally the world's business," I said.

"Fine, but *I* want to know, so get reading or I'm grabbing it out of your hands and running away."

"Okay. As long as you're sure you want to hear this."

She glared at me.

I took a breath and began to read.

Chapter Fifteen

My dearest Stanley,

I hope this finds you well, along with all the old gang back home. It's been a non-stop hoot of a time up here, despite the unnatural cold. I am warmed by the lights of Broadway, of the coffee houses of the Village, the worlds of art and culture in this grand and dazzling metropolis. I finally feel like I belong here, not least because audiences have been so kind, despite the ridiculous nature of this latest play. I swear the writer must have been lost in the clouds half the time, and spent the rest wallowing in the gutter.

But never mind the script, the performance fooled the audience well enough. They simply believed it to be a witting comedy, as opposed to an unwitting one, and you know how I love the chance to overdo it all—it is my specialty!

I continue to wish for your visit, as I am now prepared to show you many sights (and sites!) and introduce you to the most interesting people. I know you hesitate, but fear need not be a leash or a prison, dear Stanley—it can indeed be a stimulant, even an intoxicant, particularly when mixed with fine and colorful liquors as they do at the Stonewall. My neighborhood is most lively; creativity is a lifestyle here.

So, come! Do come. Treat these recent years of despair as an opportunity, leave behind that dreadful scene that no longer appreciates you, and make your way here, to flourish among like-minded souls!

You say your face, your childhood scars, limit you, but I believe it gives you character, and something unique, and I have never found it to be a face to push out of bed, not even at sunrise, at which time the necessity of such measures most often becomes suddenly apparent.

On that inappropriate note, I shall end. I sense destiny in you. I wish only for you to sense it in yourself! All will be well in the end.

Yours most ravishingly,
Adaire Fontaine

"Okay, so now I'm almost getting a reverse stalker scenario," Stacey said. "Beautiful Hollywood starlet stalks homely former acquaintance from back home? Has that been done before? On Lifetime, maybe?"

"Probably on Lifetime, yeah. Anyway, they were clearly friendly with each other, not just acquaintances or passing members of the same cast. And she came back from the grave to let us know about it."

"Why us?" Stacey asked.

"Maybe the movie did it. Also, I reached out and offered her my help during that EVP session. I hope I didn't promise something I can't deliver."

"Which means we should screen more of the old movies, right?"

"If there are more with Chance Chadwick, or Adaire

Fontaine, or both…"

"'Both' would be *Hotel Island*, but I didn't see that in here earlier…" Stacey peered into the steel cabinet holding the film reels. "We should probably watch anything directed by Antonio Mazzanti, right?"

"True."

"Ha!" She gave me a wicked smile. "You just agreed to watch *Body in the Basement*."

"You can screen it, but I don't have to watch it. I'll find other work to do."

"Oh, come on!" Her face fell.

"They aren't paying us to just sit around watching movies, Stacey."

"I mean, they're paying us in gift certificates and popcorn and pizza—"

"That was your idea."

"I have no regrets. Maybe I'll have my birthday party here."

"And I'll just pay my rent with pizza," I said.

"If your landlord tries this pizza, that could possibly work."

"Good point. Is there anything else we could screen?"

"Oh. Wow." Stacey took in a sharp breath as she lifted another reel. "This is really interesting. You know, his whole collection of films here is pretty impressive. The studios don't like leaving these out in the wild. Usually, you lease them and return them."

"What's that one?"

"This is the one that really earned Mazzanti his reputation. *The Heart of Man*."

"With the shapeshifting devil in Venice?"

"Oh, yeah. But here's the problem…" She unspooled a long stretch of it, showing me lots of lumps and bumps. "It's totally worn down. It's been repaired a bunch of times, which means it's been watched a bunch of times. This one probably won't survive another spin through the projector."

"It might be worn down because Stanley watched it again and again?"

"Possibly."

"So he might be emotionally connected to it."

"I see where you're going. I'd save it as a last resort, though." She put it back delicately. "How about *Bootlegger Boulevard*? It's a later Chance Chadwick film."

"Okay. Got anything with her, though?" I couldn't help wondering if Adaire might reach out to me again, or if that moment had been my imagination. It certainly didn't match the video evidence Stacey had taken, and when in doubt, I'd been trained to go with the evidence. Otherwise, the world of ghosts and the supernatural grows murky and confusing fast.

Stacey gave me a half-grin. "You're turning into a fan, aren't you?"

"We have to follow up *The Body in the Basement* with something less awful."

"Okay. *Legend of the South* it is. Our double feature for tomorrow night is set. Jacob's going to freak."

"I'm glad he's coming. Maybe he can help us figure out why this place is overrun with dead celebrities. Plus, he can watch that horror movie with you."

"Come on, you might enjoy it! You can sit in my car with us if you're scared."

"Pass," I said. "I'm not third-wheeling it with you and your boyfriend at the drive-in."

"You could fourth-wheel it and invite Michael, too."

I hesitated. "Nah. I still try to keep him away from all this. After his sister and everything."

Stacey nodded. We'd barely managed to save his sister from possession by the murderous ghost of Anton Clay.

Who was now gone and buried at last, I could reasonably hope. The drive to protect the living against the dead was still ingrained in me, though, a life's purpose, a calling I could never shake, because not enough people out there know the dangers of the paranormal realm, or how to combat them. And those who know are still wise to avoid some of those entities rather than face them.

We returned to the van, settling in the back to watch and listen to the monitors.

It had been an extraordinarily active night, between the farmhouse and the ghost of Adaire—or the one who'd chosen to look like Adaire, I reminded myself.

After the movie, the drive-in went quiet again. No thumps from the farmhouse, no ghost movies on the screen.

With just a preliminary look at the night's recordings from the sunken projection house, Stacey found ice-cold spots and giant spikes of electromagnetic activity while *Pocketful of Aces* had played on the screen. It looked like Cigar Man—Stanley Preston himself, by my guess—had been up and around the previous night but hadn't been moved to come out and haunt us. Maybe he'd gotten absorbed in watching the movie, too.

An hour passed with no further activity. Then another. Stacey and I walked out to do EVP sessions, asking questions around the areas we suspected of being most haunted, including the projection house, the game room in the concession stand, and the farmhouse, but the entities seemed to have gone to ground after the night's excitement.

Eventually, we broke camp and headed home relatively early. We left the van there, collecting data from the various cameras and microphones for us to study later. Stacey dropped me off at my apartment at about two in the morning. I was exhausted, an aftereffect of the adrenaline spikes from encountering ghosts and dodging foosball tables.

I barely managed to text Callie and Benny to explain the situation, in case they wondered why the picture frame from the game room was now in a garbage bag, waiting to be repaired or tossed out.

When I stretched out on my bed and closed my eyes, I could still see Adaire Fontaine's immense gray eyes regarding me from up on the big screen.

Calvin called early the next morning. Okay, it was almost eleven, but it felt early because I was still asleep. My blackout curtains kept the time a mystery until I checked my phone.

"As requested," Calvin said. "Police reports, fast-tracked to your inbox. I hope you like badly slanted PDFs."

"Who doesn't? Thanks. Maybe I can finally start to make sense of all this."

"Case is going that well, huh?"

"It's a strange, weird mess. Especially…" I caught him up briefly, mainly emphasizing my two apparent encounters with the dead movie star.

"You're sure it was her?"

"I'm only sure it looked like her. It definitely had her eyes."

"She did have famous eyes, didn't she?"

"When the big screen darkened and she just looked out at me, it was clearly different from what Stacey recorded on her camera. Yet I was watching the same projection at the same time. It wasn't like one of us was watching the edited for TV version."

"I do have a thought, but I'm not sure if it's a useful one."

"It can't hurt to try."

"You've heard of sympathetic magic, right?"

"I was a weird goth teen obsessed with ghosts, so yes. It's how voodoo dolls are supposed to work. You make an image of someone, and attack the image, or do whatever you want to do to that person."

"Yes, but a popkin or 'voodoo doll' might include magic by contagion, like hairs taken from the original subject. Think instead about images. That could be some of the oldest human attempts at magic, painting prey animals on cave walls. Making sculptures of animals and attacking them, or even dressing up like an animal in a sacred dance. All to prepare for the hunt, the hunt that provided sustenance and life."

"Okay. And I can apply this information by...?"

"The idea is that an image of a thing contains some mystical connection to it, and affecting the image can affect the reality."

"But it can't. Can it?"

"I only bring it up because it might be a factor when you're talking about people obsessed with images. Or with films."

"Like Stan Preston. Or Adaire Fontaine, or any of them, really. The crazy director, Mazzanti. They all had some deep personal relationship to the world of the movies."

"Adaire Fontaine may have put quite a bit of her soul into her films along the way," he said. "When you played that old movie, it gave her an opening to reach out to you."

"So, is Adaire haunting the drive-in or not, do you think? Or did she just drop down off the screen to show me her letter and postcards?"

"Either way, we can assume she had a reason for contacting you."

"Yeah, I've got a couple of ideas about that. I call one Stanley the Psycho Killer. I call the other Maybe Something

Else."

"You might work on clarifying that second one," he said. "Sometimes the obvious answer isn't the correct one. But then, sometimes it is."

"Okay. I'll just keep kind of driving around in circles and getting attacked by dead movie-star ghosts until something comes up, then."

"That's the spirit. I have to run. I'm at my daughter's house. My grandson is crawling now. He likes to stick his foot in his mouth. I'll send you a picture."

"Sounds great," I said. It was a little weird to hear the formerly gruff and distant homicide detective say anything like that. Maybe the Florida and family life was softening him up a little. That was probably the best thing for him.

When he hung up, I opened my laptop to read about the dead.

Chapter Sixteen

Later, after looking at police reports, my private investigator data-fusion database, and assorted publicly available information, I called Stacey to give her the rundown.

"Anything suspicious?" she asked. "Murders at the drive-in?"

"No murders there, but some deaths. Starting with Stanley's mother-in-law, Ruby Jackson."

"The cane lady."

"Yes. She had emphysema—that device we found in her room was an old-timey nebulizer, meant to blow medicine into her lungs. And it was her cause of death in 1955. You'll remember she opposed her daughter's marriage to Stanley, thought he wasn't up to the standards of Nancy's first husband who died."

"Are we suspecting Stanley for causing the tractor accident?" Stacey asked. "If he's maybe a murderer?"

"It sounds like Nancy met Stanley later, in her wild-widow phase, spending late nights with the arts and theater crowd, so I'm not sure about that. But we know Ruby went on to oppose Stanley's idea of turning the farm into a drive-in."

"But conveniently for him, she died."

"Exactly. If she was near death anyway, maybe it wouldn't have taken much to push her over the edge. And if the 1950s local police don't look too closely, on account of her known multiple medical conditions—"

"Old Stan Preston could have gotten away with it," Stacey said.

"Then in 1959, Adaire Fontaine was strangled to death. It's not the exact same, but it's similar, isn't it?"

"Well, if he got away with it the first time, he might do something similar the second time. Are we thinking he murdered his mother-in-law, then later went to Los Angeles and murdered Adaire Fontaine?"

"It's possible. And usually, a murder or tragic death is behind a haunting. So far, we don't have any obvious murders except Adaire's. Okay, jumping ahead to 1998, Nancy died of cardiac arrest while sitting in the passenger side of Preston's car, watching a movie on the big screen. They were alone, the theater was closed that night. I think the drive-in was sputtering pretty badly as a business by then, anyway."

"Do we know which movie?" Stacey asked.

"We do not. They were in his 1984 Buick Riviera convertible, which the police report describes in detail more than anything, like the policeman who wrote it was thinking of buying one for himself. Preston said they were watching a movie together and she just passed away. Seventy-one years old. Preston went on to live here on his own for about fifteen more years, then died of hypothermia."

"What? How?"

"Apparently out here watching a movie on a freezing cold night. They found him in front of the screen, the projector still running like nobody had been around to turn it off."

"Screening *Pocketful of Aces*. That's the one Benny found on the projector when he bought the drive-in, and it had been closed since Preston's death."

"It was closed years before Preston died. He just kept on living here anyway."

"That's some real dedication," Stacey said. "He must have loved this place."

"Or couldn't afford to move."

"Yeah, there's that. Hypothermia while watching a movie alone. That's sad. Now I feel bad for him. Unless he actually was a murderer, obviously."

"Obviously. Finally, we have a report that the stepson, Zeb, died in an airboat accident in Louisiana and was partly eaten by alligators. That sounds… interesting, I guess… but not directly related to the case."

"Unless he was doing a *Legend of the South* airboat tour, maybe? If that exists? Wasn't there a real flooded plantation that inspired that movie?"

"I have no indication he was on such a tour… or that they exist… but I guess anything's possible. That was in 2010, after their mother Nancy had died, but a few years before Stanley did. Stanley was elderly by then, though. I doubt he was out arranging his stepson's death in a swamp at that point, unless he has a clear motive to, which I don't see, either. If Stanley murdered his mother-in-law, it was to gain control of the farm. If he murdered Adaire Fontaine, it was some kind of obsessive-stalker thing based on their past relationship and maybe her national fame."

"And we don't know that he committed any murders, really. We're just guessing."

"Right. We need to get inside Stanley's mind and try to figure out what he was thinking and what he might have done. I guess it's time to watch the home movies."

"I hope they're not too creepy."

"That's why I've been avoiding them."

In the afternoon, Stacey picked me up and we returned to the drive-in, where we met up with the family at the concession stand.

The mood felt less friendly than before.

Callie emerged from the kitchen and told her husband to take Daisy and Gumby to play outside. Then she looked us over without too much warmth.

"Can you explain the damage in the game room a little more?" She removed the kerchief from her head and shook out her braided hair. "There's damage to the wall, and the corner of the foosball table is bashed up. I'm sure it'll still work fine, but it seems like things are getting more dangerous, aren't they?"

"We always have to be extra careful with entities capable of throwing objects around." I drew out the yellowed postcards and letter from my laptop bag. "I believe she was trying to show us these. We have a lot to catch up on, if you have a minute."

"I don't have much more than a minute. We're putting some final touches on the kitchen. A million things to do before the grand opening, but what's fun is doing them with no time or money or energy." She sighed and dropped into one of the booths. "So, what's up?"

We caught her up, showing her the correspondence we'd discovered and our recordings from the night before. My footage of the foosball attack was pretty short and low-quality, but the audio of the entity saying "Look at me" made Callie shiver. She read over the postcards and letter from Adaire Fontaine, her jaw dropping.

"So, the drive-in owner and Adaire Fontaine really were an item at one point?" Callie asked.

"It's possible," Stacey said. "Adaire obviously felt warmly about him, but she was known to be friendly and flirtatious all around, so it's hard to tell how serious it was."

"It was serious enough for Stanley to keep these. And hide them," Callie said. "He must have been hiding them from his wife, right?"

"He left them hidden even after his wife's death," Stacey pointed out. "And there's another possibility. They could be evidence potentially tying him to Adaire's murder."

"You think he murdered Adaire Fontaine?" Callie looked shocked. "The owner of this grungy middle-of-nowhere place?"

"That's one possibility," I said. "We know Adaire was murdered, and Stan Preston had some kind of relationship with her, and possible obsession given how he placed her posters all over the drive-in. And we know violent and tragic deaths can lead to a haunting. But it's possible he didn't do that at all, and that the real history is something we still have to uncover."

Callie shook her head slowly, taking it all in. "Does that mean Adaire Fontaine is haunting this drive-in? It seems like a really bleak place for her to end up."

"That's just what I said!" Stacey told her.

"I don't know whether she's here permanently, if at all," I said. "All we know that she, or an entity posing as her, wanted this information found."

"She didn't reach out to Benny and me, though." Callie sounded almost disappointed. "I mean, we would have helped. If you're going to have a ghost, it may as well be someone cool like her."

"It might be that playing *Aces* on the big screen gave her the opportunity," I explained. "There's an idea that an image of someone can, under the right conditions, have a little of their spirit or soul in it."

"Like the old idea that taking someone's picture can steal their soul," Stacey said.

"And if there's any grain of truth in that idea, it's most likely to apply to this kind of situation. An actress like Adaire would be pouring her spirit and emotion out deliberately, trying to transmit it through the medium of film," I said. "This is another idea we're looking at as we try to find some clear pattern or order to the haunting here."

"From what you're telling me, this place is crawling with… actual ghosts. Dead people, wandering around everywhere." She gestured to the parking lot outside, the sky painted late-afternoon orange. "And they come out at night. Next you'll tell me the drive-in was built on an old graveyard. Or someone was murdered here."

"We haven't found any sign of that," I said. I didn't add that, around Savannah, lots of things were built on old graveyards. "We have someone coming out tonight who's extra sensitive to these entities."

"Like a psychic?"

"Right. He'll help us map things out a little more clearly."

"And you plan on playing more of the Stan Preston's favorite movies tonight," Callie said. "Benny told me. *Legend of the South* and *The Body in the Basement*."

"Yes, we'll see if it helps bring out the ghosts while our psychic is here."

"Then I have one request. Play *Legend of the South* first. I've seen the poster for *Body in the Basement*, and I don't want to be outside while that's on the screen. And I definitely don't want to risk Daisy seeing it."

"Of course," I said, though for selfish reasons I'd hoped to get the horror movie out of the way first and then have the period-piece costume drama to help wash the first one out of my mind. I had to respect the client's wishes, though. "First, we're heading to the top floor of the screen tower, playing some of the old home movies we found up there."

"Okay," Callie said. "Well, this is bad news overall, because there's so much happening here. I hope it doesn't get even worse."

"We'll get it straightened out," I said, hoping I could keep my word on that.

Chapter Seventeen

Stacey and I again ascended the concrete stairs to the screen tower's less-than-hospitable third floor. We ducked through the musty curtain of the haunted-castle doorway frame and into the dark little room beyond. Stacey hesitated, looking over the dusty equipment on the shelves and the disorganized spools of film on the desk.

"Everything okay?" I asked.

"Yeah, I'm just worried about what we're going to see on Preston's home movies here. Hopefully nothing that scars us for life." She nervously studied the archaic home projector, rubbing her scalp through her short blonde hair. "It'll just take a sec to figure out. I don't want to break this thing. It's basically prehistoric. Dinosaurs probably watched movies on this thing."

The only seating was the worn, icky-looking armchair where Preston had spent untold hours viewing his home films and whatever else he did up here alone in this hidden room. Neither of us wanted to sit there, so we cleared the assorted Halloween decorations off the black coffin and carried it in to use as a bench. It was sturdy enough to hold us both. We'd considered the Santa sleigh, but it was too rickety.

"There better not be anything too scary on these," Stacey said, not for the first time. "Should we go get popcorn? Or maybe that pizza Callie offered to make us?"

"If there *is* anything disturbing on Preston's home movies, maybe it's better to watch them on an empty stomach."

Stacey blanched and nodded.

The flickering eight-millimeter movies were in color but had no sound. Most focused on the theater itself. We saw the heyday of the Nite-Lite Drive-In's glory days, with rows of *Titanic*-sized automobiles with bench seats and tail fins squeezed in between the speaker poles. At night it was like a miniature carnival, crowds of people chattering, long lines at the concession stand, colorful lights guiding their way.

Summertime scenes on the lawn were full of minor attractions like pony rides and clowns, and once a guy in a Superman costume, inexplicably wearing a ski mask and driving a tractor. In one video, a mob of boys received cap guns as a promotion for some cowboy movie. A battle ensued among the children, full of smoke and howls as the boys hunted and shot at each other, parents cringing and covering their ears.

Another video lingered on a long line of 1960s-era cars and trucks waiting to enter the drive-in, as if Preston just wanted to brag about how popular it was. And it did seem popular.

We glimpsed his family incidentally in these scenes, his wife Nancy working the concession stand with her son Zeb and daughter Leah, all in the striped and bow-tied costumes that Leah had complained she was embarrassed to wear in front of schoolmates. None of the family members looked especially happy with the roles Preston had assigned them. Nancy looked particularly glum. Doling scoops of popcorn into paper bags and pouring fountain drinks probably wasn't the glamorous life she'd expected from fast-talking Preston and his big theater dreams.

One home movie captured a couple minutes of a Christmas morning. The boy and girl were in their early or middle teen years, both looking sullen. The film focused mostly on panning across the pink plastic tree and glittering decorations around the house. It was hard to believe the farmhouse had ever looked habitable, much less in living memory.

"Is it just me, or does it seem like Preston spent a lot more time filming the drive-in than his own family?" Stacey asked.

"It sounds like he never really got close with his stepkids, beyond using them as labor," I said. "Leah didn't seem to like Preston at all, and she said her brother never got into Preston's good graces despite trying."

"Man, their dad dies in a tractor accident, then they get some dude who's totally cold as their stepdad. Then their grandma, who took care of them while Mom was out partying, dies right after that. That's all kinda sad."

Another reel showed a view out of a moving bus window, which Stacey quickly identified as Hollywood Boulevard. "That's Grauman's Chinese Theater, home of countless movie premieres. This is basically a touristy look at Los Angeles."

Another one, also viewed from the bus window, provided glimpses of immense, ornate mansions through front gates and palm trees.

"Looks like one of those celebrity home tours," Stacey said. "I wish there was sound so we could know whose houses these are."

After the celebrity home tour, we watched a reel of Preston's wife and stepkids on the beach. The two teenagers seemed to almost be having fun for once, until they noticed their stepfather filming them, at which point they frowned and walked glumly away.

Preston turned the camera on his wife instead. Dressed in a brightly pinstriped bathing suit, Nancy waved, smiling under her sunglasses, though it looked forced. Maybe their marriage had grown strained, or maybe she was thinking about going back to the concession stand after vacation was over, back to endlessly popping and scooping popcorn for lines of impatient snackers.

Nancy took the camera and turned it back on her husband, giving us a look at Stan Preston around age forty, going saggy and gray. He was still rocking the big Chance Chadwick mustache well into the 1960s, though Chadwick himself had died back in 1957. His swimsuit was almost inappropriately European.

Another reel returned us to Hollywood Boulevard, but on foot instead of a tour bus, filming the Walk of Fame stars embedded in the sidewalk. Stacey pointed out such notable names as Burt Lancaster and Joanne Woodward.

The next reel gave us a view through a high, wrought-iron fence, into a garden with a swimming pool, the back yard of a bright pink mansion with elaborate white trim reminiscent of pastry icing.

The person holding the camera—Preston, presumably —was on foot, apparently spying on the house.

"Isn't that one of the mansions from the celebrity tour?" I asked Stacey.

"Yep. In fact, let me check…" Stacey looked up

something on her phone. It only took her a few seconds to find an image of the pink mansion, located on a current Hollywood tour company's website. "It's hers."

"Adaire's house?" I guessed.

"The 'Adaire Fontaine Murder House.' She was renting it, but yep, that's where she lived."

I shivered. "Maybe Stanley Preston took a little detour from his family vacation to murder Adaire Fontaine."

"Hm. But not so much. This reel was filmed with a Super 8."

"And?"

"Those didn't come out until the 1960s, and Adaire Fontaine was murdered in 1959. This film had to be made years after she died. Maybe he was just going for a trip down Murder Memory Lane, as psycho killers do." Stacey checked her phone as the reel ended. "Jacob's on his way."

"Is it that late already?" I checked my own phone. "Callie's got dinner for us. Pizza."

"I'm going to blimp up if this case drags on too long. That pizza's too good to resist. I can't wait for Jacob to try it." Stacey set up another reel. The Super 8 reels were short, only three minutes each, their silence and faded colors giving them a strangely ephemeral quality, like half-remembered dreams.

The next reel showed a four-story stucco apartment building, not the fanciest place by any means. Plywood tagged with graffiti patched one ground-floor window. Dark concrete stairwells receded like caves into the building, the exact opposite of inviting.

"That doesn't look like a stop on the Homes of the Stars tour to me," I said.

The handheld camera wobbled and shifted. Pedestrians passed on the sidewalk, in the foreground and background. The camera holder was watching the building from across the street.

A woman emerged from the apartment building. She wore a definite late-sixties California style: orange-tinted sunglasses, sandals, and a threadbare shift dress with a swirling, psychedelic rose print. It was hard to tell her age at this distance, especially with the grainy, faded film, but I got the impression of a young adult, twenty to thirty years old, curvy with long dark hair.

"Who is she?" I asked. "Stacey, get a digital of this."

"You got it." Stacey drew the small digital camera from her belt. "It's going to be awful quality, though."

On the silent, wobbly Super 8 film, the woman stopped to mooch a cigarette off some disheveled guys lingering at the corner bus stop. She hurriedly smoked a part of it and passed it back as a bus arrived. She climbed aboard, and the reel ended.

Stacey's phone buzzed again. "Jacob's here," she said. "Let's go collect him. He's been dying to see the drive-in." She shut down the projector and hurried out through the curtained haunted-castle frame.

I lingered, looking at the suddenly dark portable screen, trying to make sense of what we'd watched.

Chapter Eighteen

"Okay, first off, this place is amazing," Jacob said as he climbed out of his accountant-gray Hyundai. It was getting dark, and a few exterior lights were lit, mostly around the concession stand. "I mean it. I can't believe y'all are getting paid to hang out here."

"It gets pretty weird late at night," Stacey said, greeting him with a hug. She introduced him to Benny and to Gumby, who Benny held on a long leash. The dog wagged at Jacob, acting much friendlier to him than he'd been to me, but I tried not to be jealous of the dog's clear preference.

"Even better. Weird is good." Jacob adjusted his glasses. An accountant at a CPA firm, Jacob was not a particularly stereotypical kind of psychic. He was more of a buttoned-down and responsible guy—I mentioned the Hyundai already—who was into classic science fiction and fantasy novels and cheesy Mystery Science Theater movies.

Maybe it was the bad movies that formed the basis of Jacob and Stacey's otherwise unlikely relationship, making up for her insistence on dragging him into kayaking excursions and camping trips on their days off.

"Weird is good, that's a great philosophy," said Benny, with his red suspenders and his puffy newsboy hat. "You're really a psychic, huh?"

"Some people prefer the term 'sensitive,'" Jacob said. "Not me, though. I prefer 'psychic.'"

"Whoa. How's that work?"

"I'm just somewhat more aware of the dead than the average person. And the dead are sometimes more aware of me, which is annoying when I'd rather be left alone. Speaking of the dead, I understand we'll be viewing *The Body in the Basement?* The mostly banned murder movie?"

"It's a double feature," Stacey said. "We're starting with *Legend of the South.*"

Jacob winced. "I believe *Legend of Boggy Creek* was mentioned? We should watch that instead. There's nothing like it. It's all about this Bigfoot creature in Arkansas, part fake documentary, part docudrama, part inadvertent self-mockumentary."

"Yeah, I could definitely line that up—" Benny began.

"No, thanks," I said. "While *Legend of Boggy Creek* definitely sounds like… well, a pretty weird movie… it's not related to our case."

"And the other two are?" Jacob asked. "Wait, isn't *Legend of the South* with Adaire Fontaine? And we're also watching *Body in the Basement*, with Portia Reynolds, directed by Antonio Mazzanti? The director who murdered them both? We're having a murder movie double feature? Y'all are twisted."

"We are not!" Stacey told him in mock anger. "You're the *Boggy Creek* fanboy."

"Benny," I said, "like I mentioned earlier, we need Jacob to walk through the tower, including your apartment. It's better to do it after dark, but at the same time we shouldn't be tramping through talking about ghosts while Daisy is there—"

"We've got it figured out," Benny replied. "I'll set up some cartoons ahead of the feature, and we'll sit out on the lawn and watch those with Daisy. You guys can psychic around the tower while we watch the 'toons, then text us when you're done. Daisy will probably fall asleep on the picnic blanket before then."

"Sounds good," I said.

"But then we have to miss the cartoons!" Stacey said. "Just kidding. That totally works for us."

"Excellent. Now, who wants pizza?"

"Look at the concession stand!" Jacob marveled as we approached the enormous Purple Pizza Eater with its smiling dragon sign. "Tell me the pizza is actually purple."

"It's not actually purple," Stacey said.

"We could probably pull that off, though." Benny scratched his beard thoughtfully. He opened the concession stand door and gestured for us to enter, bowing a little like a proper butler.

"If anybody could, it's y'all." I stepped inside, into the aroma of warm freshly baked crust and melted cheese— and, of course, popcorn.

"Hey." Callie glanced at Stacey and me quickly, then even more quickly at Jacob before looking down at the counter again, as if she were especially shy around new people. "I've got a couple pizzas coming up for you to try, but if you hate them, I can make something else."

"I doubt it'll be possible for us to hate them," Stacey said.

"Pick a spot. I'll bring them out."

"Who's playing foosball?" Daisy came skipping out of the game room, a *Darkwing Duck* comic book in her hands.

"I will, champ," Benny said.

"You always lose-ball." Daisy looked among us carefully, then pointed at Jacob. "You wanna play?"

"I mean, kind of. There's a foosball table?" Jacob turned to look.

"It's a little dinged up," I said.

"Daisy, they're here to have dinner and work," Callie said.

"We could probably handle one game while we wait, though." Stacey looked at me. "We'll play teams. Daisy already picked Jacob. So that leaves us."

I shrugged and followed them in. Daisy whispered some kind of secret instructions or strategy to Jacob.

As we played, my eyes kept drifting to the blank spot on the wall where the *Pocketful of Aces* poster had been. Adaire Fontaine, or at least an entity who wanted me to believe it was Adaire Fontaine, had gone to a lot of trouble to make those old pieces of correspondence known, but I still wasn't clear why. Was she trying to tell me Preston was innocent of her murder? Or guilty? Or was I confusing the whole situation by focusing on her murder? Maybe I'd rushed into some assumptions that kept me from seeing the big picture.

"Ellie! Look alive!" Stacey snapped. I glanced down to see the ball whizz past my goalie, who was clearly sleeping on the job, and down out of sight through the goal hole. I spun the little character uselessly, seconds too late.

"Lose-ball!" Daisy announced triumphantly. "And no spinning."

"You made us lose-ball," Stacey told me with an accusing stare, while Jacob and Daisy high-fived each other.

"Okay, Daisy, it's time for cartoons on the lawn."

Benny waved his tablet, from which he could control the digital projector upstairs if needed. "Let's go grab Blankety."

"Blankety! Yes!" Daisy, still the reigning foosball champ, ran after her father as he walked out the door.

Stacey, Jacob, and I returned to the main concession stand room, where Callie was at one of the booths, setting out two steaming pizzas on elevated metal plates.

"This one is just avocado and bacon, and that one is kind of a spicy Southwestern style with grilled chicken and peppers and olives and queso, and the sauce is frijole-based with jalapeno. It's not even really a pizza. If you don't like it, I can just make a regular cheese pizza or whatever." Her voice was fast and nervous, her eyes flickering among us.

Jacob gaped at the meal as he and Stacey dropped down into one side of the booth. I took the other. Since I had no date tonight, I could sprawl all I wanted. My fingers ran over the years of hand-carved names, smiley faces, stars, peace signs, and the occasional scratched-out phone number on the table.

"I didn't realize it was crazy gourmet pizza night," Jacob said. "This looks amazing. Definitely the Southwestern for me."

Callie watched nervously as we took slices. I picked the bacon-avocado one, and no surprise, it was as good as everything else she'd made.

"Oh, man." Jacob shook his head after the first bite. He looked out the window, almost wistfully, at the parking lot and the huge outdoor screen where a Grape Ape cartoon played. "This place is basically paradise, you know that? I'm never leaving. Are you guys going to be adding condos out here?"

Callie laughed. "Don't suggest it to Benny, he might try. In the olden days, they did have drive-in movie motels. You could lie in bed, turn on a speaker box in your room, and watch the movie. Believe me, we've learned about every type of drive-in there was, trying to take every idea that worked and avoid the ones that didn't. Learning why so many have failed but some stay in business."

"I'll tell you what, if you keep making pizza like this, I don't see how you can fail," Jacob said, and she blushed. "Do you have somebody to do your taxes?"

"Don't we have to make money first?" she asked.

"Absolutely not! Losses can be your friend." He fished out a business card and passed it to her. "I will personally do what I can to help this place on the financial end."

"Okay, thanks." Callie headed outside to join her family.

"I guess we'd better hurry so they can put their kid to bed," I said.

"Fine, but we're taking the rest of these pizzas to go," Stacey said. "All of this is going into my stomach while we watch *Legend of the South.*"

"You'd better have it finished before *Body in the Basement,*" Jacob said. "I don't think that one pairs well with food."

"I'm getting creeped out the more I think about it," Stacey said. "I mean, it was weird enough watching *The Heart of Man* with my film-nerd friends in school, knowing the filmmaker was a murderer. But *Body in the Basement* stars Portia Reynolds, one of the women he actually murdered. Maybe we shouldn't watch it."

"I want to watch it less than anyone else," I said. "In fact, I might keep night watch on the monitors instead."

"Oh, come on," Jacob said. "Of all the people I know, I can't believe the two of you would be afraid of a horror movie."

"But it's the murder movie," Stacey said.

"He didn't kill her while making it, though, right?"

Jacob asked. "Not like Adaire Fontaine?"

"It was never proven that Mazzanti murdered Adaire," Stacey reminded him.

"Yeah, but come on. Everybody knows it." Jacob looked around the purple concession stand, smiled at the *Rocky* poster. "This place is great," he said, yet again.

We loaded our leftover pizza slices into a take-out box, wiped down our table so Callie wouldn't have to, and headed out to the parking lot. My heart was nervous, my stomach heavy. I should have kept it to one slice, but I'd failed at doing so.

Behind us, the family sat on a large checkered picnic blanket on the lawn—close to the concession stand, I noticed with approval, nowhere near the back gate and the farmhouse. Callie waved at us. Daisy fell over in laughter at the antics of the befuddled Grape Ape and his sidekick Beegle Beagle.

We dropped our leftovers in the cooler in the van— always good to have a cooler for long, late-night stakeouts —and continued on to the screen tower. The night was overcast, but the reflected Grape-Ape glow from the screen helped light our way. It was warm outside, but we wore jackets as protection against possible supernatural attacks. I don't like to go poking around in haunted spots without a layer of leather protecting at least some of my more vital organs.

We rounded the corner and opened the steel door in the side of the tower.

"This is so cool." Jacob gazed around the interior, looking at the steeply slanted wall, the mountain bikes and Rollerblades, the camping gear, then beyond the mud room space into the long theater office, the walls papered with movie posters, surfaces cluttered with paperwork and junk exhumed from Preston's apartment on the second floor. "I didn't know you could go inside the old movie screens like this. Mind, blown."

"I thought it was pretty neat, too," Stacey said. "And, hey, they're a nice couple. They're fun and outdoorsy."

"Bad movies and camping," I said. "Y'all should double date." I was sort of joking, but Stacey nodded with a "hmm" and looked like she was seriously considering it.

"Okay…" Jacob took a deep breath and walked forward, holding out his hand like Baby Yoda using the Force. I think that was deliberate. "I've got a lot of flickering impressions here. This was a workplace, obviously, people in and out, money being counted. I'm sensing one guy at the middle of it all. But it's all just quiet trace memories here. I doubt your clients are having trouble in this room."

I nodded, not so much because he was right—he was —but to let him know I was listening. When a medium is surveying a location for the presence of the dead, it's best not to interrupt their thoughts and impressions, but instead pay attention and take notes.

Jacob looked through the open door to the playroom with its picture books and stuffed animals now neatly organized on low shelves, a rainbow rocking horse, a kid-sized painting easel. He nodded and kept moving. "I think this floor is fine. Let's go up."

We walked through the clients' second floor apartment next, the most awkward part of the evening. Jacob trailed his fingers along the recently painted walls and occasionally leaned his head against them, as if listening to some hidden presence crawling through hidden spaces.

"I'm getting that same guy from downstairs, but stronger," Jacob said. "He lived up here, right? But it didn't look like this. You can tell it's been recently renovated. Before it was kind of a beige old-man sort of place, that's the impression I'm getting. He lived here alone, for years. I see him as very elderly, feeling himself shrink, feeling himself get weaker year by year... but still, this apartment wasn't really his focus. It could just as well as have been a motel room. His real interest was more..." Jacob frowned up at the ceiling. "There's a third floor, isn't there?"

"There is," I said.

He sighed, and any trace of good humor left his face. "I guess we'd better get it over with." He trudged back to the stairwell door like he expected gloom and doom ahead.

Chapter Nineteen

The bleak, unadorned climb to the third floor was a good prelude to the shadowy chaos that waited inside. We let Jacob lead the way, following his supernatural senses.

He opened the door, flicked on the scattered overhead bulbs, and stood inside the dim room shaking his head at the old movie theater decorations.

"I really don't know what's creepier, the actual haunted castle flat or that Santa Claus." He pointed to the Santa Claus mannequin sitting in the sleigh, with its unnerving permanent plastic smile and staring eyes.

"The *Body in the Basement* poster is worse than both." I pointed to the faded promo pinned to the wall, with its image of rotten fingers poking around the edges of the basement door as someone—The Body, presumably— made their way up from below into the pleasant-looking suburban hallway above.

"Uh, maybe we shouldn't watch that, after all," Stacey

said.

"No chickening out now," Jacob said. "This area is probably your most active. The male entity I mentioned earlier, he's really focused up here more than anywhere else in the building. He's not here right now, but he comes and goes. A lot. His energy is like…brown slime all over everything. Your clients should stay away from this floor. This is his territory."

Jacob poked around, moving aside junk to reveal more junk. He lifted a child-size cowboy hat hanging on a shoddily painted plywood space rocket, put it back. Nudging aside some tiki statues, he dragged out a wooden treasure chest painted with a skull and crossbones and opened it, revealing books and papers crammed inside the gold-painted interior. "Hm," he said, but continued poking and exploring elsewhere.

I dug into the treasure chest. I hadn't seen it before—Jacob had found it crammed behind a cutout of a palm tree with a sand-colored hill at the bottom, like those tiny deserted islands where any number of forlorn cartoon characters have found themselves marooned over the years.

The chest held technical specs for the Super 8 camera, celebrity magazines, and a few underground-type newspapers of the late 1960s and or early 70s, stiff and crumbling with age.

Below these were a couple of biographies. One was called *The Rough Bunch*, after the nickname given to Chance Chadwick and his circle of brash, hard-partying young actors and musicians of the late 1940s and early 1950s. Those were the type of people Stanley Preston and his wife Nancy had aspired to be, in their own way, among the smaller stages of Savannah's theater and arts scene.

A casual flip-through revealed many dog-eared pages, some with notes hand-scribbled in the margins. All of the marked pages mentioned Chance Chadwick or had pictures of him. In each role, he wore a similar outfit topped with a fedora, cutting a similar figure, regardless of whether he played a mobster, con man, detective, or spy.

While Jacob and Stacey wandered off through the haunted castle cutout, through the curtain to Preston's hidden film-viewing room, I flipped through another book crammed into the treasure chest, one that interested me far more.

Legendary Lioness: The Adaire Fontaine Story featured on its cover an image from Adaire's most popular movie, *Legend of the South*, in which she wore an immense curly red wig and the wide, many-layered antebellum dress currently on display at the Savannah Historical Association.

Inside the book, someone, presumably Stanley Preston, had added a number of hand-drawn notations, circles, and scribbles between the lines and in the margins, creating a real serial-killer bulletin-board-of-obsession look.

In the black and white picture section at the book's center, he'd circled a squat, balding man with solid black-circle sunglasses and a long beard, dressed in a tuxedo. On his arm, in a dress studded with glittering stones, was the stunning Adaire Fontaine, her face as inscrutable as the Mona Lisa.

Adaire Fontaine and director Antonio Mazzanti at the Academy Awards, 1959, read the caption. Adaire would be murdered later that year. It was one of the last pictures in the book.

"Mazzanti," I murmured.

The room grew colder.

I looked up, sharply aware that I was alone, though Jacob and Stacey weren't far away, just beyond the curtain. Unless they'd tiptoed past and left me alone while I was looking through the books, but surely they wouldn't have done that.

Holding the Adaire book in one hand, I rose from where I'd been squatting. I widened and strengthened my stance, ready for an attack, and drew my flashlight in case I needed it.

A dark figure stood silently watching me, unmoving, back in the cluttered shadows. It was so still that at first I thought it was Santa the Dirty Mannequin, but the shape was all wrong. It was the outline of a man wearing a fedora.

An acrid cigar smell filled the air. A pale glow rose, barely illuminating the face.

Chance Chadwick remained back in the shadows, as he had when we'd glimpsed him before under the screen, his face even paler than it had been in black and white. Under the brim of his hat, his eyes were locked onto me, his expression flat and emotionless.

"Why are you here?" I asked, keeping my voice low. If the entity was a fragile sort, I didn't want Stacey and Jacob responding to the sound of my voice and possibly chasing it off.

Of course, it could also have been the malevolent, aggressive sort, so I kept my grip on my flashlight instead of reaching for a voice recorder.

The entity didn't move. It stood like a statue, as though merely observing me.

I held up the book in my hand, with Adaire Fontaine on the cover. "Did you know her? Is she here with you?"

The apparition continued to stare at me, its eyes never blinking, as though they had been painted on, like the face was a death mask rather than living flesh. Its uncanny lack of movement, and the coldness of its gaze, made it completely impossible for me to enjoy what could have been a handsome apparition of the dead movie star.

"Why are these books hidden here?" I asked. "What

was Stanley Preston doing? Did he murder Adaire Fontaine?"

A loud bang sounded next to me, making me jump.

The treasure chest had slammed shut, as though he wanted me to look no further.

This, of course, could only make me want to look much further.

When I turned back to look, he was no longer in the distant shadows, but right in front of me, his bloodless, pale face inches from mine, staring at me with those painted-on death-mask eyes.

Up close, the whole face seemed even more artificially smooth, mask-like.

"Are you really Chance Chadwick?" I asked. "Or Stanley Preston, trying to look like Chance in death, just like you did in life? Is that it?" The air grew freezing cold around me, so fast I could hear the crackle of ambient humidity hardening into frost, coating everything in the room. Suddenly it was winter up there.

I pressed on. "Did you start obsessing over Chance when Adaire co-starred with him? Did you watch *Hotel Island* and *Pocketful of Aces* and think, hey, that should be *me* starring in those movies with her instead of him? Something like that?"

The face shifted in front of me. Cracks and pits opened along both sides of it, turning the face that had charmed a postwar generation into a moonscape across both cheeks, partly concealed by the big mustache. The nose, chin, and forehead shifted in subtle ways, the hairline receded, the fedora and suit shifted from solid, smooth black to ratty gray plaid.

It was a different man who stood before me now. Only the mustache was truly the same.

"Stanley Preston," I said.

He reached up and touched the craggy side of his face, seeming shocked to find how it had changed, how the face below the mask had revealed itself.

"Pox scars?" I asked.

His face twisted into an expression of rage.

"Ellie!" Jacob burst out from behind the curtain and swept the room with one of our tactical flashlights in flood mode, filling the gloomy storage area with white light that chased away all hint of shadow. "It's coming for you."

"Yeah, it was." I'd been on the edge of clicking on my own light, but still holding back, waiting to see what else the entity might reveal, intentionally or otherwise.

The entity was gone.

"Are you okay?" Stacey asked, swinging her own light around. "Jakey said you were under attack."

"It was the Chance Chadwick apparition again," I said. "Only now I'm pretty sure it's just Stan Preston, hiding his insecurities behind a Chance Chadwick image, like he did in life."

"Well, that kinda makes sense. Then who's behind the Adaire Fontaine apparition?"

"I'm not so sure about that." I looked at the biography in my hand. The pirate treasure box had slammed shut hard enough to crack and splinter its lip. "But it looks like Jacob uncovered a treasure trove of possible clues for us. We can get some insight into Stanley's movie-star obsessions." I showed them the heavily marked Adaire biography.

"Shiver me timbers!" Stacey said. "That *is* obsessive. What do we do now?"

"We stick to the plan," I said. "Wait for the hour to grow later, and until then, we go to the movies."

Chapter Twenty

Jacob was chivalrous enough to insist on carrying the wooden treasure chest down the stairs for us, which I tried to counter-insist he didn't have to do, but I didn't try very hard to stop him.

We—I mean, he—lugged it out to our van in the middle of the parking lot, where I could paw through it at my leisure.

Benny and Callie saw us emerge from the screen tower and met us halfway, Benny carrying a sleeping Daisy on his shoulder. Callie skateboarded ahead to speak to us. They must have stashed the picnic blanket somewhere, maybe inside the concession stand.

"How did it go?" Callie rolled to a stop, speaking in a stage whisper. Benny continued onward, carrying their slumbering child toward their screen-tower apartment, by either prior arrangement or unspoken mutual understanding between the parents.

"We encountered the third-floor entity again," I said. "All of you should stay away from the top floor for now. Stacey, want to take Jacob somewhere? Maybe get the movie going?"

"Oh, yep." Stacey took his arm, and they headed for the concession stand. Jacob, as our psychic consultant, needed to be kept from hearing too many details of our case, but I had to catch Callie up on everything.

"Do you think we're safe in the apartment?" Callie asked me.

"Well, the fact that the third-floor entity hasn't come down and bothered you all this time would indicate he's not that interested in the first two floors of the tower. That's what our psychic said, too. Just avoid the third floor completely for now," I said. "If it's Stanley Preston, like I suspect, he might even be glad you're getting the drive-in going again. It was his dream, and his life's biggest accomplishment, and all that. Still, I wouldn't leave Daisy in the tower, or anywhere without an adult present anymore, even with the baby monitor."

Callie nodded. "Okay. But why would Preston be scaring off customers if he wants the drive-in open again? Or is it another ghost doing that?"

"If it's Preston, maybe he's not doing it on purpose. He's just freaking people out as he looks around."

"Could it be Adaire Fontaine?" Callie asked, a smile twitching the corner of her lips. "I mean, an actual movie star ghost, that could be good for business, right? If only she'd stop sneaking up on people."

"I'm hoping the entity will sneak up on us, sooner or later," I said. "That's part of the reason we're screening movies while our psychic is here. Maybe whatever's haunting your parking lot will come out tonight. Then, hopefully, we can identify it and figure out how to remove it."

"Sounds good to me." Callie frowned at the screen tower. "I wish we had somewhere else to go live, but we just don't."

"I'm sorry it's not going faster. Removing a ghost requires understanding who it is and why it's here, understanding its story. That can take time, unfortunately."

"I'm sure it's not easy work," Callie said. "I feel crazy just finding out ghosts are not only real, but that our place is crawling with them. I can't imagine what it must be like for you, dealing with it all the time."

"You get used to it," I said, which was only partly true. There are always new horrors revealing themselves, new depths of the soul to face.

Callie skated away toward her haunted home. I wished her a good night, but she shook her head like that was an incredibly absurd comment under the circumstances.

The wide second-floor window of the concession stand glowed, and a black and white studio logo appeared on the screen, bouncing and flickering. This dissolved into a bright blue sky, and the view panned down to the vast Mississippi River.

I climbed into the van and turned on the radio. A chorus of voices singing an old-time work song rose from my speakers. On the screen, slaves hacked through a field of sugarcane.

A well-appointed carriage drawn by four white horses, driven by a slave coachman in fine livery, traveled along a road through the cane fields.

Inside the carriage sat three extremely well-dressed people—a middle-aged man and woman and their daughter, played by Adaire Fontaine.

The mother character made it clear they were on their way to a ball, and it was imperative that Adaire's character make the right sort of impression on the most important gentlemen. The father broke in occasionally to mention each potential suitor's bona fides—this one was a banker, that one owned a sugar mill.

The daughter seemed less than interested in this talk, her eyes straying to the fields and laborers.

The contrast of worlds couldn't have been starker between the inside and outside of the carriage. Within, a young woman born to wealth and comfort prepared to be courted and married in a way that would only increase her wealth. Without, suffering people with little hope for the future toiled under the scorching sun, among mud and mosquitoes, enabling the leisure and luxury enjoyed by the others.

Legend of the South was a truly famous movie, probably Adaire Fontaine's most famous, though not the one for which she'd been Oscar-nominated.

Stacey approached, and I lowered my window.

"Jacob's in my car," she said. "Are you sure you don't want to join us?"

"Splitting up might be better. The idea is to try to get stalked by the parking lot phantom. Don't tell Jacob, though."

"Well, come on if you want. I know you've got a hot date with those old papers, but maybe you'll get bored." She nodded at the pirate chest I'd moved up to the shotgun seat. "Want me to have Jacob peek into the projection house out here?"

"Only if he brings it up first."

"Gotcha. He asked what it was, but that's all so far."

"Okay. See you at intermission if nothing jumps out and attacks us."

"Let's hope it does!" Stacey waved and walked back to her car.

I watched the movie for a while, part of me hoping that it would darken in the strange way as *Pocketful of Aces* had, that Adaire Fontaine would look at me or reach out to me with another message of some kind. I left my window open so I could listen for approaching footsteps. If Adaire walked up on me, or perhaps something much worse, I didn't want to be caught by surprise.

I'd heard of *Legend of the South*, seen bits and pieces, and knew that a great flood would eventually destroy everything in sight. The movie was visually beautiful, saturated with bright colors, filled with swamps and rivers, flowers and fine clothing, but the story droned a bit as Adaire Fontaine's mother focused on shopping her around to eligible men. Adaire's character was secretly in love with an unacceptably low-born blacksmith in town, a handsome fellow who could sing and dance in concert with everyone at the local tavern as though they'd all rehearsed and choreographed things ahead of time.

Soon I was rummaging through the pirate chest again.

One standout item was a faded, fragile page from the *Los Angeles Free Press*. It was dated 1969, and everything about it reminded me of *The Great Horned Owl*, the long-defunct underground newspaper I'd grown familiar with during a case in Atlanta.

Preston had saved one sheet of the paper. The square boxes along the edges advertised head shops, upcoming concerts, and something called a "People's Theater Troupe" that performed in a public park.

An interview with the film director Antonio Mazzanti took up most of the page.

Under the headline THE FORGOTTEN WORLD OF ANTONIO MAZZANTI was a picture of the director, looking much rougher than he had on the Academy red carpet a decade earlier with Adaire Fontaine at his side. Mazzanti was balding and graying, had developed a paunch, and wore a stained, ratty t-shirt under a partially buttoned outer shirt. He still wore the pitch-black circular sunglasses and the excessively long beard, though it had gone gray and ratty. He looked like he hadn't seen the inside of a bath or shower in days. He sat in a dim, dingy-looking bar with filmy, dusty windows behind him.

Turning my flashlight to its dimmest setting, I began to read.

RIKER'S WATERHOLE, NORTH HOLLYWOOD - The famous director, once hailed as a groundbreaking young visionary, sits in a rundown bar and thinks about the past, his once-legendary place in the filmmaker pantheon somehow lost in recent years.

"This isn't a bad spot," Antonio Mazzanti says, over a chipped glass half-filled with cheap brown whiskey. "We filmed *Biker Banshee* here, a lot of it. The bar scenes. Did you see that one?"

No, I must have missed it, I tell him.

He begins to tell me the film's story—something about an undead female motorcyclist—but soon loses the thread, and it's clear he doesn't recall much about the 1966 biker horror flick he directed.

"You didn't miss much," he concludes. "The result always falls short of the vision."

Is that the advice he gives young film students who make their pilgrimage to visit the famous director?

"I tell them stick to your vision, forget what the guys in suits and the bean-counters have to say. Forget what everyone says and go with what's inside you."

Is that good advice for success in film?

"No, unless you are brilliant. But maybe someone brilliant will hear it."

What about the rest of them? The non-brilliant?

"Anybody coming out here to ask me the secrets of commercial success is madly off-course. I can't speak to commercial success. Only to artistry, only to the creative demon raging within. Without the demon, you will make nothing. Perhaps you will make fine commercials for laundry soap, but you will make nothing that cuts deep, nothing that leaves a mark on the soul."

Many would say *The Heart of*

Man leaves such a mark. How were you inspired to make a film about the devil prowling Venice in the 1700s?

"That is how it came to me. Is the devil out there, or in here?" He touches his chest. "Can we ever separate ourselves from evil? Is it with each of us, always? The voice of temptation is born as a whisper, but grows stronger each time it is fed. Each time it *feeds*. And the desire to purify the world, to purge all evil, this leads to the greatest evils of all, no?"

He asks me if drinks are included with the interview—he previously asked me this on the phone. He orders a whiskey to replace the one he's finished, which does not appear to be his first of the day. It's a hot afternoon outside, and the rattling air conditioner in the bar's window is doing nothing to cut the burn from the air.

I ask him about *Stanzas for Regina*, the story of an Italian immigrant woman, an elderly widow, her mind decaying along with the bug-infested tenement apartment around her as she looks back on her life. Is this in any way about his family?

"My parents immigrated from Italy," he said. "My father was a steelworker like Regina's husband. My sister died of tuberculosis like Regina's daughter. Why do people ask stupid questions?"

Does he have plans to do more films like his early movies?

He laughs.

"You're like everyone," he says, his voice slurring now. "You think those two films are grand works of art, and the rest is trash. When will you make another *Heart of Man*, they ask. Nobody ever asks about the underlying themes in *Biker Banshee*, or when will I finally make another *Body in the Basement*." He laughs and orders yet another drink. "The hidden curses and dark secrets of us all."

With that, we both know the time has come to raise the subject, radioactive but inevitable, that will perhaps always be intertwined with Mazzanti.

"It has been nine… ten years," he says. "There is nothing I can say I have not said countless times, to police, to journalists, to those who stop me on the street and ask. Of course I do not know who killed her. Of course I would never have wished her dead. She was a rare light, a divine presence in a dark and despicable world. She was to be the shining jewel in my finest film. *House of Gold* would have been an expression of great human truth, forged in the fires of passion and desire and suffering, yet it was only a finely wrought setting for her talent to glow, to illuminate. To destroy her would be to destroy all that was good in the world. I have truly loved no one since. Her loss left me broken inside."

Does he believe Adaire Fontaine's death affected his work?

"Another tired question," he says. "You are asking me, are my later movies trash because of my pain and loss from her death? Did my talent die with her?" He smiles as he says it, but it doesn't last. He appears to be staring into space, lost behind his trademark solid-black sunglasses, his drink forgotten an inch from his lip. "Perhaps," he finally says.

Is there any truth to the
rumors of his struggles with
alcohol and drugs?

"Of course not. That's not
the problem. My enemies at the
studios spread those rumors
about me." He checks his shirt
sleeve, buttons the wrist to hide
marks I've already seen. "The
problem is these false rumors
about Adaire Fontaine. Not only
did I lose the greatest love of my
life, but at that very moment of
profound loss, I gained a
reputation as a monster. I was
suspected and investigated, never
arrested. I would never have
harmed her. Her death is the
dark cloud over my life in every
way. Perhaps I am already dead,
and drifting now through Hell."
His words hang in the smoke-
filled bar, where heavyset bikers,
mostly men, erupt in raucous
laughter at the next table.
Perhaps the once-great
filmmaker, the grand auteur
turned fallen idol, has spoken
the truth of the human
condition once again.

"Hey, bleak closing paragraph," I mumbled as I set the
article aside and began chewing it over, trying to see how

any of it might apply to our case. Why had Stanley saved this particular article?

One of our working ideas was obviously that Stanley Preston was the true murderer of Adaire Fontaine, considering that we seemed to be encountering both of their ghosts and one of them was the victim of an unsolved murder. To biographers and the media, Stanley would have been too marginal a figure to notice, a meaningless background blip in a tale full of romances and flings with prominent movie stars, musicians, and a professional athlete or two. Yet Stanley was someone who could have gotten into her home without a struggle. He could also have conveniently skipped town without a trace after the murder, since he didn't live in Los Angeles in the first place.

I read the interview again. Was there any sign here that Antonio Mazzanti would murder two actresses less than a year later? He was clearly a broken-down version of his former self. He also clearly obsessed over dark things, over evil and the devil, and claimed to have demons within. Maybe he had committed the murder of Adaire Fontaine after all, and it haunted him, and in time he'd given in again to that urge to kill, murdering actresses Portia Reynolds and Grace LeRoux in their apartment.

Then it hit me.

I texted Stacey: *What if Stanley Preston wasn't a psycho killer, but was trying to solve Adaire's murder?*

Ooh, you think so? she replied.

He seemed to be studying the case years after it happened. Like he was trying to puzzle it out.

I don't suppose he wrote his thoughts down for us somewhere? That would be convenient.

I'll keep digging.

As I looked through the press coverage—all revolving

in some way around Adaire, Mazzanti, or Chance Chadwick —I thought about Stacey's last question. Stanley Preston had only died a few years earlier, a very old man living in his crumbling ruin of a theater. If he had indeed solved the mystery of Adaire Fontaine's murder, he'd had plenty of years in which to make his knowledge public.

Perhaps he'd found something he'd chosen to keep secret. Or perhaps he believed he had solved it, but nobody in the news media was interested in the opinion of some random drive-in owner from the other side of the continent. Anything he said would have been just one more crackpot theory for the pile.

On the screen, Adaire Fontaine strolled along a boardwalk clad in a wide, flowing antebellum dress and a parasol, presumably by the Mississippi or one of its tributaries. She walked with her unacceptably poor blacksmith beau, played by 1950s heartthrob Phineas Darby.

In the world of the film, it began to rain. Adaire's character opined they should get inside, but the handsome blacksmith insisted, in a somewhat less than logical claim, that the best method for avoiding the rain was to dance through it.

I saw where this was going—he started demonstrating dance moves, and she copied him, then outdid him with a flourish. Soon it was more of a dance-off between them, their shoes clomping rhythmically on the boardwalk, each trying to out-jump or out-spin the other, in a kind of musical-theater mating dance.

To cornball things up a little more, a small crowd of local river folk formed to watch the dance—first a group of three fishermen came up the boardwalk, pointing and gaping at the two dancers, then three washerwomen with laundry baskets entered from the opposite direction, doing the same.

Soon enough, the fishermen flung aside their buckets and poles, the washer-women dropped their wooden baskets of damp clothes, and everyone joined in the dance.

I'm having doubts about the historical accuracy of this film, I texted Stacey.

If there's any place where people are spontaneously breaking into song and dance, it's Louisiana, she replied, and I guessed she had me there, though the scene wasn't set in New Orleans.

I checked the monitors in the back of the van. My eyes were quickly drawn to the camera feeds from down in the projection house. The night vision showed nothing out of the ordinary, but the thermal showed a vast, deep cold spot down there, near the projector. The cold spot was as still as a winter pond, as though the entity were sitting in place, perhaps watching the movie on the big screen through the front porthole, perhaps waiting its turn to project one of its ultra-late-night ghostly films.

Eventually, I returned to my seat up front. I considered texting Stacey about the cold spot, but when I looked over the top of the sunken building to the window of her Escape, I realized she was locked in an embrace with Jacob, doing things that teenagers of yesteryear had surely done in the relative privacy of the drive-in.

Swinging my sun visor down and around to block off as much of my side window as possible, I returned my attention to the movie, still hoping for a message from Adaire, or at least an appearance by the parking lot phantom.

Soon the great flood swept away the plantation and the town, in a visually stunning climax of destruction that had wowed audiences back in the day and was still pretty impressive. It must have been done with very well-crafted and painstakingly detailed scale models, because it didn't look fake at all.

Adaire ended up on the rooftop of her flooded mansion with a group of people, the waters rising around them, all distinction between aristocrats and common men and slaves wiped away by the flood, a sentiment expressed by an elderly slave in an earnest soliloquy, his straw hat over his heart, an uplifting moment.

Then the floodwaters rose and swept them all away, leaving no trace of the plantation, only water to the horizon. The screen went dark.

Chapter Twenty-One

Being a more upbeat film, it didn't end there. The sun rose to find Adaire and her young blacksmith floating on a broken balcony, right in the heart of New Orleans, where they and the other rooftop survivors were lifted up by the locals, who immediately pulled them into a jazzy song and dance number. With her parents' plantation destroyed and her family impoverished—as well as those of her various approved gentleman suitors—Adaire's character was at last free to marry the man she loved. Naturally, New Orleans had a parade about it.

Stacey knocked on my window as the credits rolled, and I hopped out to greet her.

"Okay, it was pretty good," I said.

"How about that flood scene, huh?"

"Impressive, like people say."

"Jacob's ready to check out the old tomb. I mean the projection house."

I looked over her shoulder to see Jacob slowly circling the low brick pillbox structure. He knelt to look into the two portholes where the projectors had cast their relatively low-powered, short-range images in the earliest days of the drive-in.

"There's a major cold front down there," I said to Stacey, in a low voice so Jacob couldn't hear. "I think Preston might be stirred up by the movie starring his favorite actress. I'll go down to guard Jacob. You stay up here and make sure that creepy little door doesn't slam shut and trap us in there."

"Yikes, good point. But I'm going with him. You hold the door up here for us," Stacey insisted.

"I'm not comfortable putting you in potential danger —"

"You're always putting me in danger, so relax. I want to watch out for him. If it was anyone else, I'd probably let you go ahead."

I was surprised, but she seemed pretty firm in her stance, so I went with it.

We joined Jacob at the projection house, where he was running his fingers over the cracked bricks.

"This is your problem right here, ladies," he said. "That guy up in the screen tower? He's down here, too. But his energy's much stronger down here."

"Could he come up to the parking lot, do you think?"

"Yeah, he feels like the whole theater is his. He used to work here, or maybe he ran it, or even owned it... he's definitely territorial..."

"Is he dangerous, though?" I asked.

Jacob shrugged. "You saw him upstairs. He's not something you'd want in your home or workplace. Especially if they're the same place." He toed the strange half-door with his shoe. "I guess we have to go down in there. I've known it since I first saw this weird little building. It's been hanging over me this whole time."

Stacey kicked open the little half-door and slid down inside, followed by Jacob. I sat down in the doorway, propping the door open with my body.

As the thermal camera had indicated, it was frigid down there.

"Okay," Jacob whispered. "I think this is his lair. He especially likes to stay over there, by the projector." Jacob reached out to touch the massive antique machine and shuddered visibly on contact, like it was freezing cold, or like he was getting an electrical shock, or both at the same time.

He was quiet a long moment.

"This is bigger than I thought," he said, his breath coming out in frosty clouds. "There's a troupe of them… and they perform up there, on the big screen, acting and reenacting the same roles over and over… I don't know if that makes any sense…"

"It does," Stacey and I said.

"Oh."

"Are they dangerous to the living?" I asked, my usual top concern.

"Potentially. But I'm not sensing anger right now. He— the main guy—is annoyed at us for being down here in his space, especially me for touching the projector." Jacob drew his hand back. "Just like he didn't want us up on the third floor. But I'm not sensing hostility toward the family, your clients. If anything, he's glad to see the drive-in restored, to see movies on the screen again."

"What about the rest of them?"

Jacob shook his head. "They're drawing away. I don't think he wants another confrontation like upstairs."

"They're happy, though?"

"They're active, they're energized. I think they're feeding on the rejuvenation of the theater."

"By scaring customers?" I asked.

He shrugged. "Maybe. But this spot right here is the real center of the haunting, more so than the tower, though the guy spends time in both places. And just because they're not attacking now, it doesn't mean they're friendly. You saw what happened up in the tower."

"Yeah, I did notice the ghost getting right up in my grill in a threatening way," I said. "That hasn't slipped my mind yet."

"I wouldn't rest easy just because they're leaving us alone right now. They are watching and waiting. I'm not sure what they're waiting for. And to be honest, I'd really like to get out of here, posthaste."

"Did you seriously say 'posthaste'? Like, out loud?" Stacey asked.

"If you don't start heading for the door, I'll start saying '*tout suite*.' On the reg."

"Okay, I'm moving. This is all too painful for me to hear." Stacey started toward me, and I scooted back to clear the doorway.

She climbed out on her belly, the only way to exit that stupid sunken building, and Jacob followed close behind. I let out a little sigh of relief when they were both outside.

Stacey brushed dirt from her jeans. "Okey-doke. Let's go load up our low-budget creature feature, *The Body in the Basement*."

Jacob cast a glance back at the small door. Maybe he was feeling less enthusiastic about the prospect of subterranean horror movies.

The concession stand's warm yellow lights and funky polka-purple interior were a welcome relief from the dark place we'd just left. The baked-in scent of popcorn exuded from everywhere.

"This is more like it," Jacob said.

"No moody dead people here?" I asked.

"Not exactly, but I'm picking up lots of trace memories. This was a very dense focus of activity for many years. It was long ago, but it still echoes with the thousands who came and went. People here for a good time, for a night out with family or friends, for a date… and more specifically, they came into this building for snacks, for the refreshment phase of a fun night out. Definite good feelings in this building. This is where you want to hang out. Not those other buildings, avoid those."

"Good to hear there's a bright spot at the drive-in. I'll go load up tonight's awful horror movie." Stacey headed around the corner, to the back hallway with the bathroom doors and the employees-only stairs to the second floor.

Jacob wandered over to the game room. "They need more here. Retro video games, at the minimum. Pinball, ideally."

"That's what Benny wants eventually. I think it's a budget issue." I followed him at a distance.

"Yeah, I could see that. Maybe they could go low-budget first, like a ping-pong table, or bumper pool…" He touched the hole punctured in the drywall, then glanced at the smashed corner of the foosball table. "Looks like somebody was a sore loser."

"Something like that."

Jacob looked at me. "What did you see in here?"

"Who says I saw anything?"

"Sometimes I can tell things about the living, too."

"That makes one of us. I never understand the living," I said.

"What did you see, Ellie?"

"Should I tell you?" I asked. "Couldn't it unduly

influence your psychic-vibe action?"

"Okay, you can tell me later. You clearly want to."

I laughed. "I actually do, yeah. Stacey better not have mentioned it."

"Not a word."

"What secrets are we keeping from Stacey?" Stacey ambled into the room, hands on her hips.

"None," I said. "You and I are keeping them from Jacob."

"Oh." Stacey looked at the damage he was inspecting. "Yep. Now the movie's about to start, so I say we pile into my car, because the van's a real back-breaker."

"We should split up again," I said. "Ghosts are more likely to approach isolated individuals. Maybe even into three cars."

"Well, that's no fun," Jacob said.

"And that really hasn't been the rule around here," Stacey said. "The parking lot phantom scared off that whole family in the packed van, right? If anything, this entity might be drawn to a larger crowd."

"I shouldn't be hearing this. I'll meet y'all outside. After I grab one of those honey basil sodas." Jacob headed out.

I considered what Stacey had said until he was gone. "Yeah, that's a good point."

"And do you really want to watch *Body in the Basement* alone?" Stacey added.

"That's a *great* point. But we should keep an eye on the monitors."

"The people who got stalked weren't watching monitor arrays. We need to imitate what they were doing—watching the movie as a group."

"Okay. It's worth a try. Plus, your car really is more comfortable."

"I know! So come on, it's starting."

We piled into Stacey's Escape, a hybrid SUV, roomier and with far better seating than the van. I stretched out in back, doing my best to act like a regular person out with friends for a night of innocent fun. It was weirdly hard for me to pretend that, for some reason.

Legend of the South, the evening's first movie, had been a sweeping, high-energy epic, packed with song and dance and romance and tragedy, all the ingredients believed to make a grand movie in those days.

The Body in the Basement had... none of that, as I shortly had the displeasure of learning.

Chapter Twenty-Two

On the screen, the camera panned across an average, unassuming suburban house from Anytown, USA—but I knew from the movie trailer that all was not as it seemed, as least once you got to the basement door.

Soon the camera view entered, somewhat Peeping-Tom fashion, through a window into the bedroom of Portia Reynolds, playing a teenager dancing to a boppy song on her radio, at least until her character's stern-looking parents entered and insisted she turn it down.

As luck would have it, her parents were traveling out of town for the weekend, but she was not to have any guests, and certainly no parties.

"Oh, mother, how can I have any parties when I've no friends in this awful town that's so strange and odd? I wish we'd never moved here!" Portia Reynolds emoted tearfully. She was definitely pretty, shorter, dark-haired, and very curvy, where her roommate and co-Silk-Strangler-victim

Grace LeRoux had been tall, blonde, and willowy.

Was it possible that Portia Reynolds was the woman in the sunglasses we'd watched on the Super 8 reel as she left her apartment and climbed aboard the Los Angeles city bus? It was very possible.

"You will make friends," Portia's movie mom assured her.

"But not this weekend!" the movie dad added, gruffly.

I pulled out my phone and looked up Portia Reynolds, a girl-next-door type, apple-cheeked and smiling in her publicity photos. She'd been twenty-five when she starred as a teenager in *The Body in the Basement*, thirty when she died five years later. She'd only had three minor roles after *The Body*, all in low-budget movies. Maybe she'd worked on the stage in that time, but I had the impression of a struggling young actress. If not for her murder, she might have moved on into a quiet post-acting life. She had only gained fame with the manner of her death.

Her apartment building was easy to find because it was listed on multiple macabre Hollywood tours, including a "Hollywood Murder Tour," a "Movie Star Death Tour," and one ghost tour.

There it was. The four-story stucco apartment building with the cavelike stairwells. A recent Google street view image showed it even more rundown than in the stalker home video we'd seen, where it hadn't looked all that inviting, either. Garbage was strewn down one set of stairs; bars had been added to the ground-floor windows.

"Hey! Are you seriously looking at your phone, Ellie?" Stacey asked, alerted to my distraction into other activities by the light from my screen.

"I was just researching," I said. "It's about the movie, don't worry."

"Well, you're missing the plot. She's going to have

friends over on Friday night even though her parents told her not to."

"What a shocking twist."

"Are you done with your phone yet?" Stacey asked, rather demandingly.

"Yes, done." I touched the power button to darken the screen. "Let's watch the banned murder movie, hooray."

"That's the spirit!" Stacey turned back to the screen.

I checked out the window for any actual spirits who might be wandering the parking lot, but I didn't see much. My gaze lingered on the dark shape of the sunken projection house, only a few feet away. It wasn't hard to imagine the odd little door silently opening, letting some undead thing slither out.

To take my mind off that, I focused on *The Body in the Basement.*

Portia Reynolds, twenty-five years old, lay on her stomach dressed in a plaid jumper on her bed, hair tied back in a huge bow, stocking feet kicking excitedly as she chatted on a big phone with a coiled wire. "We'll play records, drink pop, and have the grandest time!" she gushed.

The view cut to another actress, also in her mid-to-late twenties but playing a teenager. "I'll telephone the boys!" she said.

"Agnes!" Portia gasped. "We can't have boys at a party without adults around! They're apt to get fresh!"

"What if the boy is Tom Hooper?"

"Tom Hooper?" Portia gasped. She did a lot of gasping in this movie. I supposed that was appropriate, considering the director would eventually strangle her to death in real life. "But he's the finest fella on the whole football team! And class president! Why, they don't come more popular than Tom Hooper!"

"And the scoop around school is he's got the hots for you."

"For me?" Portia gasped, again. She was on her feet, looking at herself in the mirror, turning this way and that. "I would be the luckiest gal in town!"

"You'd better act fast, because the latest scuttlebutt is Myra Finklestein has the hots for him."

"But she's the prettiest gal in school!"

"Then I propose you invite him to the party. Or you could end up the loneliest gal in town."

"Gee whiz. Darn that Myra Finklestein, always getting her pick of the pack! You had better telephone the boys after all." Portia hung up the phone and looked dreamily out the window, a doo-wop song crooning over her radio. "Tom Hooper. He's such a fine-looking fella!"

The camera view pulled back and away from her, then panned down, down, down, to a narrow basement window. A movement flickered behind the glass, as if somebody lurked in the basement, hiding, listening, waiting.

I texted Stacey a link to the image of Portia and Grace's apartment building.

Up in the driver's seat, Stacey's phone buzzed. She gasped like Portia in the movie and whirled around to look at me.

"I knew it! He was stalking her! Which means—"

"Are y'all texting each other? Really?" Jacob asked. "That's not allowed at movie theaters."

"Drive-in rules are much looser," Stacey argued.

"Could you two keep it down up there? Some of us are trying to watch a movie," I said.

"Very funny." Stacey shook her head and looked back at the big screen.

The movie was bad, but at least the pace was quick. Before we knew it, the Friday night party was in full swing.

Portia and a couple of school gals in bright dresses with matching headbands showed off a repertoire of top 60s dance moves—the swim, the hitchhiker, the mashed potato —along with three fine-looking fellas in high school letter jackets and pomaded hair. Things were starting to get wild.

The camera panned down to the floor… then passed below it, to show the trusses of the basement ceiling bouncing and shifting as the groovy teens twisted and twirled and bopped. Dust spilled and cascaded down to land with a dry rattle on a row of widely spaced boards, which barely covered a sunken pit in the basement's dirt floor.

One board slid abruptly to the side. It was startling, even though I should have expected it.

Dirt-coated fingers reached up from below.

Back upstairs, the teen shindig continued.

Then the music ended abruptly, and the lights went out.

"Hey, what gives?" asked the girl called Agnes, stepping back from her dance partner. "Are you fellas trying to pull a fast one?"

"Oh, foo! The radio's gone out, as have the lights!" proclaimed Portia Reynolds, though the room hadn't darkened much, if at all.

"It's bound to be an electrical problem," one of the letter-jacketed footballers was bright enough to figure out. "Where's your fuse box?"

"It's down in the basement," Portia Reynolds said. "But I never go there. It's ever so frightening. I wish we had no basement, but we have one, and it's frightening."

"I'm not frightened of some loopy basement!" the footballer proclaimed. "Why, my pop's an electrical man. I can fix it up lickety-split. Where's your flashlight?"

"I wouldn't know. I suppose my father must have one in his toolbox. Oh, I'm ever so frightened!"

"Don't be frightened." The handsome Tom Hooper embraced her. "We'll keep you safe. We're football players, after all. Nobody tussles with us."

"Oh, will you, Tom? Will you really?" She returned the embrace, with much batting of her eyelashes.

The electrician's boy, armed with only a flashlight, reached the end of the hall and approached the basement door, made of patchwork, decaying wood that blatantly didn't belong in this otherwise peppy suburban home. It looked like it had been transplanted from a rickety old barn, maybe even a rickety old slaughterhouse.

The teenage boy—well, the actor was easily thirty—eased open the door and looked into the basement below. Now that he was alone, his brave front wilted.

"Say," he called over his shoulder. "Say, Mickey! You want to give me a hand?"

The third footballer strolled up, looking cocky, until it was his turn to gaze down into the basement. The camera angle on this was from deep inside the basement, looking up the sagging wooden stairs toward the two boys in the doorway.

"What's the big idea?" asked the one called Mickey. "I thought you said your pops was an electrical man."

"He is. It's not the fixing I need help with, see, it's holding the flashlight. I need both hands to work."

"Shucks," Mickey said. "Well, it's a sorry thing to ask a fella to do, that's all I'll say." But he followed the other guy down the stairs into the basement.

The camera lingered on the basement door, which gradually pulled shut of its own accord, sealing them inside.

"Well, they're dead," Jacob commented.

"I think they'll be fine," Stacey replied. "After all, his pop's an electrical man, see?"

"I wonder what's down in the basement," I said. "What

if it's a body?"

"Seems like a reach to me." Jacob scratched his chin thoughtfully. "What gives you the idea there could be a body in the basement?"

On the screen, handsome quarterback Tom Hooper struck a match and used it to light a candle that Portia Reynolds held in a decorative candlestick. She trembled and sighed as Tom touched his flame to her wick. They stood alone in the dining room, the other girls elsewhere in the darkened house.

"Oh, thank you, Tom," Portia said, watching her flame grow.

"Look here," Tom said, as he continued to light her candles, "I know this is a heck of a time to ask, but—aw, for Pete's sake, you're a swell gal, and well, what do you think about going steady? As in you and me?"

"Oh, Tom!" Portia gasped. "Do you mean it?"

"Would a fella ever lie about a thing like that?"

"Of course not, Tom. Not a nice fella like you."

"I am a nice fella," he said. "You can bank on it, honest."

"I'm just going to say it," Stacey piped up. "I don't think Tom's really looking for a long-term relationship at all. I think he's into Myra Finklestein."

"But the Portia Reynolds character is too naive to see it," Jacob added. "She only sees what she wants to see."

On the screen, a long, almost wolf-like pained howl sounded from the basement, like one of the football guys had gotten seriously hurt down there. The two other girls, having joined Portia and Tom in the candlelit dining room, grabbed each other, screaming, while Portia grabbed on to Tom.

"I'd best go check on the fellas." Tom took a candlestick and started off, but Portia grabbed him and hauled him back to her, in a way that seemed fairly unsafe to do when the guy was holding a burning candle.

"Yes, Tom," Portia said. "My answer is yes. I will go steady with you."

He looked at her, and then they embraced and kissed long and hard, in a way that seemed awkward and forced between the actors. The two girls in the background seemed unsure what to do during the scene.

"Oh, Tom," she sighed, as he pulled away to join the other guys in the basement. "Don't get hurt down there."

"I'll be fine, my little bunny-tail," Tom said. "It's just a basement."

"That's what you think," Jacob whispered.

So quarterback Tom Hooper journeyed down into the basement alone, his path lit only by his candle, the stairs creaking beneath him. There was no handrail at all. That basement was not up to code.

"Fellas?" Tom asked, descending into the concrete-and-dirt land beneath the house. "Mickey? You there?"

"You're a dead man, Tom," Jacob said.

"He is not!" Stacey argued. "He'll be fine."

"He's thrown his last touchdown pass," Jacob said.

"He has not! There's hope for Tom. I believe in him."

Soon, Tom called for Portia to come to the basement door.

"Look at this," he told her, pointing to the obvious pit in the dirt floor that had been loosely covered with boards. A few of those boards had now been thrown aside. "It's like something came up through the ground. Now there's a hole in the floor."

"Tom, what are you saying?" Portia gasped from the basement door.

"Well, see for yourself. It's your basement, after all."

She came down the stairs, and they looked into the pit

together.

"It looks like something was buried here," Tom said.

"There's nothing buried there now," Portia said. "How do you suppose it became unburied, Tom?"

"It's about the size of a... well, I don't want to say it..."

"A body?" she gasped.

"I didn't want to say it. But why would there be a body in your basement?"

"Shucks, I for sure couldn't tell ya. We only just moved here over the summer. Tom, where's Mickey? And his best pal Ricky?"

"It seems they've gone missing."

"Missing!"

"It's a goof, I'm telling ya," Tom said. "Those two guys are always off goofing around together. They get into all kinds of tomfoolery. Betcha they're in a closet somewhere, just waiting to bust out and give us a scare."

I checked my phone to see how much longer until the movie ended. It was going to be awhile.

So far, nothing had emerged from the sunken projection house to harass us, which would almost have been a nice distraction from the film at that point.

On the screen, the movie characters continued to get separated and attacked. We didn't see the assailant, but instead watched those scenes through the assailant's eyes. All we saw was a dirt-encrusted hand, turning doorknobs, walking down halls, grabbing people when they were alone.

Agnes, the delinquent friend who'd encouraged the presence of boys at the party, was killed while sneaking a bottle from the parents' liquor cabinet.

The other girl, who'd gone upstairs to take a bath in a leap of logic understood only to horror-film makers, was found dead on a bed, muddy handprints all over her white bathrobe.

Portia screamed at each dead body they found. Soon it was just her and Tom, following muddy footprints down the hall to the closed basement door.

"Don't go in there!" Stacey said. "Get out of the house!"

"They're so dead," Jacob said.

"No! There will be a happy ending!" Stacey insisted.

"There's somebody in the basement," Portia Reynolds said onscreen.

"Which is a good reason to *leave the house*. How stupid can you be?" Stacey asked, but Tom just nodded, opened the basement door, and led the way down. Portia stuck close behind him.

The movie was actually getting to me at this point, and I was scared of what they would find in the basement. Partly, this was because the director, perhaps facing budget limits, had kept whatever inevitably cheesy monster costume they were using mostly off-screen, other than the muddy hand, giving it a bit of a *Jaws* or *Evil Dead* approach.

Also, I have encountered many genuinely evil and terrifying things in basements, so my sympathies for characters walking into them ran high, and my fears about such situations deep. My hand instinctively went to my flashlight as I watched the characters onscreen descend into the basement. I expected something awful to leap out at them from beneath the basement stairs or the dark pit in the floor.

"Mickey?" Portia whispered, stepping ever closer to the pit, her ankle within grabbing distance of anything that might lurk within. "Is anyone here? Anyone at all?"

Something shifted inside the car.

Stacey and Jacob didn't seem to notice it, but I did. The night had gone darker somehow, like a large shadow had been cast across the back of the car.

I turned and looked out the rear window.

There was only darkness, aside from the glow of the projector on the concession stand's second floor.

"Hey, Stacey?" I said. "Didn't we leave a light on at the concession stand?"

"Shh, it's getting good," Stacey whispered.

I looked from the blacked-out concession stand to the tomb-like projection house nearby. As far as I could see, nothing had emerged from there, but I couldn't see much.

Then I heard it, right behind me.

Tap. Tap. Tap.

I stiffened, feeling my blood almost curdle at the sound of it. Before I turned, before I looked, I thought I could almost recognize the sound, the cadence of the three taps.

They came again, apparently too soft for anyone to hear but me, with the movie blasting over the SUV's sound system, or maybe it was an auditory apparition meant for me alone.

Tap. Tap. Tap.

Feeling queasy, I forced myself to turn and look out the side window, trying to prepare myself mentally for whatever awful thing awaited outside the glass.

I failed to prepare myself adequately.

Right outside, rapping the crook of her cane against the window, stood a woman who was undeniably dead.

Ghosts can appear all kinds of ways. Sometimes, like with Stan Preston, it was a matter of personal wish fulfillment. He'd always wanted and tried to look like Chance Chadwick. Other times, they make themselves look larger and more imposing than they did in life. Sometimes they attempt to fool you by pretending to be something they are not.

Sometimes, though... they look like they crawled out

of the grave, and this was definitely one of those. Clumps of wiry hair clung to her skull. Her eye sockets were empty, just as poor Daisy had described them. I could see the hollow where her nose had been, her empty eyes, and her teeth through a hole in the side of her face. She wore a double strand of pearls, which clinked against exposed collarbones. The remnants of a stiff, high-necked dress clung to her deteriorated body.

"Ruby Jackson," I said to the windowpane between us, my breath frosting it up despite the previously warm spring night outside.

I rolled down the window, removing the barrier. She was close, as close to me as Stanley Preston's apparition in the tower had been, but more frightening. I could smell her cloying perfume, barely covering the underlying scent of deep decay.

As I opened the window, a voice in my head spoke to me the way Stacey had to the movie characters just before they went down into the basement—why expose myself to greater risk?

But I guess, like Portia's character, and like Tom Hooper, I just had to know.

"Ruby," I said. "Are you the one who's been scaring people in the parking lot? You never wanted the drive-in built. You never wanted your daughter to marry Stan Preston—"

Ruby's decayed hand lunged at me through the open window, in much the same way The Body's dirty, decayed hand had grabbed and killed the victims on the big screen.

My lungs felt painful and heavy, packed with some thick, sticky fluid that threatened to drown me. I tried to draw a breath and failed, which kicked off some serious panic.

Ruby Jackson, Preston's disapproving mother-in-law,

had emphysema, among other health problems, and now she was attacking me with her memory of it.

I tried to call out for help, but that flooded-lung condition fought against me.

Ruby watched my struggles with no sign of mercy.

Finally, I managed to loosen my flashlight and blast it at her, searing the apparition with bright light.

"Hey!" Jacob and Stacey called out in protest, but at least they finally turned to see what was going on in the back seat. Apparently, Jacob's psychic abilities ended where his absorption into a bad movie began. He'd told me before that he sometimes resorts to playing death metal, tuned to a low volume, to blot out the voices of the dead that he can hear late at night. He doesn't particularly like the music, it was just what worked.

Jacob charged toward me now, leaping between the front seats.

"Begone! I cast thee out!" Jacob bellowed, like a bouncer at the Renaissance Fair.

Stacey skipped through channels on her car radio, away from the drive-in's 89.3 FM broadcast, skimming until she reached a local gospel station. Then she blasted her Escape's sound system at full volume from every speaker, like we'd all just teleported into the middle of a rousing church service.

I continued blasting Ruby Jackson's ghost with light, but Preston's late mother-in-law showed no sign of retreating, or even of letting me catch my breath. Jacob continued to rebuke the spirit, shouting at it.

Stacey leaped out of the car and circled around outside, illuminating the ghost with a tactical light in each hand, until she was behind Ruby. Blinding white saturated the ghost from all directions. No shadows, no darkness.

Under the intense glare, Ruby looked more desiccated

than ever, the white light shining through a thousand cracks and holes in her body, her skull visible through the remnants of her skin, her pearls gleaming like polished bone.

She finally trembled, though, withering under the onslaught, and after a moment she was gone—no dramatic exit, not so much as a good-bye.

I took a deep breath at last. Stacey opened the door where the horrifying entity had stood and wrapped her arms around me as she made sure I was still alive.

Chapter Twenty-Three

"Well, that would certainly chase away customers," Jacob said.

We stood outside the van, in a loose circle so we could watch for anything sneaking up on us. I kept my eye on the concession stand in the distance, where the yellow interior light had sputtered back to life above the popcorn machine.

"Are we now thinking Ruby Jackson, the mother-in-law, is the parking lot phantom?" Stacey asked.

"It makes sense. The entity certainly looked like her pictures in the farmhouse," I said.

"Except a little more rotten," Stacey said.

"Gross, but true. And she had the cane, obviously. She never wanted Preston in her family, never wanted the drive-in built. She had to die before he could do it, that's how much she opposed it."

"Should I be hearing this?" Jacob asked.

"It's fine. We're pretty clear on who that entity was. If

you want to show off your psychic range, see if you can sniff out her lair," I told him.

"So I'm a bloodhound now?"

"Aw, bloodhounds are cute," Stacey said. She touched Jacob's cheek. "With their flappy, mushy faces. Go sniff out the evil mother-in-law ghost."

"Are we sure she's evil?" Jacob asked.

"She literally just tried to kill Ellie, so yeah, I'm putting her in column 'E' for evil. That doesn't mean the other ghosts here are nice. They're probably all evil in different and deadly ways. That would be our luck," Stacey said.

Jacob took a breath and turned slowly around, like he was trying to pick up a radio signal using a weak antenna. "I didn't sense her in the screen tower, or down in the projection house, or the concession stand..." He looked at the Purple Pizza Eater and narrowed his eyes. "Wait. What's behind there?"

"Oh, just stuff," I said lightly.

He nodded and strode off toward the concession stand.

Stacey and I fell into step several paces behind him, letting his Spidey senses lead the way.

We rounded the concession stand to the lawn beyond it. He turned to look up at the screen, where The Body pursued a silently screaming Portia Reynolds, its mud-crusted hand reaching for her. It was all soundless, since we hadn't activated the concession stand's outdoor speakers.

"Pretty good view from the lawn," Jacob said. "Could be nice to stretch out here and watch the movie, maybe better than sitting in your car. But something's not right." He walked to the back fence, and we followed him as he trailed his fingertips from plank to plank along the weathered wood panels, making a steady *bump, bump, bump*.

He slowed at the gate, despite how featureless and hard

it was to find on this side of the fence, especially at night. After some poking around, he pushed it open and led us through, into the realm of the gardens in the shadow of the overgrown farmhouse.

Stacey followed, taking video for our records. I released the gate gently as I joined the two of them on the other side. The latch fell into place with a clack like the lock of a prison cell door.

I really did not like that farmhouse, and now had a personal vendetta against its long-dead occupant. She wasn't just threatening our clients' business, she had tried to kill me, to make a ghost out of me. Then I could have been stuck haunting the old drive-in for eternity. No, thanks. Not even with Adaire Fontaine to keep me company.

"I don't have to tell you this place is active, paranormal-wise." Jacob led us into the dark inner space of the house, where spindly tree limbs grew in through ivy-shrouded windows.

We kept our flashlights off inside the house, relying on the trickle of moonlight from the open front door and the windows. Jacob looked among the decayed remnants of furniture and into the kitchen with its sloping floor and rusty pipes.

The sound came from upstairs, just above our heads. *Thump. Thump. Thump.*

Stacey and I glanced warily at each other, recognizing the banging of Ruby's cane.

Jacob stared at the ceiling. Another triple thump sounded, dislodging dust from above that spilled down on us, not unlike the *Body in the Basement* scene where the teenage dancing awakens the corpse buried under the house.

"She's moving." Jacob followed the course of the sound to the bottom of the stairs, where he stopped and looked up.

Even before we joined him, the look on his face told me he could see her.

I saw her, too, Ruby, leaning on her cane in the shadows above, watching over the second-floor railing, her rotten features mercifully hidden in the gloom, at least for the moment. Hopefully, she wouldn't move into the moonlight so we could see her better.

"We're only trying to help," Jacob said, as though already in the middle of a conversation with her. "Nobody wants—nobody—" I had the impression he was being interrupted. "Okay! But that's not why—these are different people. You're not listening—"

Thump, thump, thump. Her cane rapped the floor.

More dust rained down on us, along with rusty nails.

"Hey, watch it!" Stacey shouted, pulling a nail from her hair. "You hit me in the head. Now I'm going to get brain tetanus."

"What is she saying, Jacob?" I asked.

"She wants us gone," Jacob said. "Not just the three of us who are here in the house, but all the living, from this whole area. She wants everyone gone and the theater buildings destroyed."

"So she's a possible threat to the family?" I remembered what Daisy had told me about the dead woman's voice calling her over, luring her through the gate. This infuriated me, so I edged around to look Ruby in the eyes, or at least in her shadowy face up there. "Ruby Jackson," I said, in as commanding a tone as I could manage, "you have to move on. You don't live here anymore. You're dead. You've been dead a long time—"

The dead woman slammed her cane down three more times.

More pieces of the second floor pelted us—chunks of

dry-rotted wood, more dust, more nails, leaving open holes above.

"I know it can be hard to let go of the past," I said. "You didn't want your daughter's second marriage to happen. You didn't want the theater to happen. But that's all water under the bridge, that's ancient history. Did Stan Preston murder you over it? That's what we're here to find out. We want to help you."

"Oh," Jacob said.

"What?" I whispered.

"When you said that name, she got very angry," Jacob said. "Maybe we should go—"

The cane rapped three more times. Each sound was like a thunderclap, shaking the house to its foundations. The floor rumbled beneath us.

Above, a sizable support truss broke loose above and came hurtling down. Jacob pulled Stacey aside as it crashed into the floorboards where they'd been standing.

Balusters cracked and fell, shattering some of the stairs on impact. One broken baluster came spinning at me like a baseball bat thrown aside by an angry player. It sailed over me as I ducked. It went on to strike the wall behind me with a loud crack. It could easily have been my skull instead of the wall.

"Let's go!" I shouted.

We bolted for the front door, pelted by chunks of the ceiling and pieces of the walls as Ruby's cane thudded and thudded above. The house shuddered like it was going to shake itself apart and come crashing down around us before we could escape.

We raced out the front door.

A loud creak sounded above. A porch beam or two had given way, and now one end of the porch roof came rushing down to crush me.

I leaped toward the front steps and the gardens beyond, trying to reach the yard before I got buried in an avalanche of rotten woodwork.

Before I was clear of the porch, though, something struck me across the backs of my legs, something that felt very much like a hard cane swatted across my calves by someone with a lot of pent-up anger to express.

The impact swatted me down like a fly, knocking me to the porch stairs as the porch roof crashed down behind me.

"Ellie!" Stacey ran toward me. Jacob was standing up, brushing dirt off himself, having apparently made a similar desperate jump but with more success. "Are you okay?"

"Maybe." I looked back. One end of the porch roof had fallen all the way down and could have squashed us as we fled out the front door. The tacked-on widow's walk railing had come down with it, and a loose baluster had struck me across the back of the legs like a cane.

Now the porch roof blocked the door and formed a rickety, ivy-shrouded ramp up to the second-story door that had opened onto the movie-viewing area. Anyone stepping out that door now would fall a few feet before landing in the ruins of the old bench, or maybe impaling themselves on the rusty speaker pole.

I could see nothing but darkness inside the open door, but I felt like Ruby was watching us from in there, hoping she'd harmed us.

"Well, she's no Casper," I said.

"Casper? She's not even Beetlejuice." Stacey helped me up. "She's more of a Freddy Krueger."

"What's your professional opinion, Jacob?"

Jacob replaced his glasses, which had flown off when he'd jumped to avoid the collapsing porch roof. "I would say there are better than even odds that this house is haunted."

"Okay, that's all we needed. Guess you can head home," Stacey said.

"And miss the end of *Body in the Basement*? Not a chance." He looked up at the open door that had once been a dormer window. "Ellie, after you said the name that made her angry, but before she lashed out and tried to bring the house down on our heads, I picked up a clear, burning image from her. A memory, one she clings to with a lot of fury."

"Tell us, Mr. Weiss," Stacey said in a newscaster tone, holding up her handheld video recorder. "What was this memory?"

Jacob closed his eyes. "A man is standing over her. She's gagging, choking, trying to breathe, but can't... she's dying. He's watching."

"What does he look like?" I asked.

"Big mustache." With his fingertips, he traced big swoops coming out on either side of his nose. "Little scars all over his cheeks. He's wearing a coat and tie, a fedora. There's a lot of cigar smoke in the air, which isn't helping her breathing situation."

"Then what?" I asked.

"That's it," Jacob said. "Just that image. I think it was close to her death, and she holds on to it angrily."

"So... did he kill her?"

"That's pretty much the idea I'm getting. She wants revenge, too. She wants to destroy him, to destroy everything he ever made... which, I think, is maybe the drive-in? Because the guy she's obsessed with is, I think, the one haunting the tower and the projection house. It's like they're both dead, but their hatred lives on."

"Aw, how sweet," Stacey said.

"It seems like Ruby is the one stalking and frightening

customers," I said. "Maybe we should advise the clients to go ahead and tear down this house. Down to bare earth."

"And burn it," Jacob added. "Then have the ground where it stood blessed, and grow some plants or trees there to break down any lingering dark energy."

"I think our clients might like that solution. I know Callie would."

Warily, watching over our shoulders, we left through the gate and returned to the drive-in's lawn. Though I couldn't see her, I was sure I could feel Ruby's rotten eyes on us as we walked away.

Chapter Twenty-Four

As Jacob hoped, we did return to the parking lot in time to catch the climax of *The Body in the Basement*. The formerly pleasant interior of the Portia Reynolds character's home was now a wreck, with muddy handprints on every wall. The Body pursued Portia's character and her boyfriend Tom, who both looked battered and muddy but so far still alive.

Jacob raced ahead to Stacey's car to hear the audio.

By the time I climbed into the back seat, the speakers were full of shrieking and screaming. The Body had tackled Portia Reynolds to the carpet, and now we got our first actual look at The Body that wasn't a camera point of view and a single muddy hand.

"Whoa," Stacey said. "The Body is a woman?"

"A muddy woman," Jacob said, in a tone so carefully neutral it made Stacey scowl a little.

She scowled because the actress playing The Body

appeared to be wearing nothing but a skin-tight layer of dirt and mud, and she was wrestling Portia Reynolds on the carpet, dropping the whole movie to a new and sordid low. Portia had a butcher knife and was doing her best to stab The Body as it attacked her, but with no luck. Both women kept crying out and screaming, their legs tangled together.

"What's the stupid boyfriend up to?" Stacey asked.

As if to answer her, the Tom character appeared on the screen, gawking uselessly at the fight. "Jeepers," he finally said. "You're telling me the body in the basement was... Myra Finklestein? The prettiest gal in school?"

"That's right!" Portia Reynolds gasped, while losing her wrestling match with the dead girl.

"But, golly, how?" Tom scratched his head, as though resolving this mystery was far more important than helping his girlfriend or perhaps going crazy with fear over the knowledge that an aggressive corpse had just murdered everyone in the house.

"Because she killed me!" The Body hissed.

"That's right! I killed her!" Portia flipped The Body/Myra Finklestein on her back and straddled her, gaining the advantage in their wrestling match, and held the butcher knife high, preparing to kill Myra. For the second time, apparently. "And my friends helped me bury her body in the basement!"

"Smokin' heck!" Tom said. "Why would you gals go and do a thing like that?"

"For you, Tom." Portia looked up at him, and her face and voice softened. "I knew she would steal you from me. But only if I let her live."

"Jeezum crow, that makes you a murderer!" Tom stepped back. "I can't go steady with a murderer!"

"Then I'll kill you, too, Tom!" Portia released The Body and charged at Tom, knife high. Tom cringed, cornered, not a particularly tough character in general.

However, the death blow never fell. Tom opened his eyes but maintained his cringing posture.

The Body had Portia by the neck, and now dragged her down the hall, toward the open door to the dark basement. Portia struggled, screaming, but couldn't break free.

"This is extra disturbing knowing the director actually strangled her five years later," Stacey whispered. "No wonder they pulled this from distribution."

Onscreen, The Body dragged Portia down into the basement, leaving a trail of muddy footprints on the carpet. The odd patchwork door slammed shut, sealing them inside together. Screams sounded from below.

Tom gaped, then turned and ran out the front door and away down the street.

The movie lingered on the open front door after he departed. Then the view slowly panned down to the basement window, where something shadowy moved, and another scream sounded.

The credits rolled.

"And now she becomes nothing but… a body in the basement," Jacob intoned. "Man, they should have worked that in at the end. I mean it's kind of implied, but it feels like a missed opportunity."

"I'm just glad it's over," I said.

"You didn't like it?" Jacob asked. "It had strong female characters."

"Who were murderers and undead revenge corpses," Stacey said.

"Yeah, but that was progressive for the time."

"Tom Hooper got off scot-free," Stacey said.

"What did he do wrong?" Jacob asked. "Other than cringe a lot?"

"He was clearly trying to short-term Portia's character.

Maybe he was ready to sock-hop her, but no way was he taking her to the prom."

"I think it's interesting that both this movie and *Biker Banshee* featured vengeful spirits of murdered women," I said.

"Oh, do they have *Biker Banshee* here?" Jacob sounded hopeful.

"No," I replied quickly. "But it's a recurring trope in Antonio Mazzanti's later movies, after Adaire Fontaine's death. If he killed her, maybe this is his way of expressing guilt. He might have felt haunted by her ghost. He might have *actually* been haunted by her ghost."

"And he's dead now, too, so if he's a ghost somewhere, their ghosts could be attached, right?" Stacey said. "Connected by the murder. We see that all the time. But on the flip-flop, if he didn't kill her, he probably had lots of personal trauma about the situation."

"True. He was close to her, she was murdered, he was suspected, and there was never any justice."

"Sounds like a recipe for a dark, self-destructive path to me," Stacey said.

"Which matches what I read in the article. You should read that."

"At this point, I have to mention that all normal psychic medium consultant procedures have been tossed aside here," Jacob said. "I'm happy to keep helping, but I know too much about your investigation to be completely objective, possibly."

"That's okay," Stacey said. "We can still use your services as a bad-movie consultant. For which you will be paid in popcorn, pizza, and drive-in date nights."

"I can live with this."

"Come on, I need to shut down the projection booth now." Stacey opened her door. "And from now on... I prefer not to walk around this theater at night alone, like, ever again."

Chapter Twenty-Five

"Basically, here's the deal," I said to Callie and Benny, as they worked on the Herculean task of trying to organize the first-floor office/storage/everything area. Daisy sat beyond the closed glass door in her playroom, wearing headphones and playing a keyboard, while watching a piano lesson on a tablet. "Aside from Ruby's lifelong opposition to the drive-in's very existence—"

"—and deathlong, too, because she has *not* let it go since dying," Stacey said, "even though that's usually a great opportunity to let go of things."

"—anyway, aside from the need to deal with her, there's also this little troupe, as our psychic consultant said, who appear to be bound together, willingly or unwillingly, possibly led by Stan Preston. Or it's possible he's not in charge, that he's a captive of the group, we don't know. The more complicated part of our job is flushing them out, getting them to move on. We may be able to trap one or more of them. Our first goal is just to identify them, though."

"How are you going to flush them out?" Callie asked. She was polishing a desk while Benny looked, rather slowly, through a heap of rolled-up movie posters from a cardboard box, tossing some and keeping others. Sunlight leaked in from the lone window. We'd summarized for them everything we knew so far, including our experiences the night before.

"We're working on a couple of ideas. It would be ideal if y'all could be elsewhere for the night while we try it out, though. Because if it works, the paranormal activity here could grow extremely intense. I'd feel safer if you were off the property altogether."

They looked at each other nervously.

"Is it that bad?" Benny asked.

"It could be," I said. "I know it's a hardship to stay away from home—"

"Nah, no way," Benny said. "It's warm enough to camp by the beach. Maybe Hunting Island?"

"Or Edisto Island," Callie said. "It's quieter."

"Oh, I love Edisto!" Stacey told them. "Have you ever been to Ossabaw? It's *completely* wild, if you're looking for that…"

After some discussion and checking the weather, Cassie and Benny decided they could indeed go camping the following night.

"Great," I said, glad I'd been free to tune out the camping portion of the conversation. "Until then, keep the drive-in closed. Don't show a movie on the big screen tonight, for the public or for yourselves. Leave some exterior lights on. Continue to stay away from the farmhouse, the old projection building, and the third floor." I glanced upward, and Callie shivered.

"How long until this is over?" Benny asked.

"I'm not sure," I said. "We won't stop until it's safe here."

"And that includes destroying the farmhouse, right?" Callie asked, smiling just a little through her visible anxiety. "I'm definitely a 'yes' vote on that."

"Burning it down would be your best bet." I told them. "Don't do it on your own. I know some guys at the fire department who can help."

Stacey and I returned to the farmhouse during broad daylight, flashlights on the whole time, climbing up into the back door since the front was blocked with the end portion of that fallen roof. The back steps had rotted away, so we had to boost ourselves up a few feet, fairly awkwardly, to get up into the doorway.

We wasted no time in rescuing our gear and hightailing it back out of the house, with no plans to return. Ruby's ghost didn't show up to harass us in there, fortunately, but we could feel how the whole upper floor was less steady after she'd broken a main truss down on us.

We spent that night back in routine observation, watching the silent, vacant theater for activity, and also reviewing some of the heaps of data already collected. This primarily confirmed what we'd observed before. Passing cold spots and occasional small orbs in the screen tower's third floor indicated a haunting, but cameras on the first floor and in the stairwell picked up no activity.

The farmhouse was quiet, too, especially compared to the previous night.

Heaviest activity occurred down in the sunken projection house. Immense recurring cold spots and glimpses of shapes on the night vision reminded us that Jacob had called it the center of the haunting, though that had been prior to visiting the farmhouse.

It stayed relatively quiet that night—no parking lot phantoms, no fully formed apparitions or psychokinetic activity, not even a ghost movie on the big screen. It was as though, after all the action of the previous night, the entities had withdrawn to their own corners to watch and wait, and perhaps to plot their next moves.

The night had a calm-before-the-storm quality, with much tension in the air. Stacey and I did nothing to provoke or even interact with them; we had plenty of provocations in mind for the next night.

We made it an early night by our standards, leaving at about two-thirty in the morning, our gear programmed to keep recording until sunrise.

"Why do I feel like we're going into some kind of battle tomorrow?" Stacey asked when she dropped me off at my apartment.

"Maybe we are," I said. "We have a lot to prepare."

She nodded. We'd discussed a plan to attempt to confront Preston and whatever spirits were with him, based on what we'd learned from our investigation. It was a strange case, requiring a less than standard approach.

By the time we returned the next day, the feeling of tension had only grown. The sky was gloomy, and the gray clouds pressed low, crushing out some of the wide-open space feeling inside the theater.

"The forecast said it would be clear," Callie told us when we caught up with the family loading up overnight supplies into the camper on the back of Benny's aged, battered Toyota Tacoma. "I'm a little worried."

"No worries," Benny said with a smile that seemed almost too confident about the weather. "It'll pass. And it won't follow us all the way to Edisto Island."

"I'm super jealous. I wish I was going there," Stacey said. "Oh! Not that hanging around your drive-in isn't cool, too."

Callie smiled. "I think it'll be good for us. A night back in nature, away from…" She swept her arm, indicating the whole drive-in theater. "Everything."

"Hopefully, we'll have some things sorted out when you get back," I said.

We got to work, and at some point, they drove off.

Later, as the sun sank away behind the tall pines surrounding the drive-in, Stacey and I stood in the center of the parking lot, among snaking cables, a bundle of which trailed off to the concession stand.

"I've put together some Crazytown arrays of cameras for ghost hunting, but this may be the Crazytownest of them all," Stacey said.

"Looks like… Stonehenge," I said. "A little smaller, though."

We'd set up a widely spaced array of cameras and other gear in a circle around the old projection house, placing each one several yards back from it. Hopefully, this would minimize damage if the entities turned hostile.

We had also placed ghost traps in stampers in front of the cameras closest to the projection house's small door. These offered candles, fairly weak ghost bait but better than nothing, inside the cylindrical traps. If a ghost charged one of the cameras—or perhaps was drawn to the cameras, if we're talking about dead actors—it might trigger an automated trap and get caught inside. It couldn't hurt to try.

Even if we didn't capture one, we'd hopefully get images or other information about the entities, helping us identify them.

"Okay, time to test out ye olde integrated control system upstairs." Stacey looked reluctantly up at the big second-story window of the concession stand, where the two cameras stood, the flashy new-generation digital camera and the clunkity, middle-aged thirty-five-millimeter, the drive-in's twin engines of entertainment, retro and cutting-edge.

The ancient ruin of the first-generation projector, abandoned long ago down in the projection house, did not factor into our plans.

"I know Jacob told us the concession stand was the least haunted place, the happiest place, but I still don't love the idea of going up there alone," Stacey said.

"Neither do I. Wait for Jacob to get here and he can stick with you."

"Oh, no, he needs to be down here on the front lines with you." She set out candles on top of the projection house. With its tomblike shape, it looked like we were preparing some kind of cemetery séance.

Headlights glowed along the circuitous driveway. Jacob had arrived.

He parked next to Stacey's car and walked over to our bizarre tableau, which only grew more bizarre as we lit the candles.

"You two definitely look like you're out here summoning the dead," he said.

"That's the general idea," I told him.

We grabbed folding camping chairs from Stacey's car and placed them back in the drive-in's fourth row so we could watch the door to the projection house and the big screen at the same time.

Then Stacey departed for her post on the upper floor of the concession stand. Jacob watched her until she was inside, then dropped into the camping chair beside me.

"Ever seen this one?" I asked.

"*The Heart of Man*? Nah. I like some old movies, but the kind where you can see the strings on the flying saucer," Jacob said. "Not so much the high-art, avant garde stuff. Like, you know that Andy Warhol movie that's just a single eight-hour-long shot of the Empire State Building? I could only sit through half of it. How about you? Are you a big Mazzanti fan?"

"Nah, I prefer directors who don't murder people."

"Stacey said she knew people in film school who said Mazzanti being a serial killer just added authenticity and power to his films," Jacob said.

"It makes it hard for me to watch them. I had to force myself to keep watching *Body in the Basement*."

"To be fair, most audiences responded the same way. *Body in the Basement* only has eleven percent on Rotten Tomatoes, and probably deserves worse."

"What about *Heart of Man*?" I asked.

"I'll check." Jacob looked at his phone. "Eight-five percent."

"Do you think it's really that good?"

"Or film critics don't want to look clueless by panning a film that was considered a groundbreaking work for its time. How many people are going to fact-check them by digging up this weird old movie and actually sitting through it?"

"Good point."

The drive-in's exterior lights went down—not that we'd had many on—and the enormous screen glowed to life as the film began to play. The logo of a long-bankrupt movie studio appeared briefly on the screen and then disappeared, much as the studio itself had.

With our client family gone, we'd cranked up the outdoor speakers at the concession stand to top volume so we could hear the move while we sat outside.

The Heart of Man was… difficult to summarize. Also, nobody had mentioned it was all in Italian, with English subtitles. Visually, it was stunning—the crowds wore black capes and tricorn hats and the white, smooth-featured bauta masks that freed citizens of Venice to engage in wild pleasure-seeking activities without harm to their reputations. Palaces full of columns and statues, sumptuous gambling parlors full of masked men and women, and ornate Gothic buildings of stone that seemed to float impossibly on the water added to the film's dreamlike quality. The music was operatic, sometimes rich and melodic, sometimes painfully discordant, as if to create confusion and disorientation.

The story began with a young priest in a confessional, inside a gorgeous cathedral full of gold and fine art.

A wealthy, aristocratic man entered to confess. His list of offenses grew alarmingly long and strange, reported with laughter rather than shame or any sign of guilt, in a way that clearly disturbed the inexperienced priest.

"I have rebelled against my creator," the man said. "I have led a third of his forces into insurrection. I have been banished. I have tempted men to all manner of sin. I have offered the cup of evil to all, and all have drunk, and my cup overflows still."

Then he described the priest's own sins—a coin stolen from his grandfather, a moment when he'd spied on women bathing in a river, a time when he'd thrown a rock at a sick, limping dog. Laughing, the aristocrat left without requesting or receiving absolution.

The priest emerged and pursued the aristocrat out of the church to the carnival-thronged streets.

From there, the movie became a confusion of sights and sounds and strange music, masks, costumes, crowds. The plot became unclear as the priest wandered from one baroque scene to another in pursuit of the devil, who changed forms again and again, played by different actors and actresses.

At least, I think that was the story.

"Anything happening?" I asked Jacob in a low whisper.

"Yes." He nodded at the projection house. "It's like a boiling cauldron in there. Building up to something."

I walked over to the eight-millimeter projector, loaded with one of Preston's homemade Super 8 movies. We'd brought a box of them.

The images projected silently, aside from the clatter of the little projector, right onto the brick wall of the projection house. They weren't particularly easy to see that way, but I was more interested in getting the attention of the ghosts than in getting a clear view of Stanley's creepy home videos.

The first reel showed the footage of Adaire's pink and white Beverly Hills mansion that had been taken up close, years after her murder, peering in through the wrought-iron fence at the swimming pool and gardens.

"That's doing it." Jacob spoke in a hushed, serious tone and rose from his chair. "You should come over here by me."

"Yeah?" I started to make my way across from the little 8-millimeter projector. "Is there an entity here now?"

He nodded, but he didn't really have to tell me, because the night air grew cold as I passed close to the corner of the projection house on my way back to Jacob and the camping chairs. In the Georgia humidity, this brought a condensation of fog, pale clouds arising from nothing.

The candles burning atop the projection house snuffed out as if blown by the wind, but the night was still. Like the ambient warmth in the air, the candle flames had been absorbed by an entity hungry for energy.

The apparition formed in front of the low door to the projection house, delicate and transparent, like an image woven from spiderwebs and threads of ice.

She was barely there at all, yet the power of her gaze captivated me from so close, her large gray eyes taking me in, her mouth showing just a hint of a sardonic smile.

"It's really her," Jacob whispered, still standing over by the camping chairs, several paces away. "It's the ghost of Adaire Fontaine."

Chapter Twenty-Six

Adaire regarded me coolly, her eyes flicking up and down as she took me in. Even as an ephemeral being who'd been deceased for decades, she had a strong presence. I felt like she was judging me, perhaps unfavorably.

"You've got a lot of stones coming back here, honey," she finally said.

"I was hoping to hear from you again," I said.

"This place isn't what it looks like to the regular stiffs, you know. He made it into something else."

"Who?"

"You're not dim, so you know without me saying."

"Right. We don't want to evoke him."

"Honey, I have one question. Can you get me out of here or not? Like what you said in the billiards room."

"Oh…" I remembered my EVP session, how I'd introduced myself and offered to help her move on. And apparently she wasn't familiar with foosball. "Right. Is that why you sent me the message? Because I actually have more questions—"

"I've only got one. When's the next train out of this lousy burgh?"

"Do you feel stuck at this theater?" I asked.

"It's a prison. You think I like being trapped here, playing out the same tired routines, the same story over and over?"

"You play the same roles over and over?" Jacob asked.

"He makes us do it." She pointed at the big screen. "Up there. I've got a reprieve tonight, since you're showing one of his favorites. I don't have to play Beretta Wagner from *Pocketful of Aces* for the ten thousandth time. And of course he always plays Ramblin' Jim Scarsdale in place of Chance Chadwick. That's the entire purpose of the production, so he can play Chance. He's like Nero playing the harp in *Quo Vadis*, forcing everyone to praise him, only it's like that every night here. Stanley only wishes he had Chance's chops."

"Ellie, are you talking to Adaire Fontaine right now?" Stacey asked over my headset. "Am I missing Adaire Fontaine live? I am never getting over this."

"I'm sorry," I said, to both Stacey and Adaire. "Adaire, if you want out, the best way is to recognize that you're dead. There is another side, and it's always there when you're ready to move on."

"It's not so easy," she said. "He's got a hold on me."

I nodded. "Did he kill you?"

"You know he did."

"There's something else you can try." I walked softly over to the nearest ghost trap, where candles burned inside. We'd already established that she liked feeding on candles. "This can seal you up. It'll be a confined space for a while, but you'll be separated from him while I deal with him. It'll weaken him. Then I can release you wherever you like, when this is all over."

"The Hollywood Forever cemetery by Paramount. I always liked it there."

"Hollywood Forever?" I asked.

"That's where she's buried!" Stacey exclaimed over my headset.

"I'm being told you're buried there, so it sounds ideal," I told Adaire.

Adaire looked at me a long moment, as if deciding whether to trust me, then started toward the glowing cylinder of the ghost trap, where she would ride in leaded glass spattered with candle wax.

"It's no Cadillac," she sighed, "but any ride in the rain, I suppose—"

Then she jerked back violently, as though she wore an invisible collar and someone had yanked hard on her leash. She made a choking sound and rose from the ground, kicking and struggling, then went limp and faded away.

As her apparition faded, her assailant grew visible, his hand where her throat had been, as if he'd choked her and then absorbed her, one ghost controlling the other as they sometimes do.

While she had reminded me of a delicate lattice of ice, somehow alluring even in death, he was a low, thick, shadowy beast, attired in layers of darkness.

I recognized him from his picture in the newspaper interview, balding, his beard long and unkempt. His eyes were solid black circles—not his trademark sunglasses, I realized, but camera lenses, seemingly implanted in his eye sockets by some macabre act of supernatural plastic surgery. They rotated, zooming in on me.

"You wish to interfere with the show," he said, an Italian accent clear in his voice. "But, no. The show must go on."

"Antonio Mazzanti," I said.

"You did murder Adaire Fontaine! I knew it." Jacob walked toward the apparition, and toward me. He must have seen the choke-grab, too, and how Mazzanti had pulled her back from the trap as she'd attempted to willingly enter it. To escape from Mazzanti's clutches, it seemed.

"All true art is murder." Antonio Mazzanti gave Jacob an eerie smile.

"Well, *The Body in the Basement* certainly murdered ninety minutes of my life," Jacob said.

Mazzanti started toward him, looking offended.

"Stacey, now!" I said.

The Heart of Man ended abruptly as Stacey shut down the thirty-five-millimeter projector.

Then she turned on the digital.

I appeared up there, a giant two-story version of myself, every pore in my skin roughly the size of a hubcap. Yikes. And I thought the undead lady in the farmhouse was scary.

Next to me was the ghost of Antonio Mazzanti, his features blurry, his face like a bearded skull.

Mazzanti looked up at the screen tower, perhaps noticing his movie had been cut off, or sensing something else was happening.

He gaped at his enormous face.

"You're dead, Mazzanti," I said. "It's time to move on. Long past time. There's nothing else you can accomplish here. Let go of your life."

The apparition in front of me seemed to fade a little. The giant version of him on the screen deteriorated, a corpse dressed in a formal black-on-black suit, maybe the one Mazzanti had been buried in.

"Accept the truth," I continued, since this self-awareness approach seemed to be working. "Accept that you—"

Mazzanti's ghost moved fast, like a momentarily flicker of film, or maybe a jump cut. He was suddenly right in front of Jacob, strangling him as he'd strangled Adaire. I don't know why he didn't attack me first; maybe he felt Jacob was a bigger threat because he was psychic. Or because he was a man. I kind of resented that.

"Stacey, light up Jacob!" I shouted, while reaching for my flashlight.

Something grabbed my wrist and stopped me. It was invisible, but I could feel it—ice-cold, smooth, soft but strong enough to bind me.

Silk.

I felt it at my throat, too, like a silky serpent had slithered under my shirt and coiled its way up to my neck to strangle me.

I couldn't breathe.

Stacey cut the digital camera, but only for a moment.

Benny had told us that the digital camera cast about forty-five thousand lumens of light. That was a tremendous amount, far more than the three thousand thrown by the extremely bright tactical flashlights Stacey and I carried. With an output like that, the projector could be used as a small ghost cannon, helping to temporarily run off negative entities if things got too hairy.

Stacey switched it over to a beam of white light, roughly the brightness of an exploding sun, and blasted it on Jacob and the entity assailing him.

Jacob winced in pain and clenched his eyes shut. The light seemed bright enough to blind someone from behind, after shining through the middle of their skull.

Mazzanti howled as the light burned through him,

reducing him to a cloud of dark spots floating like black spores in a sea of light. He released Jacob, who staggered away gasping for air.

I would have liked to stagger away gasping for air myself, but the silk bonds around my arm and neck prevented that. The Silk Strangler still had me caught.

With my free hand, I frantically grabbed at my neck, scraping my skin with my fingernails, but it was no use against the supernatural restraint.

The scarves snapped taut and pulled me down, smacking me hard against the drive-in's blacktop. Then they hauled me forward across the rough surface.

I could see them, long silk scarves like ropes around my limbs and my neck, dragging me toward the little half-door into the sunken projection house. The door was open, the space inside waiting for me like the mouth of a hungry grave.

My cold silk bonds dragged me inside, and I fell fast and hard to the dirt-encrusted brick floor.

The little door above slammed shut, blocking out the white light and trapping me in the darkness alone.

Chapter Twenty-Seven

I could see nothing, but as it turned out, I wasn't alone in there, after all.

Alone would have been better.

Hands touched me—cold, clammy hands, and too many of them. I felt like Sarah falling down the well of hands in *Labyrinth*, getting grabbed all over.

"She's here," a female voice rasped.

"She's so warm," said another, her voice creaky and dry.

"Okay, ladies, get off me," I said. Though the silk was still coiled around my throat, it wasn't choking me at the moment, now that it had stopped dragging me across the ground.

Silk scarves at my wrists prevented me from reaching for my flashlight or holy-music defenses—even if I could, it would have been wise to hold off. We'd provoked these spirits deliberately to learn about them, so chasing them away, as Stacey had done with the projector to protect Jacob against Mazzanti, was a last resort.

The dead ladies did not get off me or move away. It

was a small space down there, but they could have allowed me a little more room. Their cold skin smelled like mud and gone-over meat.

A red glow flared above me, illuminating the face of Chance Chadwick like a fire-hued spotlight on a stage. The tobacco smell mingled with the smell of death and decay. He blew out smoke and looked me over like I was an item on a store shelf and he was trying to determine my value.

In the glow, I caught glimpses of the women flanking me, holding me in place, and what I saw made me glad I couldn't see much. They were like dead bodies risen from the earth after a lot of time. They looked drained, while he looked healthy and almost alive. He'd been feeding on these ghosts, controlling them; long silk scarves bound them, too.

"Stanley Preston," I said. "You're the Silk Strangler? You murdered Portia Reynolds and Grace LeRoux?"

The women stirred and groaned at the sound of their own names.

"Snap your traps," he barked at them. Then to me, he said, "They call me Chance."

"Who calls you that? These ghosts? Because your name is Stan Preston. Your disguise doesn't fool me. You *wanted* to be Chance Chadwick, but you…" I thought of what Adaire's ghost had said. "Ultimately, Stanley, you just didn't have the chops."

His face glowed red with rage, his teeth chomping on his cigar. The pits of his pockmark scars began to appear on his face, as if his makeup was wearing off, melted by his anger.

I tried to get up, but the ghosts of Portia and Grace held me down.

"I don't understand," I said, trying to keep my voice steady and strong while horrible things held me captive. Showing fear could give him power over me. Then again, standing up to him could invite a violent attack. "I saw Mazzanti re-enact his murder of Adaire Fontaine outside. How did you get mixed up with him? Why is he here, at your theater?"

"You ask a lot of questions for a dame," he said.

"Excuse me?"

"I'm the captain of this riverboat," he said. "I'm the ringmaster of this circus. Don't let anybody tell you different."

"Huh." His insistence, out of nowhere, that he was the one in charge gave me the idea that he was defensive about that for some reason. "I thought you just worked here. Antonio Mazzanti, he's the famous Hollywood director, the genius. Everyone says so. Surely he's the one in charge. Who are you to be running a theater?"

He looked furious, but he didn't attack, not just yet. I could feel it coming, though. "This is my show. I pick the actors and the performances. He directs… but only when I tell him to direct."

"And when does the show finally end? When does the last curtain fall, so you can all go home?"

Preston—and it was definitely Preston now, his face scarred, pitted and not so strikingly handsome in general, his fedora and suit ratty instead of finely tailored, more Sears catalog than Rodeo Drive—took a long, glowing pull on his cigar. This lit up the room a bit, like a temporarily flaring candle, and I saw in more detail the emaciated, dirt-covered forms of the actresses who held me, their arms and legs like sticks, their faces sunken and cadaverous, as if he'd worked them to the bone in their afterlife.

I held back a scream, only because of long practice and experience.

"The show never ends," Preston answered at last. "The show must go on."

"Forever? Nothing lasts forever, Stanley."

That triggered him. He glared with sudden fury, casting fiery light and twisting shadows all around.

"I was old when death came for me," he said. "I knew it was coming. I had time to prepare. To plan. When I died, I did not wish to go to heaven or hell. I wished only to go to the movies, forever."

"You died of hypothermia in the middle of the parking lot watching *Pocketful of Aces* on the big screen."

He smiled. "My favorite film. We act it out again and again, Adaire and I, and the others. Adaire is headstrong. It's fortunate we have a director capable of wrangling her. Like all beautiful and talented women, she is difficult, but worth it, for the sake of the picture. But things have grown busier lately. Our audience is growing. I'll be expanding our little troupe."

I didn't like the sound of that. "Expanding it how?"

"I'd like a new girl. These are so... used up." He gestured at Portia and Grace. "I don't need another grand, volatile beauty like Adaire, either. One of those is enough for any ensemble. I need a supporting actress, a dull plain-Jane type." He looked me over. "Like you."

The actress ghosts stirred and hissed like serpents, their bony grasps on me growing more aggressive and clawlike.

"Not her," one said.

"She's nothing," the other rasped.

"Uh, no, thanks," I said. "I don't think your lady friends are happy with that idea, either."

"Actresses are jealous sorts. An actress will never welcome the new girl, because it makes her the old girl. I'm also thinking of adding a child to the troupe, for greater variety. Have you seen the little blonde one running around the theater of late? So spirited. So pretty. I could make her a star."

This brought more angry hisses from the rotten actresses. Preston smiled, basking in their suffering like it warmed him.

My guts, already roiling in a storm of fear, turned ice-cold at what he said. He wasn't just talking about killing me and forcing me to play in his theater of souls. He wanted Daisy, too. And no doubt more to follow, if he wasn't removed from this place. It seemed that Ruby, as bad as she was, wasn't even the biggest threat to the family here.

"Leave her alone," I said, my voice so cold I might have already been a member of his undead troupe.

"Did that touch a nerve?" He smiled. "Good. We can use that. Bring all your passion to your performance. We need refreshing. My girls are so drained and have so little left to offer. They can barely perform even the smallest roles anymore. And they've gone so ugly over the years."

The actresses snapped and hissed, but at least loosened their grip on me in their fury at his taunting and insults, which seemed to be a constant part of their relationship. Silk scarves had coiled over their mouths, preventing them from speaking. They were prisoners here, as much as I was.

"I refuse," I said.

"As did these two," Preston replied. "But I can be very persuasive."

The silk around my neck constricted.

The scarves binding me, as well as Portia and Grace, all originated under the sleeves of his worn-down suit coat. He had us leashed like dogs.

I looked up toward the small door above, cloaked in darkness now. Maybe Antonio Mazzanti was keeping Jacob and Stacey busy, because they sure weren't showing up to rescue me. Or maybe they were outside the door, unable to open it, and Preston's control of this little reality down here was so absolute that he could block out everything from the outside world, creating his own little bubble where he was a king, or even a petty would-be god, insisting that all things bend to his will.

He was powering this little paranormal fiefdom with the ghosts of the murdered actresses. And now that people were coming to his drive-in again, he was planning to murder more, increasing his power, and presumably the scale of productions he could mount. They might become more than faint glimmers on the big screen late at night.

He had to be stopped.

The silk tightened again.

"Wait," I said, because that's certainly one thing you want to communicate when someone is preparing to murder you. Every precious second becomes another steppingstone toward possible survival. "Preston, I thought your favorite movie was *The Heart of Man.* Antonio Mazzanti's masterpiece? You played it in your projector until it was almost falling apart. The film's probably already broken out there tonight."

I was fishing, but I sensed some sort of conflict between the ghosts of Preston and Mazzanti, as if Preston felt the need to prove himself against the famous director. Also, he'd surely watched *Heart of Man* to death for one reason or other.

My fishing hook must have caught on something, because Preston's ghost glowed a fiery red, and anger twisted his features. His pockmarks expanded to deep canyons and holes in his flesh, exposing him to the bone, exaggerations of what they'd been in life.

"He is nothing!" Preston shouted. The dead actresses gasped and pulled away from me toward the walls of the little half-underground room, as if worried they'd be caught in his wrath. Portia's gasp was quite familiar to me after I'd heard it dozens of times in *The Body in the Basement.*

"I thought he was brilliant," I said. "He was a genius, and you were just a failed actor, who became the owner of a failed theater. Your marriage sounds like a failure, too— you ended up living in the screen tower, while your wife stayed in the farmhouse. Is there anything in life at which you didn't fail?"

Preston barely looked human anymore; he was smoldering, his face pure hatred.

"He was no genius," Preston said. "I watched it again and again, searching for the genius, and it *wasn't there*. He's a charlatan. *She* is the true talent, and that's why he wanted her for his own. He had no right to take her from me. And what I could have been—if only I hadn't been trapped here —"

"You were never trapped," I said. "You were just a coward."

He glowered at me. The actresses huddled against the walls, making themselves as small as possible. I was trying to work my hands down toward my utility belt, but the silk still bound them in place.

Then the red glow receded, and Preston shifted back into Chance Chadwick form—cool, calm, collected, the standard character type played by Chadwick, commanding every situation with a combination of street smarts, fast talk, and charming of any relevant ladies.

"You think you're a real smart cookie," he said, in Chadwick's voice. "Truth is, your head's full of nothing but crumbs. I got genius inside of me, too. Life dealt me a bum hand, but death's been good to me. You'll see. Sit back and watch the show, plain Jane."

He turned the ancient projector toward me, away from the closed porthole through which it once projected movies onto the screen outside.

The ancient reels turned slowly, rattling. No film had

been loaded into the projector, but that didn't seem to matter to him.

The projector lens glowed, not a bright white light, but a deep infernal red, the hue of Preston's cigar, like the eye of a demonic beast, staring into me.

Pointed directly at my face, the red light burned into my eyes. Closing my eyelids didn't help much at all.

The hellish light filled my skull… and then the movie began.

Chapter Twenty-Eight

The movie was black and white, and it unfolded all around me like a dream.

A young Stanley Preston stood at the front window of the farmhouse's front bedroom, in its full posh Hollywood Regency glory, sparkling and glittering. The window looked out onto the section of roof where he would one day put a bench and a drive-in speaker. Cows and goats roamed where the parking lot and screen tower would be.

"Life had knocked me down a few times, but I had moxie," his voice narrated, from somewhere inside my head, an arrangement I disliked immediately and immensely. "I had visions for the future, but someone stood in my way."

The young Preston left his bedroom and walked down the hall, past his stepkids' rooms, to the partially ajar door at the back of the house. The voices of his wife and small stepchildren rose from the kitchen below; he ignored them.

Smoking a cigar, he peered into the bedroom with its rough-hewn but solid furniture and the narrow iron frame bed where his mother-in-law slept.

"She was stuck in the old ways, while I was getting a jump on the future. Maybe I got cheated of my chances as an actor, but now I'd make the world's greatest theater, and I'd be a big shot in a whole new way. If only I could make her understand. But I couldn't. She was the enemy.

"I hatched a plan, but I wasn't sure if I had the stones to carry it out. She was sick already, bad sick, but she could have hung on a few more weeks, months, who knows? All I knew was, if I wanted my theater open by summer, I needed her dead by January. I waited until the day after Christmas, out of consideration for my wife. No reason she should lose her mother just before Christmas. That would toss a real gloomer on the whole holiday."

The young Preston stood trembling in the doorway, plainly consumed by fear, puffing his cigar in a fast, nervous way.

"I didn't think I could. But then I remembered—I'm an actor. I don't have to be brave. I just have to pretend. Play a character with nerves of steel, nerves I didn't have."

As I watched, young Preston morphed into Chance Chadwick, confident and fearless, a sardonic look in his eyes, like he was above everything around him.

"I thought of Ramblin' Jim Scarsdale from *Pocketful of Aces*, the gambler so confident he could walk through a viper pit of crime bosses and crooks, double-crossing them all without breaking a sweat, and wisecracking along the way to really let you know he was in charge. Chance Chadwick, there was a man's man. And on his arm—the world's greatest beauty and talent, my old flame, Adaire Fontaine, playing Beretta Wagner, the moll who falls for him. Playing it beautifully, like she did everything. I could see myself as Chance Chadwick. I'd always been a big fan."

In his Chance Chadwick guise, the young Preston

stepped into the room where Ruby slept.

"When she woke up coughing in the middle of the night, and first thing in the morning, she needed that medicine." While his voice spoke in my head, he opened the drawer in her nightstand and removed the nebulizer used to pump medicine to her lungs. Then he took the walking cane from beside her bed.

He hid the nebulizer in her closet, then shut the closet door and hung the cane on the doorknob.

Then he retreated to the doorway, checked his watch, and casually puffed his cigar, watching.

Ruby stirred, gagging, sounding like her lungs were brimming with fluid. Hacking and wheezing, she reached for her nightstand drawer and opened it.

Preston, as Chadwick, watched with a look of wry humor as she rummaged desperately through the medicine bottles for the nebulizer that wasn't there.

She looked at the floor around the nightstand, checking to see whether it had fallen. Her wheezing intensified. A thick gurgling rose from her chest.

Then she reached toward where her cane had been and found that it, too, was missing. It was heartbreaking watching the horror and pain on her face.

Finally spotting her cane on the closet door across the room, she pushed herself to her feet and walked, badly stooped, gasping for air, her face darkening in the black and white movie world like she was running out of air.

She collapsed halfway to the closet, then used the last of her strength to crawl on hands and knees. She reached out, her fingertips barely brushing the cane's surface. Then she collapsed completely.

She shuddered on the floor, too weak even to gasp, too little air left to cough and wheeze.

"Then I made my move," Preston's voice said inside my

head, while I watched him tiptoe into the room, puffing merrily on his cigar, and gently lift a pillow from the bed. "The final crush to put her out of her misery."

Ruby looked up from the floor and saw her son-in-law standing over her with the pillow in his hands, preparing to finish her off. I would have looked away if I could, but I was caught inside this illusion, a captive audience to the narrative Preston seemed eager to present.

Terror flashed in Ruby's eyes as she understood he was going to kill her.

Then her eyes shifted, staring blankly, and all tension left her body.

"In the end, her sickness offed her," Preston narrated. "Luck was on my side that day. I told myself it was probably an act of mercy, anyway, ending her suffering. Now I just had to cover up the deed. Thinking like Chance kept me cool-headed like that. She was already going stiff when I picked her up."

He returned the woman's body to her bed, tossing the blanket over her but not bothering to close her empty, staring eyes. He replaced the nebulizer and cane where he'd originally found them, then left the bedroom and closed the door behind him.

Then, Preston-as-Chadwick looked directly at me, like a character breaking out of the story to address the audience, and grinned around his cigar.

"When my wife found her dead ma, she howled like a wolf caught in a bear trap," he told me.

A scream sounded from inside the bedroom.

The door opened, and young Nancy Jackson Williams emerged sobbing and threw her arms around Preston, who remained in cool, collected Chadwick mode.

"She's gone!" Nancy sobbed into her husband's shoulder. "She's really gone!"

He embraced her and murmured words of comfort... but he also looked over her shoulder and shot me a big, triumphant smile. Happy, jazzy, big-band music rose all around us.

Suddenly, I was at the drive-in's grand opening, which I recognized from the big newspaper spread, and it was packed. There was a festival atmosphere, with a band playing live music in front of the screen while the crowd waited for the sunset.

Stanley Preston walked among the crowd, shaking hands, smiling, posing for photographs, and generally soaking up the attention from the mobs of people who'd come out to his theater. He was in his real form, feeling no need to pretend to be a Chance Chadwick character that day.

I didn't see his wife Nancy with him. Maybe she was inside the concession stand, feverishly serving the throngs of people who streamed out holding hamburgers, fried chicken, cotton candy and ice cream cones.

"Life was fine as frog's hair after that," Preston narrated. "The drive-in was the way of the future; I was sure of that. Business boomed, crowds packed the place every night, and it looked like I was turning into a real big wheel in the movie biz, after all. Never mind the directors who wouldn't put me onstage. Here, I ran the whole show. And I guess that made me the real star.

"Then, in '59, the news hit me like a sucker punch to the heart."

On the screen tower, a jittery newsreel reported the murder of Adaire Fontaine, including footage of the same mansion I'd seen on the Super 8 stalker reel, and clips of her most famous movies, *Legend of the South* and *A Soldier's Dame*.

"I could say she was the love of my life, but that's not

enough," Preston narrated, while I watched his 1959 self stare in horror at the news. "She was a goddess, cut from finer cloth than most everyone, so fine I was lucky to touch it at all, before she went on to glory and forever out of my reach.

"Who had destroyed that? Who had murdered that? Who had taken the light from my sky and snuffed her out? Who had dared? I knew I would never be the same. My soul went dark that day."

Personally, I figured his soul had gone dark sometime before he'd started plotting his mother-in-law's murder, but I found I couldn't speak. This wasn't an audience-participation performance, it seemed.

"I obsessed over her murder. People said it was the director, Mazzanti, but he never went to prison. Typical. Some Hollywood bigshot gets away with murder, and there's no justice for the victim. Years went by, and nothing happened. Like nobody even cared anymore. She was just some wild girl from Tifton who ran away to California and got herself offed. People forgot about her. But I cared, and I didn't forget.

"So, I kept thinking, what would Ramblin' Jim Scarsdale do? What would Chance Chadwick do? I cooked up a new plan. It wasn't easy, but it was nothing Chance Chadwick couldn't handle."

I found myself in a crowded cafe, and judging by the clothing and hair, we were definitely in the late 60s or early 70s, and a long way from the rural South.

Stanley Preston sat at a table by a window, out of place in his white seersucker suit. He'd grown out a goatee and really had some Colonel Sanders energy going.

Across from him was the voluptuous Portia Reynolds, dressed in orange bell bottoms and a flowery blouse, a slender pink silk scarf around her neck, her dark brown hair long and freshly ironed. She hung on Preston's every word as he spoke, beaming and fluttering her eyelashes at him.

"I picked her because she'd starred in a Mazzanti picture a few years earlier, just like Adaire was doing when he killed her. That tied her to Mazzanti, you see. I found Portia Reynolds in the phone book. A two-bit actress with a failing career can't afford to be too hard to find.

"I told her I was a playwright from the Deep South, and I'd just signed a three-picture deal with Warners. Before I knew it, I had her eating out of my hand."

Soon I was following them, in a long Scorsese-esque tracking shot, up through the dim stairwell of an apartment building—which, unfortunately, I also recognized from the stalker video—through her apartment door as she unlocked it and led him inside.

She poured him a drink and put on a record. "Mississippi Queen" by Mountain filled the air, perhaps her subtle tribute to his alleged reputation as a great Southern playwright.

Portia danced, and Preston filmed her with his Super 8, and I tried to scream at her to get out of there.

Instead, she was flirtatious, willing to put on a big performance for the chance at a role in a Warner picture. She drew him through a beaded curtain into her bedroom.

She lay back, and he straddled her, still filming her. She pointed at the camera and laughed, shaking her head; she didn't want him filming what came next.

But she was wrong about what came next, because Preston grabbed her silk scarf and pulled, strangling her with it, filming her death throes.

"Things were going real smooth, smooth as silk," Preston said in my head. "Until a new wrinkle walked in. Portia's roommate, another nobody actress named Grace

LeRoux."

The willowy blonde actress giggled at first, thinking she'd walked in on an intimate moment, then screamed as she realized Portia wasn't moving.

"Well, that was one heck of a cock-up, but I put it to rights," Preston's voice told me as he chased Grace LeRoux, catching her before she could flee the apartment. He tied her to her own bed with a couple of Portia's scarves, then tied another one around her neck.

He stopped to change his camera to a fresh reel, then filmed her murder, too.

"Once that was all squared away, I was glad the other girl showed up," Preston told me. "Two murders was a much bigger story than one. I added an occult angle, something that could point to Antonio Mazzanti, since his films were known for that." He painted blood-red pentagrams on the wall, and inverted crosses, and the words *Satana sarà vittorioso.* "That means Satan will be victorious. I translated it from Italian using a dictionary at the library. Again, Mazzanti."

Preston quickly tossed the apartment, stealing anything of value—jewelry, cash, even their bank books with their checks—and made his exit. "I went straight to the airport. Before anybody found their bodies, I was across the continent, back home like nothing ever happened. That was the nice thing about my secret ability to become Chance Chadwick. He was the original smooth operator, always able to bluff his way out of a jam, always a step ahead of the other guy, with an ace hidden in his pocket, a scam, an exit strategy. The real Chance was dead, had been dead for years, but that just made it easier for me to become him. Because nobody else was filling his spot in the world, you see?"

Sounded crazy to me, but he still wasn't letting me

speak, even when seeming to ask me a question. What a narcissist.

"Now, don't think I wasn't sweating bullets for weeks after that." The view changed to show him back home, sitting at the kitchen table, reading a newspaper article headlined 'SILK STRANGLER' MURDERS CONTINUE TO BAFFLE LAPD. Preston looked like his normal self again, a little slouchier and grayer than I'd seen him before, his goatee trimmed back to a mustache again.

The kids had grown up and gone, the kitchen was looking a bit rundown, and Nancy did dishes in the background. She was talking, but Preston paid her so little attention that none of her words made it into his memory that I was watching.

"I kept expecting them to come for me," Preston said, while his past self jerked and looked up at a sudden loud knock on the door. But it was only the mailman. "Funny thing is, nobody ever did. People suspected Mazzanti, considering his history with Adaire Fontaine and Portia Reynolds. But they didn't arrest him. That was all right, though. Chance and I had a plan for that, too."

I stood in a dim, smoky biker bar that seemed weirdly familiar, until I realized I'd seen a picture of it in the *Los Angeles Free Press* interview, where the now-defunct underground newspaper had caught up with the once-celebrated director near the end of his life, drinking himself to death at his favorite watering hole.

Preston, looking more Chance Chadwick than ever despite the fact that fedoras and Chance Chadwick mustaches were both long out of fashion by 1970, approached the balding, unhealthy-looking director where he sat alone in the back of the bar, eyes hidden behind round black sunglasses.

Mazzanti frowned as he approached, but Preston took

out a twenty and placed it on the table.

"I told him I was a big fan," Preston's narration continued. "The biggest. I showed up in my best suit and insisted on buying him a drink, anything he wanted. He ordered a tall glass of whiskey. I'd read up on him and knew he was hard up for cash, and a dope fiend besides, so I hoped he'd look at me as a mark to milk. And he went for it. We had a drink, he said he liked my Chance Chadwick look, he laughed when I did my Chadwick impression, he said it was spot on, the greatest he'd ever seen. 'You should have been in pictures,' he said. The great director, he actually told me that. I could have done anything Chance Chadwick did, if I hadn't gotten such a raw deal in life.

"Keeping to my plan, I drop a few hints that maybe I'm a junkie, too, and next thing you know we're in the hotel where he's living, and I'm forking over hundreds of dollars, buying all the heroin his dealer could bring."

The scene cut to a dreary, rundown hotel room full of dirty clothes, scattered trash, and more than one ashtray overflowing onto the carpet.

I have to say this was turning into one of the bleakest movies I'd ever seen, because I then had to watch Mazzanti shoot himself up with heroin.

"I watched the process slowly, the spoon, the lighter, all of it," Preston narrated, while the 1970 version of him sat in the hotel room chair and stared. "When he was good and high, I started talking about her. About Adaire. I just wanted to hear him admit it. And he did. He admitted to killing her.

"When it was my turn, I cooked up a big needleful of that junk myself, doing just what he'd done, and I jammed it in his arm and shot him up again. And I kept doing it until none was left. I wanted him blacked out, unconscious. If he died, that was fine, I could live with that.

"Then I planted the evidence."

Preston unloaded, from the pockets of his jacket, the jewelry and bank checks he'd taken from Portia Reynolds and Grace LeRoux after murdering them, dumping them into the top drawer of the hotel room dresser, among Mazzanti's socks and underwear.

Then he took one of Mazzanti's cigarettes and lit it. After a couple of puffs, he positioned it carefully under a floor-length window curtain.

"I'd timed it back home, and I had about four or five minutes before the cigarette burned down to where it would light up the drapes. Chance Chadwick used the same kind of trick in *The Nightingale Job*, only the cigarette lit a dynamite fuse instead of a window curtain." Preston headed out the hotel room door, leaving it cracked behind him. "I beat feet to put that place in the rearview—the rearview of a cabbie zipping me to the airport so I could fly the coop before the law dogs came sniffing."

Preston's narration fell silent. I thought the movie might end there, but a little more followed.

I found myself in Preston and Nancy's bedroom, watching them sleep by the full moon. That was awkward, though fortunately they were fully dressed in flannel nightclothes.

"And that was that," Preston said. "Mazzanti was found dead, but the evidence was there, and everybody knew he was a murderer for sure. I finally got justice for Adaire. But I had problems back home."

I hoped this wasn't going to delve too deeply into any kind of marital issues with his wife, and fortunately it didn't.

"The people I killed, I kept having dreams about them," Preston said. "And then something else made it worse."

A *thump, thump, thump* echoed through the house.

Preston's eyes opened. Nancy remained asleep, utterly at peace.

It came again—*thump, thump, thump.*

He sat up and got out of bed.

"Somebody was in the house," he told me. "Only problem was, nobody but us lived there anymore. And I knew that sound… but it couldn't be. She'd been dead fifteen years. But that was how she summoned us, with that awful banging cane, whenever she wanted anything. Made me happy as a pig in slop to deprive her of that at the end of her life."

Preston drew a shotgun from under the bed and tiptoed down the hall, looking terrified.

Thump, thump, thump.

With the muzzle of the shotgun, he nudged open the door to the back bedroom, Ruby's room, still furnished with her belongings.

The old woman sat on the edge of her bed, as she so often had in life, banging her cane to summon assistance from a family member. The moonlight fell across her body, and her cane, but left her face in shadow. She wore a double strand of pearls and a peach dress.

She rapped the cane again, in full sight of Preston. *Thump, thump, thump.*

"You're dead," Preston said.

"We're all dead," she replied, her voice brittle.

She banged the cane again—*thump, thump, thump.* Then again, louder, faster, more violently, the end of it pounding dents into the hardwood floor. *Thump thump thump THUMP THUMP THUMP THUMP THUMP THUMP THUMP—*

Preston turned on the lamp, and he got his first good look at her.

She was dead, rotten, horrible, just as she'd been when

she approached me in the parking lot. Only now she seemed to be grinning ear to ear, too many of her teeth visible through her rotten cheeks.

THUMP THUMP THUMP THUMP THUMP THUMP THUMP—

Preston fired the shotgun. The window by the bed exploded.

Nancy screamed and ran into the room.

Ruby was gone; Preston stared at the bed where she'd been.

"Ruby bothered me all the time after that," Preston narrated. "Her cane would knock all night. Or I'd be in a room alone, and look up and see her staring at me, like she'd been there a long time before I'd noticed. She never bothered Nancy, though. Nancy never heard or saw a thing.

"That's why I moved out to the tower."

I saw him sitting in the second-floor room that was now Callie and Benny's bedroom. It was unadorned; he hadn't even hung his beloved movie posters up here. Just a bed and a chair, where he smoked a cigar and looked out the window at the highway, winding away toward Pembroke and the inland world in one direction, toward Savannah and the ocean in the other.

"Ruby's ghost left me alone out there. Nancy wouldn't join me, and I couldn't blame her. She'd lived her whole life in that farmhouse, since the day she was born. I guess we lived apart, we grew apart. That's how it goes sometimes.

"I dreamed all the time of Portia Reynolds and Grace LeRoux, Antonio Mazzanti, and most of all my beloved Adaire Fontaine, for whom I'd done it all.

"Once, I tried to explain it all to Nancy. In some crazy way, I thought it would patch things up between us. I was wrong."

I saw the two of them sitting in a Buick convertible,

both gray-haired now, Stanley in the driver seat and Nancy beside him. The top was down, and they were watching a movie.

It wasn't on the big screen, though. It was on his smaller, portable screen, set up along with an eight-millimeter projector, right in front of their car. A miniature drive-in, for one car only.

Nancy watched in horror as her husband strangled Portia Reynolds to death on the small screen.

"Before I could even load the second reel of the murder double feature, Nancy was hysterical, refusing to listen," Preston narrated inside my head.

Nancy was, in fact, pushing her way out of the car, then running across the parking lot as fast as her feet could carry her… unfortunately, she was frail and collapsed.

He hobbled over to her, no spring chicken himself, and looked down at her.

She died gazing up at Stan Preston in helpless horror, just as her mother had.

"I closed the drive-in after that," he said. "It was nearly dead, anyway. The crowds had stopped coming. I put my special movies away, since there was no one left to watch them." He dropped the reels into the black coffin stored on the third floor of the screen tower and nailed the lid shut.

Then he stood in the parking lot again. In a rapid time-lapse, he aged before my eyes while weeds grew up through the drive-in blacktop, paint peeled, and the surrounding trees grew taller and taller, walling the place in ever more completely.

A thin, feeble, stooped version of Stanley Preston stood alone, watching *Pocketful of Aces*, wearing a moth-nibbled suit and fedora that had been out of fashion for decades. It wasn't nearly enough to protect against the freezing night. Snow fell softly, piling up on the empty parking lot, collecting on the brim of his hat, while Preston spent the last moments of his life, by choice, completely absorbed in the movies.

Soft piano music arose, as though Preston's death were the truly tragic scene of the whole piece.

Then the scene faded to black.

Chapter Twenty-Nine

It was almost a relief to find myself back on the dirt floor of the projection house. The projector was off, but an unpleasant afterimage of its infernal glow suffused the inside of my head.

Preston watched me through the burning red end of his cigar.

"Was that... supposed to make me sympathetic to you somehow?" I asked.

"You see the struggles I've had," he replied. "That's just the backstory. Now you'll be part of my next act."

Someone pounded at the small door in the darkness overhead. Hopefully, one of my friends.

"Stacey?" I started toward the door, but of course the silk bindings held me in place.

"You won't be leaving that way, plain Jane." Preston pulled tight on the scarves.

"Okay," I whispered, because he was making it harder to breathe. "How about this way?"

Then I charged right at him.

His dead eyes widened in surprise.

The scarves binding me weren't actually real objects, of course. They were symbolic projections from his psyche, focusing his use of psychokinetic energy.

However, he didn't necessarily know that, and so they would behave like scarves.

Pulling away from him, trying to reach the door, meant drawing them taut and tighter around me.

Running toward him, on the other hand, made them go slack.

Preston gave me a startled look and flickered aside.

I bolted past him, raised one of the plates covering the projector portholes at the front, and screamed "Jacob! Stacey!" at the top of my lungs.

"Ellie!" Stacey dashed into view from around the corner. "Are you okay down there? What happened? We can't get the door open. Could be psychokinetically sealed. Jacob went to go look for a crowbar or something—"

"The cane!" I shouted. "The cane!"

She looked at me quizzically, but before I could say more, Preston regained mastery of his scarves and of the situation generally. The scarves snapped me back and away from the porthole, ripping me off my feet and smacking me bodily into the dirty brick floor. Again.

"Don't try to be cute, plain Jane," Preston said, standing over me. "I'm afraid 'cute' just isn't believable, coming from you."

"Ugh," I said, not so much in response to him, but because I'd realized that "The cane! The cane!" was exactly what Adaire Fontaine's character had exclaimed when the floodwater swept across the sugarcane fields, drowning the crop and bankrupting her family. I hoped Stacey hadn't misunderstood and thought I was making a *Legend of the South* reference, perhaps signaling her to go spool that movie again.

"Look who's talking about not being cute. With your hideous face." I stood and started for the portholes again, but he pulled the scarves tight. We'd pretty well switched places. I stood in his usual spot by the projector and portholes, and he stood closer to the door where I'd crashed in. After forcing me to watch his slanted and self-serving biopic, he was now blocking the only way out.

"I am more than my ugly face," he said.

"Good. Glad you're feeling less insecure these days." I moved toward him, which again slackened my bonds a little. I reached into my jacket and brought out the bulky item I'd stashed there.

"I guess this was considered portable in your day." I held up his Super 8 camera and looked at him through the viewfinder. "You remember this, I'm sure. You must be very attached to it. You used it to stalk Portia Reynolds, and to record her death. And the death of Grace LeRoux. Why did you record their deaths?"

"It… just seemed like the right thing to do. The right way to capture them at the moment of death. I thought, if I could capture that, perhaps I'd see something deep and true, and I'd have it on film."

"They say certain cultures won't let you take pictures of them, because pictures steal a piece of your soul," I told him. "My boss mentioned it. I tried to learn more, but there's not much out there. Yet this myth persists, that somewhere people believe photographs can take your spirit. I can't find an example of any sort of traditional culture that actually believes it. So why does this story persist so strongly? At first, I thought maybe it was a way of looking down on people who don't understand technology. You know, look at those simple primitive people, they don't know anything.

"Then I realized something else—you know who believes that myth? *We* do. You and I, Stanley. The modern people, the picture-takers. We're the ones who believe it, and we're just projecting our belief on nameless, non-specific primitive people. We put pictures of people we care about or admire up in our homes, as a form of remembrance or reverence. We make sure to take pictures of our most significant moments, to enshrine them as permanent images.

"And you, Stanley, you believe it more than most... the movies, the images, they're more sacred to you than real life. They always were." I started recording him with his own stalker/murder camera. "If each picture takes even a small sliver of your soul, and this camera takes eighteen pictures per second for three minutes... well, that gets to be quite a lot of slivers, Stanley. Thirty-six hundred frames on a spool."

He seemed puzzled as I advanced on him, recording.

But he was fading, though it was almost too subtle to see, as though the camera were only slicing away a tissue-thin layer at a time. He wasn't going fast enough.

"Your tank must be getting low by now, Stanley," I said, easing closer. "You've fed on poor Portia and Grace down to the bone. I know how this works. Ghosts only have so much energy. You've figured out you need to feed on the living. But we're not going to allow that. Portia, Grace, do you have anything to say to Stanley in his new, weakened state?"

The two emaciated actresses flanked him, their silken bonds slack while he focused on me. They seemed suddenly aware of just how slack their bonds had gone.

They leaped on him from both sides, biting and clawing, tearing into him like starving cannibals.

I kept recording, hoping his murder camera would

continue to drain him. It had been a longshot, inspired by my conversation with Calvin, by my research into sympathetic magic, but it seemed to help a little. Perhaps one really could capture a soul with a camera, if the soul was camera-obsessed enough.

Stanley staged a comeback, angrily flinging the actresses to either side, slamming their bony bodies into the muddy brick walls. The scarves coiled and tightened around them again, and even more scarves slithered out like he had a whole nest of them up the sleeves of his suit coat. These wrapped around and around the actresses, binding them more tightly than ever.

He had reasserted control over them, but not without a cost to himself. He was panting, tired, flickering as I continued to film him.

"Stop that!" he snapped at me, realizing that I was indeed draining him somehow. He smacked the camera from my hand and shoved me back against the wall. His face loomed close, like he meant to bite me.

Then Stacey appeared again at the porthole.

"I got it, Ellie!" she shouted. "What do I do with it?"

"Give it to me." I reached out a hand and accepted Ruby's cane as Stacey passed it through the porthole. It was solid, smooth, polished. Heavy.

I didn't have a lot of room to swing, but I brought the curved head down with as much force as I could summon.

It smashed into the side of the old projector. There was an audible crack. Several corroded components tumbled loose and fell to the floor.

"What?" Preston drew back, looking with plain horror at what I'd done. "You can't—"

I swung the cane sideways, shattering the projector's lens. I hit the antique machine again and again.

"You can't!"

"Your sob story was a big help." I kept beating the projector, bashing it and breaking it with the cane. "I thought you might have murdered your mother-in-law. But that's not exactly right. She died from her illness. And when you eventually did become a murderer, she began haunting you. She didn't want you living in her house with her daughter anymore. She preferred you living out at the screen tower.

"You may have some power over Portia, and Grace, and Antonio Mazzanti, because you killed them all with your hands. Ghosts can work that way sometimes, unfortunately. The trauma of death, the connection that's created in that moment, can go on and on. It's certainly not fair to the victim.

"But you didn't kill Ruby, so you can't control her. You can't even stop her from haunting the parking lot… running off the customers you're so desperate to prey on. She wants the drive-in to stay closed, because she knows re-opening will make you stronger and more powerful."

With a final lunge, I rammed the head of the cane into the side of the projector hard enough to knock it loose from its support pedestal. It toppled over and smashed into the floor, its metallic mass striking the brick with an echoing boom.

Preston let out a pained howl at the projector's destruction.

In the drive-in's earliest years, he'd worked down here in the dark, constantly changing reels, making sure the audience had a smooth, unbroken movie experience. Here, he'd been at the center of the process, creating the experience for the moviegoers by hand. No wonder it had been the place most heavily imbued with his psychic energy, the place his ghost had chosen for its lair.

He charged me, but the actresses were digging into him

again with their sharp, broken nails and their biting teeth, slowing him down.

I raised the cane, then slammed the end of it into the ground. Once, twice, three times.

Preston hesitated… then made a gasping, gurgling sound and dropped to his knees.

Ruby stood behind him, her hand buried in his back, treating him to the experience of her advanced disease, as she'd done for me. Now I understood, though, that she was driving customers away from the drive-in to protect them from her son-in-law and his predatory plans, like those he had for Daisy.

With the Super 8, I resumed filming him. He was much diminished when the camera reached the end of its spool. He looked like one of his captive actresses, cadaverous and weak, shivering on the floor as they stood over him. The Super 8 camera was ice cold in my fingers.

Another figure arrived, and I recognized her from her pictures. Nancy, his wife, once a hard-partying young widow with small children and a big farm. She wore a golden taffeta cocktail dress, her hair recently permed, a girl of the 1950s out for a good time. She'd died in her early seventies, but apparently chose not to wear that form as a ghost. She looked healthy and alive, hardly a ghost at all.

"Stanley," she said.

Preston looked up from the floor, then lurched forward to kneel at her feet.

"My love," he moaned.

"No," Nancy said. "Your love was for yourself, and your world of illusions, your desire to be a star. Perhaps you loved *her*—the woman whose posters you hung everywhere—but only because she reminded you of your time on the stage, the foolish time in your youth when you believed you would be famous, that the world would know your name.

"In life, I saw you through a glass darkly, and myself, too. We were both chasing glamour. Illusions. But now I see clearly. You only wanted to use me. I know what happened with you and my mother, how you watched her die. Do you know why you failed as an actor, Stanley?"

"Because I didn't have the chops," he gasped.

"You lack heart, Stanley. Heart and soul. You had nothing to bring to the stage, no truth to express through performance. You're empty, Stanley. Truth is, there's almost nothing to you at all."

He gaped at her. And indeed, he'd been reduced to nearly nothing, a faint apparition, exposed as what his wife of more than forty years knew he truly was—a low, miserable thing with almost no soul at all.

Then he was gone.

I looked among the apparitions there, four women Preston had either killed outright, or to whose deaths he'd significantly contributed.

I felt like I should say something to them, but before I could think of anything, a loud crack like a gunshot made me jump. The dead didn't respond, not jumpy at all. Show-offs.

The half-door ripped away from its hinges as Jacob finally succeeded in prying it open. He flung the door away, put aside a hammer and crowbar, and reached out a hand for me. The glow of the film projector from the concession stand could have been a shaft of sunlight falling into that dark place. I was glad to see it, but I hesitated.

Nancy and her mother Ruby had already gone, their business concluded, without a word to me. I found this a touch rude, considering Ruby had literally thrown a porch roof at me. An apology would have been nice, but at least she didn't attack me this time. I had to settle for what I could get.

Portia Reynolds and Grace LeRoux remained down there, shivering and looking lost, as if seeing sunlight for the first time after years in a dungeon.

"You can take off the scarves," I told them. They did, sliding the silks from around their necks and arms, then dropping them to the dirt-covered floor, where they turned into nothing at all.

"That's the way out." I pointed. "After you, Portia and Grace." Hopefully, adding their names would help.

Jacob, probably seeing all of this clearly, moved aside from the doorway, leaving their pathway to the open air wide open.

Sharing an uncertain look, they started toward the open door together.

They faded before they reached it, the open door signifying their chance to move on, to leave this world for the other side.

Unlike them, I had to climb the loose rungs in the wall, so I accepted Jacob's hand to get me up through the weird door and back on solid ground.

I stood, brushing off dirt.

"Ellie!" Stacey started to reach out and hug me, then realized I was coated in floor filth and switched to sympathetically patting my back instead. "I was so afraid for you."

"Thanks for the getting the cane." I looked around. "What happened to Mazzanti and Adaire?"

"We aren't a hundred percent sure about that, because Mazzanti disappeared by the time I ran down here to check on Jacob. But since *Heart of Man* is playing on the big screen… and the thirty-five-mil was switched off when I left… I'm guessing we can find the ghost of Mazzanti up in the projection booth, playing his old hits."

I looked from the screen tower, where there was some odd scene involving a goat in a museum and a woman strumming a harp, over to the concession stand, where the square of the projected movie glowed on the glass window upstairs.

I sighed. "We'd better go deal with him."

"We've got your back," Stacey said. "Let's do it."

I dropped the abnormally cold Super 8 camera into a ghost trap and sealed it. Then, reluctantly, having already taken repeated full-body poundings, I started toward the concession stand to see about the other murderer haunting this theater.

Chapter Thirty

"I'm going in first," Jacob said, opening the employees-only door to the stairwell.

"You don't have to be a macho man," Stacey told him. "This isn't a Village People concert."

"I'm the lead investigator, I go first," I said, but they both argued against that immediately.

"You're totally battered, Ellie," Stacy said. "You should stay down here and drink a slushie. Maybe hold it against your bruises."

"I'm going first because I'm the psychic," Jacob said.

"And I'm second. Let's go." Stacey shoved him into the stairwell, ending the argument.

Reluctantly, I went up last, my flashlight drawn and ready.

Jacob stood at the closed door to the projection booth on the second floor, listening. After a moment, he nodded and opened it.

A shadowy figure stood by the projector, its back to us, facing the big screen as if watching *The Heart of Man* out on the big screen. The audio was playing in the room, too, but it was in Italian and so didn't clarify the plot for me.

My eyes weren't on the movie, anyway.

The figure turned to face us, pale and ghostly, her apparition as delicate as woven threads of ice.

She didn't wear her *Pocketful of Aces* dress anymore, but a long traveling coat, gloves, and a striped head scarf and oversized sunglasses, like she hoped to travel anonymously.

She removed the sunglasses, taking us in with the large gray eyes that had entranced so many audiences from so many screens.

"Hoooooly cow, it really is Adaire Fontaine!" Stacey said. "Oh, my gosh. I am such a big fan, seriously. All your movies, so great. Amazing performances. You got robbed on that Oscar. I wish you hadn't died so young, though."

"You and me both, honey," Adaire replied.

"Where's Mazzanti?" I asked.

"That chump? Once Antonio got wind of how you worked over Stanley Preston, he beat feet. Went on the lam. He's afraid Johnny Law is after him, on account of how he did me wrong, and he figures the cell they got waiting for him is going to be a hot one."

"Let's hope he's right. What about you? Are you able to move on now?"

"Oh, I've got a ticket in my pocket, don't you worry. I may have been a little bit of a sinner—well, a lot of one— but I'm sure they've seen worse. I just thought I'd have a last look at this picture. They say Antonio was a genius, but I don't see it. I'd rather think I was murdered by a genius, though. Wouldn't you? That's got more zing than getting done in by some lousy ex-lover who bristled at getting brushed off."

"I can't believe it's really you!" Stacey gushed onward. "I mean, wow. I totally love you!"

"Love ya, too, blondie. You're quite the minx," Adaire told her, and Stacey touched a hand over her heart, awed. To me, Adaire said, "And you've got gumption—I can tell about people, and I could tell that about you. You've got it in spades. That's why I reached out to you."

"I thought you said I had stones."

"Oh, you've got those, too, honey."

"Gumption stones," Jacob said. "Sounds like something my grandfather would develop from eating too much dairy."

Adaire kept looking at me like he hadn't said a word. That was probably for the best. "You take care. There's a lot of jackals out there."

"I know. You, too."

"Looks like I've got a train to catch."

"Sure you don't want to stay for the rest of the movie?" Stacey asked, clearly hoping to stretch this into a slumber party with the dead star.

Adaire glanced at the screen, where girls in angel costumes stabbed a man with daggers, getting blood all over their lacy white dresses and fluffy white wings. She shook her head. "I'm afraid I'm just not a fan of Antonio Mazzanti."

"And why would you be after he murdered you?" Stacey asked. "We can play any movies you like."

Adaire gave her a long look. "You're a good egg," she finally told Stacey. "Take care."

Then she moved past us, her sunglasses on, carrying a valise and a hatbox, items that had been nowhere in evidence a moment before.

Adaire left the room and walked out of sight down the stairs. We didn't hear the door at the bottom open or close, but when we went to look, she was gone.

Chapter Thirty-One

"I can't believe you actually solved the murder of Adaire Fontaine," Callie said, pacing among the dusty holiday decorations. Benny knelt in front of the coffin decoration, hammering the flat end of a crowbar under the edge. Stacey was outside, playing Frisbee with Daisy. Or perhaps they had moved on to lose-ball.

"Well, not technically," I said, glancing at the *Body in the Basement* poster on the wall. "Not in a way you could prove in court, or even to a reputable journalist. All we learned was that the guy everyone suspected actually was the murderer. We actually solved the Silk Strangler murders, which everyone believed had been solved decades ago."

Benny grunted as he pried open the coffin lid and eased it away, wary of the nails protruding on the underside.

We all looked into the coffin.

"Well, there it is," Benny finally said, the first one to get his voice back. "That's evidence."

Two Super 8 spools were inside. I was guessing they showed the murders of Grace and Portia. I certainly wasn't eager to watch, especially since I'd already watched them before, quite involuntarily.

In addition, there were a couple of silk scarves and a pair of sunglasses with thick, circular, pitch-black lenses, of the type worn by Antonio Mazzanti. They were likely the last pair he'd ever worn. Murder souvenirs.

"What should we do with all this stuff?" Callie asked me, looking pained.

"Good question," I said. "We can't bring Stanley Preston to justice for his murders, because he's already dead. But there's no innocent person to exonerate, either, even posthumously, because Mazzanti did kill Adaire. So... it's up to you, really."

"I hate to say it, but it would definitely attract heaps of free publicity," Benny said. "Although 'the murder drive-in' doesn't really have the best ring to it."

"No, it doesn't." Callie looked at the *Body in the Basement* poster on the wall, the basement door slightly open, the dirt-covered hand of The Body reaching out. "Maybe we'll see if the victims still have any living family members who might want to know. That's all I can think of."

They decided to replace the lid for the short term. Benny hammered it back into place.

"That's it, right?" Benny stood, brushing dust from his jeans. "No more weird dude up here on the third floor? Nobody harassing the theater patrons?"

"I think Ruby's moved on," I said. "She started haunting Preston heavily after he committed his murders. She didn't want him to grow more powerful by preying on your customers or your family. She was trying to protect you, in her very unpleasant way. But now that it's over, I'd consider getting rid of that farmhouse completely, every bit down to the soil, and replace it with plant life."

"I'm totally for that," Callie said. "More room and more light for the garden. And no weird, scary house looking down on me with an angry ghost inside. That's an upgrade."

"Same advice for the old projection house. Demolish it, fill it with earth, put some plant life down to recycle any residual psychic energy," I added.

So it came to pass that, a couple of weeks later, the Nite-Lite Drive-In hosted a real barn-burner of a housewarming party. Guests of honor included my boyfriend, Michael Holly, and a number of others from the Savannah Fire Department, who were happy to set the farmhouse ablaze for a training exercise, after bulldozing a firebreak around it.

This event, which would be staged before the evening's movie began, was interesting enough that a number of their friends came to view it, and they ended up temporarily removing several fence panels and replacing them with yellow DO NOT CROSS tape, so people could watch from the safety of the enormous lawn.

Also in attendance were assorted film-school friends of Stacey's and friends of Jacob, including their informal Bad Movie Club that met occasionally to watch only the very worst of movies.

The house was reduced to a bonfire by the time the sky started turning dark.

Personally, I kept my distance, because I have my reasons for not particularly enjoying fires at all. I hung around the concession stand with Callie, who had a cousin in town, helping her babysit and run the concession stand. I played lose-ball with Daisy and did not win, but also avoided any organ damage from her swiftly stabbing rods. And I didn't spin my rods anymore, either. Rules are rules.

Visitors thronged the concession stand, grabbing treats or ordering pizza before the first movie began, as Benny's announcements over the outdoor speakers repeatedly encouraged everyone to do. He played music to keep things festive when he wasn't hawking the wares. I didn't recognize too many of the bands.

When the outdoor lights dimmed, the projector ignited, and a huge cartoon appeared on the screen, the crowd cheered. Many were sitting in lawn or camping chairs outside their cars.

The first cartoon was a vintage concession stand ad—Benny wasn't joking with the salesmanship, but the dancing drinks and popcorn buckets really felt like part of the experience anyway.

Michael and I sat in the back of his truck, a red 1949 Chevrolet pickup that he'd restored. I wondered whether its previous owners had ever taken it to a drive-in theater, maybe even this very one. We lined the truck bed with sleeping bags and domesticated it further with pillows and blankets. It was a warm, clear night, made warmer with a hot cheese pizza from Callie's brick oven.

"This is amazing," Michael said, taking a crunchy, gooey bite.

"The pizza?"

"Yeah, the whole thing."

"They call it a package experience. I now have a lifetime VIP membership."

"They should just call it the city's best pizza place, but with a drive-in theater tacked on out back. What's the feature tonight?"

"It's a double feature in honor of the fire training exercise. There's *Firestarter*, where we watch an elementary-age Drew Barrymore destroy things with her mind. Then *The Towering Inferno*, a 70s disaster movie I've never seen."

"Are you sure you'll be okay with all that fire?" he asked. I was touched, because he knew I really wasn't.

"I'll watch the Drew Barrymore one," I said. "For the second one, I might need to be distracted."

"I'll do my best."

"I might even need to pull the covers over my head."

"Maybe I'll join you in solidarity. If the movie gets boring."

I leaned against him, enjoying his warmth, his arm around me.

We'd faced some dark things on this case, but we'd driven them out, and freed a few souls who needed it. We'd protected our clients, a struggling young family with a wacky dream. Maybe it would work out for them. I certainly hoped so.

The lights dimmed more, and the crowd grew quiet in anticipation.

Up on the big screen, the movie began.

The End

FROM THE AUTHOR

I hope you enjoyed this latest adventure from Ellie and Stacey. I've played with the idea of writing about a haunted movie theater for a while; eventually I settled on a drive-in because it's such a unique setting and usually evokes a particular period of the twentieth century. Once I learned that some of the early screens were large enough to hold storage, offices, and apartments, it was impossible to resist using that as a setting! The ruins of drive-ins can be found all over America, in various states of disrepair, some of them just signs or skeletal remnants, but a few hundred of them remain open around, still exhibiting films under the stars.

The next book in the Ellie series will be *The Lodge*, set on one of Georgia's Sea Islands, among the many abandoned Gilded Age mansions like those found on Cumberland and Jekyll Island. They'll be facing some interesting ghosts on an isolated, once-luxurious private island. Appropriately for an island/beach tale, that should be published in mid to late summer (2021).

Thanks for reading these books! Subscribe to my **newsletter** to hear about new releases. And follow on **Facebook** for more frequent updates, ghost memes, etc.:

Newsletter (http://eepurl.com/mizJH)
Website (www.jlbryanbooks.com)
Facebook (J. L. Bryan's Books)

Also, if you're enjoying the series, I hope you'll consider taking time to recommend the books to someone who might like them, or to rate or review it at your favorite book retailer. Thanks so much!

Printed in Great Britain
by Amazon

57673307R00180